A Thank y- for your supp-

We Are Immeasurable

A Novel Written By B. L. McGrew

You Are Immeasurable

This book is a work of fiction. Names, characters, places, and incidents are the products of the author's imagination or are used fictitiously. Any resemblance to actual persons, living or dead, or actual events is entirely coincidental.

Copyright © 2018 by B. L. McGrew

All rights reserved. No parts of this publication may be reproduced, distributed, or transmitted in any form or by any means, or stored in a database or retrieval system, without the prior written permission of the author.

To Nova, Devery, Carter, Elliot, Gianna and Elvi,

I LOVE YOU.

"When pain is over, the remembrance of it often becomes a pleasure." – Jane Austen

Preface (n.): a preliminary statement in a book by the book's author or editor, setting forth its purpose and scope, expressing acknowledgment of assistance from others, etc.

The word infinite is an adjective that is defined as immeasurably great. This basically means great without bounds, limitless in its greatness. It's a heady word, powerful, and intimidating but it's also beautiful. To have a word describe in just three syllables how it feels to want something so badly that you never want it to end. The other side of that is the loss of something or someone, and then the word infinite takes a dark turn. Its permanence is overwhelming, the pain will always be there *infinitely* changing small pieces of who you are until your own time is up.

I think we have a tendency of looking at life in patterns. It's like we get comfortable with whatever specific order is laid in front of us, accepting the overall complacency of life. When we read books, watch movies or whatever it may be, we subconsciously try to piece together clues that will lead to the big conclusion. What will the finale be? What is this character foreshadowing? Will this character have a happy ending? Does this character deserve one? Is he or she doomed? That's how we treat life in a sense. What will our finale be? I don't think you will find too many people who can honestly say they are prepared for any and everything life is capable of throwing at them.

We rarely consider the things that come out of left field, the things that smack you down so hard into the ground that you don't think you'd ever be able to get back up. We never take the time to actually understand that this could be our last day, our last words, our last breath.

We don't have those terrifying thoughts about the end every single day because it is too depressing to live life that way - to expect the worse out of every situation, to wait for the bad, the shocking, to wait for death. So we live, love, learn, breathe and keep breathing until we can't breathe anymore.

So, life may not be infinite, life can indeed be measured but the love you give and the love you receive is infinite. It's immeasurably great and, like love, make the mark you leave here in the world immeasurably great too, even if the mark you leave is only to be felt by one person.

One

Blind (adj.): unable to see; lacking a sense of sight; sightless

"Maya," I say exasperatedly. "No."

Finality in my tone, the annoyance is clear and saturates those three syllables.

"You never consider anything out of your comfort zone," my older *–much* older sister says to me. Knowing her, she is rolling her eyes. Her cheeks are probably red from frustration. "You're against anything that could make your life the slightest bit easier."

"I don't consider *anything* out of my comfort zone?" I repeat angrily. "Are we forgetting why we are even having this conversation?" I rebut, emphasizing the irony in her words. "…and the point is, I've gone this long without help. I don't need it now. I am not a decrepit." I almost snap –trying to keep my cool, not wanting this to turn into a huge argument. We don't argue much, but on the rare occasion that we do, it usually lasts for days.

"You made this decision to transfer schools on your own," she says. Traces of anxiety fill her words. "This is all so new. I just think this is an option that really needs to be considered."

"I've considered it," I respond immediately. "The answer is still *no,* Maya, I'm sorry." I sigh and stand up to make my way to the kitchen. "I don't need a Seeing Eye Dog," I say clearly before I walk fully into the kitchen.

My blood is boiling. She of all people should know that I am highly capable without my sight. I do so much for myself and in large part it's *because* of her. Right now I am pretty shocked that she wants me to get a Seeing Eye Dog.

Also, when she casually brought this up two months ago I was very adamant about not wanting to have one at my new school. So the fact that she has made arrangements for me to have one on my first day tomorrow is not only blowing my mind, but it's filling me with the kind of rage that if she weren't my sister, whom I love dearly, I would be throwing explicit words around like a sailor.

Fueled by my anger and frustration I know I have a couple of points to prove. I saunter to the kitchen counter and reach my hand straight up, sliding my fingers against the cool wood, I feel for the third metal handle; once I've reached it I open the cabinet and pull out a glass cup. I turn 90 degrees and walk to the fridge; I open it and touch the first shelf, then glide my fingers slightly to the left and grab a can. We kept the Sprite in the front so I move that can out of the way to grab the can behind it, it is a Pepsi. I close the fridge then turn around to walk back into the living room. I walk seventeen short strides before I make it to the couch and sit. I clear my throat and proceed to open the can and pour the pop inside the glass.

"Here, an ice cold Pepsi… I could go and get you some ice if you'd like?" my arm is outstretched holding the glass in front of me. She doesn't take it or say a word. *I'm winning this argument and proving so many points in the meantime.* "…now how would a dog help me do *that* any better than I already do?" I snap. Immediately, I feel bad for raising my voice but I cannot hold these emotions in. I despise being looked at as incapable and she knows that.

I am blind. It doesn't mean I have to be treated differently than anyone else.

I wave the glass in front of where I know she is still sitting. I know this because I can smell her strawberry shampoo, her floral perfume, and that weird hospital smell that is always on her scrubs when she comes home from work. Sanitizer? Disinfectant? I can never be sure.

She huffs and I know she is no longer just frustrated. She has entered the angry phase. She grabs the glass and I hear it slam on to the coffee table.

"Listen," she snaps, "clearly, I know you can do things for yourself. I never said you were incompetent but *you* decided you wanted to go to public school and, like I said, it's a new environment with new spaces and people

..." she stops speaking and I feel her sit next to me, placing her hand on my leg. "You know this house like the back of your hand –but this is different. You'll be alone and ..."

"I love you," I interrupt. I can hear that anxiety building up in her throat and she is wasting energy on a losing battle. "…but I'm not bringing a dog to school or anywhere for that matter. I don't even like dogs that much," I state.

"What!?" she shrieks, my comment momentarily distracting her. "Who doesn't like dogs?!" She says exasperatedly with total shock in her tone. She says the words as if I have personally offended her. "What about Cocoa? You *loved* Cocoa!"

"I was three, Maya. I *loved* everything," I state. She sighs and I sigh too because I know this isn't over.

It's quiet for a moment and I know that my sister is desperately trying to think of a way to get me to agree to this. Luckily she knows me well and knows that once I've put my foot down I do not budge. And my foot is down. My foot is slammed down and cemented in place.

"I took off work so I'll be there your first week," she says breaking the silence.

"Maya..."

"No!" she says, cutting me off. "This is a decision you're not going to make. You're my little sister and I need to see the atmosphere you're going to be in. I need to be there to help you get your routine set." She sighs for probably the tenth time in the last twenty five minutes, then I feel her slender yet warm arm wrap around my shoulders. She pulls me towards her to wrap me in a tight hug.

"I'm going to be fine," I whisper. She is extremely close to suffocating me. The way she has my face nuzzled into her scrubs is a bit uncomfortable. My sunglasses are smashing unevenly to the right side of my face, but I don't move, I embrace her back.

"I know," she whispers. "Are you sure you want to do this?" she asks into my hair. I'd lost count of how many times she's asked me this over the summer.

I'd gone to a school for the blind for the first three years of high school. At this school everything is accommodating and there are people there *just like you*, so apparently, I won't feel alone or like an outcast. The school prides itself on the fact it teaches real life experiences, that it does not enable their students by doing everything for us. All of that is a load of crap. Yes, it was and is amazing to have a place that is pretty much a safe haven for me, but once graduation comes what will happen?

The world isn't a safe haven.

There is nothing at that school that will teach me about the real world, about real people. It's a false representation of what the world is and I want to experience the real thing. I think I deserve that much.

I want to navigate this world and never use my handicap as a crutch. If I fall, I'll get back up. If I bump into a wall,

I'll move two inches to the right or left to avoid it happening again. If I realize this is the biggest mistake I've ever made and I regret every second of it, then that will be a life lesson I will learn. I've never thought like this before – I was used to my routine with very little complaints about it, but I think something about turning eighteen made me want my independence more now than ever before.

I will never tell Maya this, but I am terrified that I will crash and burn. Maybe somewhere deep down I know it is inevitable, but I have to at least try. I have to at least know I am giving something my all.

"I'm sure," I say dislodging myself from her warm motherly hold. That's what it feels like sometimes, like she is my mother and I am the difficult errant child any time we don't agree which isn't too often.

My sister is thirteen years older than I. My father met and married my mother after a year of dating. He moved into her home and brought along his eleven year old daughter Amaya. Two years later yours truly was born. I've never really viewed Maya as my sister. The word sister seems so insignificant when looking at all that she has done for me and continues to do for me. She is much more to me; she is a sister, a mother, a counselor, an annoyance, and my best friend. She's *my* Maya.

"The real issue is figuring out what to wear," I arch an eyebrow and I can all but sense her smile. I've worn uniforms my entire academic career. This will be the first time I can wear whatever I want to high school. I may not be able to see what I'm wearing, but the pride in knowing *I* chose it is what matters most to me.

She grabs my hand and we head to my bedroom. I sit on my bed and I hear her slide my closet door open. She doesn't say a word, but I can hear light thuds hit the floor; she's dumping out my closet. I want to object and tell her to chill but I kind of feel bad for how I acted about the whole *Seeing Eye Dog* thing, so I sigh and bite my tongue instead.

"Okay," she says. Her light footsteps walk towards me, and then I feel her hand under my chin.

"What?" I ask, reaching out directly in front of me to discover she is holding a shirt there.

"Yep," she says, clearly having an internal conversation. "You are definitely an autumn."

"What does that even mean?"

She laughs and I hear her walk away. "It means trust your big sister." She's back in front of me now. I can sense her leaning over, placing something on the bed behind me.

"Alright," she finally says. "Here are your options. A burnt orange V-neck with a plum colored scarf, black leggings and you can wear my Uggs because this is the kind of outfit that should only be worn with Uggs."

When she describes the outfit, I picture a billboard of a tall, skinny, bleach blonde, white girl holding a pumpkin spice latte, smiling with perfect teeth and ocean blue eyes as she waves to a friend in the distance. Not to be stereotypical, but it's what flits across my mind. Someone who is the polar opposite of me.

I am about average height for a girl. I have hips and breasts, not fat, but far from skinny. Skin –a creamy russet, lips –plump and full. My hair is wild and curly – unruly most of the time –rubber bands, hair clips nor *I* can tame it. And, I've never had pumpkin spice anything in my entire life.

Maya told me last year that my face was less plump than it had been. I still have high cheekbones but they aren't as full as they were when I was younger. Basically, she was telling me I looked like I'd finally lost a little bit of the baby fat I had stored in my cheeks.

Maya and I look nothing alike. Growing up people never thought we were sisters, the age gap didn't help much with that either. She is much lighter than me; she is tall and very slender –she has curves, but they aren't as blatantly obvious as mine. I've had these hips and breasts since I was eleven; an early bloomer. Her lips aren't as full as mine, but I remember they were always a beautiful shade of pink as if she had permanent lip gloss. Her hair has the slightest of waves; it's long and full like mine, but manageable, unlike mine.

The only thing we have in common are our father's eyes –deep chocolate brown, wide and large, but no one would know that now because my sunglasses cover mine twenty- four seven.

"What else you got?"

"Okay," I can tell that she is holding the outfits up as she describes them because I keep hearing things lightly hit the bed when she leans over me to pick something else up. "…Deep purple button up, white wash jeans and those black boots that you wore to Dory's graduation dinner."

I make a face and without saying a word she moves on and starts describing the next outfit. Four outfits later and I am *over this*. Usually my sister and I are on the same page when it comes to picking my clothes out for special occasions, but right now we are in completely different books. She wants me to look like I am about to model for some low budget teen magazine. I, however, want to look like an eighteen year old entering her senior year of high school.

I sigh and interrupt as she describes some pink blouse with a black pencil skirt. I didn't even know I owned a skirt. That had to have been something from her closet. "Maya," I say, "…can you go to my dresser and open the second drawer?"

"Sure," she says, not even two seconds later I hear the drawer open.

"Can you grab the shirt to your right? It's black," I say. "If it's not there, then it's in the first drawer," I add.

"The t-shirt?" she asks. I nod, assuming she is looking in my direction.

"No," she says, so I know this means she's unfolded the shirt. "Not on your first day, don't you want to stand out?"

I laugh, "I'm a blind girl coming in my senior year. I don't think I need to do anything further to stand out."

She sighs and I feel the t-shirt hit my lap. It is my vintage Jimi Hendrix t-shirt that I stole from my dad about seven months before he died. He didn't know I borrowed it and I never got a chance to give it back to him so essentially – I stole it.

"Dark ripped jeans?" she asks unenthused, "…and let me guess, Converses?"

I smile because of course; you can't wear any vintage shirt and not wear Converses. It's an unspoken rule.

I hear my sister grabbing everything. "It's on the chair," she says with fake annoyance. "It's getting late and we have a big day tomorrow," her nerves are evident, but I ignore it. I cannot let her know how unbelievably nervous I am as well. She'd take that opportunity and use my weakness against me to try and get me to change my mind or get a damn dog.

"Good night Maya –Me," I say.

"Goodnight Mazie –My," she says, her smile audible in her words.

I don't know when we started using those nicknames, but ever since I could remember we've called each other that.

My real name isn't Mazie either. I had a speech impediment when I was younger and could not pronounce my real name. A name that I do not go by because I absolutely hate it –but anyway, legend says I would say *Mazelda* when trying to pronounce my full name. My family started calling me Mazelda, and then eventually it progressed to being shortened to Mazie and for some reason that stuck. I like it, you aren't going to find too many people named Mazie.

I take off my clothes and decide I'm too nervous, anxious, and tired to put on pajamas. Underwear only it is. I climb into my bed and nuzzle under my warm blankets and like any teen trying to avoid stress by sleeping, my brain decides to make up scenarios - terrifying and embarrassing scenarios.

Scenarios in which I fall, I walk into the boys bathroom, again –falling, missing my chair when I go to sit, hearing the snickering of adolescents judging me and the sad and concerned voices of the teachers asking me if I'm okay in a tone one would use to speak to a two year old.

I take a deep breath and hold it for ten seconds. Maya is right. Why the hell am I doing this? I was so comfortable where I was. Everything is so predictable and I always know what to expect and when to expect it. I guess that right there is the problem. All of the things I feared, all the drummed up scenarios I allowed my subconscious to taunt me with, are all the reasons why I need to do this.

I want to fall on my face, figuratively of course, and I want to get back up on my own. I exhale and somewhat relax enough to finally drift off to sleep.

"Okay," Maya says nervously. One would think she is the blind girl at a new school with the way she is acting. "That wasn't so bad," she adds.

"The day hasn't even started," I say to her, and the clicking from my damn cane is annoying me. Or maybe it's tapping? Clinking? I never really had an issue with using it until this very moment. It seems louder, heavier, it seems to be standing out in the crowd –like me. Did it *always* make this sound?

"I meant that your counselor was nice," she corrects herself.

I can hear how crowded this hall is, I can only imagine the stares I am getting while walking next to my frantic sister, with my cane hitting the floor in loud obnoxious clicks, or taps…clinks?

Clink left, clink right and repeat. I can hear paper shuffling in Maya's hand, my poor stressed out, unhinged, overprotective sister. I bet her hands are shaking right now. I stop and grab her wrist.

"Are you okay?" she asks panicked. "Do you want to go?"

"Amaya," I say calmly. I only use her full name when I truly need her undivided attention. "I am fine, you're freaking out and that in turn will freak me out and then we will just be two freaked out weirdos standing in the middle of a high school hallway holding each other."

She sighs, but I know that she is smiling, "That wouldn't be a good first impression," she states.

"No," I answer letting go of her wrist. "It wouldn't."

We start walking again and I can feel the tension falling off of my sister. Good.

"Your first class is in room 112, then you have a free period, lunch, second class is in 120b," she continues to rattle off my schedule. Interesting how all of my classes are coincidentally on the first floor. I want to call her out on this because it's clear that my schedule is like this because of her. But since this is a new environment and there are students everywhere and she is already having an anxiety filled day, I hold my tongue.

"Mr. Pinkard," she says. "English, you love English." She adds nearly under her breath.

"I speak it fluently," I answer sarcastically and she ignores me as I hear her open the classroom door.

As I step into the classroom I hear chatter from the students getting settled in. I take another step in and then suddenly you can almost hear a pin drop. My cheeks are immediately hot and most probably reddening right now. I know all eyes are on me, but it is important to keep my composure. I knew this would happen, it's expected.

"Welcome!" I hear a deep gravelly voice say cheerfully – the contrast of his tone and his volume is a bit unnerving. Seconds pass and I feel someone grab my hand. "You must be Ezmerelda?"

I have to force myself to suppress a groan from my annoyance. One – I wonder if he does this with all of the new students or do they just come in and sit down like everyone else? Two – I hate my name and now every single person in this classroom knows what it is.

"Just Mazie," I say trying to cover the frustration in my tone with a fake smile. "This is my sister, Maya." I say lowly because I know that though I am speaking directly to Mr. Pinkard, the class is staring. They're listening to my every word, dissecting me, and analyzing me.

They're wondering what I'm doing here; they're wondering how I became blind. They're wondering if I will be an inconvenience to their everyday routine.

Some pity me –that's the worst one. I *hate* the pity –I hate the *poor blind girl* motif. I am willing to bet I am smarter than half of the people in this classroom and I am not saying that to be mean or cocky, but I have to work three times as hard as everyone else just to prove I belong.

I am a female, I am a woman of color, and I am blind. I have a lot to prove to a world that has already decided *who* I am and *how* I should be without even knowing me personally. I refuse to be put in a box.

"Nice to meet you," he says to my sister. "Let me lead you to your seats."

We don't have to walk far –*great I'm in the front of the class*. I sigh and take a seat. I hear screeching and know that they've pulled a chair up for my sister to sit next to me. I'm starting to think a Seeing Eye Dog would be better than this. They probably think she's my aide or caretaker. I don't need one.

I haven't even been in my first class for five minutes and I am already thinking that maybe I did make a mistake. I feel like a sore thumb, the blood red and thick, pulsating under the nail bed –the same rhythm as my heartbeat.

Mr. Pinkard goes about his day, explaining the syllabus, and what topics we'll be going over. My sister is so quiet, it makes me wonder if she too is feeling the energy I am feeling. Better yet, she is *seeing* it, the stares, and the whispers. She is as uncomfortable as I am.

After English I have a free period so Maya and I decide to go outside and enjoy this nice August weather.

"You're quiet," she says softly as we sit on a bench in the back of the school.

"I don't have anything to say."

"The day will get better," she tells me, sensing that my mood has shifted drastically from earlier this morning. "People, especially young people, have to adapt and get used to anything that is different from what they're accustomed to."

I don't say anything.

All of my classes are exactly the same. I walk in and the chatter stops immediately, then a teacher overenthusiastically introduces him/herself to me as if I am mentally challenged and not just blind.

I sit and hear people whisper, *who is that? I wonder how she went blind. You think she's been blind all of her life? Shouldn't she be in a special class? Shouldn't she go to a special school? I feel so bad for her.* I know that this is bothering Maya, but as we walk to each class she doesn't say anything and neither do I. This is going to be a long and interesting school year, that much is for sure.

"Overall, it wasn't that bad," my sister says as we walk through the front door of our home. I still don't say anything. I place my cane on the wall and throw my bag on the floor before plopping on the couch.

"What are you thinking, Mazie?"

"I'm thinking that not one person acknowledged my existence –*to my face* – today," I say, "…and maybe that's a good thing. I don't really like people anyway." I shrug –which really isn't the truth, but I'm upset. "Oh and apparently they've confused being blind with being deaf because they suck at whispering," I add.

"It's only the first day," she says as I hear her walk into the kitchen and open the fridge. "You'll make friends in no time," she calls out.

"I don't care about making friends," I state, which is the honest to God's truth. "I care about the fact people are clearly tiptoeing around me. Blindness isn't contagious. I want to be treated like everyone else," I sigh annoyingly.

I hear and feel her sit down next to me. "Here," she says, placing a can of pop in my hand. "People don't think that. Everything is going to be fine once you get your routine down, everything'll be what you expected."

"This *is* what I expected, Maya."

I don't know why I am so upset. I prepared all summer for this, for being the outcast. I chose this and now that it's happening I'm acting like someone ran over my Seeing Eye Dog.

I sigh.

It's quiet for a moment before I continue. "...and since when are you okay with this? I figured you'd take my mood and try and talk me into going back to my old high school."

She doesn't answer at first, "I listened to what you said," she finally begins, "and I've spent the last five years wanting and helping you be independent so that if something ever happens to me you would be prepared. One day you may decide you don't want to live here and that you want to be on your own and the second you want to put everything you've learned and accomplished to a *real* test in the real world, I completely freak out and fight you on it for the most part," she grabs my hand. "This may not have been the best first day, but you need this and I am happy you decided to transfer. It *will* get better."

I lay my head on her shoulder. "I'm never leaving here." I say under my breath and she laughs. "Not because of you, but I dig the free rent thing," I add. She laughs harder and puts her arms around me.

"Come on, help me cook dinner." She says.

My sister is right. I don't know why I am being so mopey. I would be pissed if I got bombarded with a million questions today by my peers, and yet, I'm sitting here pissed because other than the teachers, no one so much as said *hi* to me. I have one year left before I go to college, so at this moment I am deciding to focus on school work and college applications instead of silly high school politics.

I don't know why I am stressing out about it at all in the first place. I never cared about stuff like that before. Cliché of all clichés -tomorrow will be a new day.

Two

Pity (n.): a strong feeling of sadness or sympathy for someone or something

Today is my first day attending school without Maya.

Week two.

I thought I would be happier about this, but I am actually filled with fear and anxiety. Of course I would never tell her this, she'd lose her job and her mind trying to be here every day. Besides, anxiety is a normal feeling. I want to do this. My fear isn't enough to change my mind. I've let fear rule a lot of areas in my life, but it isn't going to rule this. This is the real world and I am determined and desperate to be a part of it.

Things are a little better than last week. The whispering stopped for the most part and a few people spoke to me, which was unexpected. A girl named Breanna even introduced herself to me and offered to study with me since we have English and Math together. She seemed friendly and overly chipper, the Maya kind of chipper, the kind of chipper that would be borderline annoying if she wasn't a genuinely good person. Those are the vibes I get from Breanna.

I am still going to just focus on school work and college applications though. I am no longer going to be distracted with worrying about things that honestly don't matter in the long run. Anybody I meet in this school this year, I won't know a year from now.

Mr. Pinkard told me that the English department decided to use grant money to have an extensive collection of Braille books added to the school's library. I am so grateful for that. I am the only blind student in the school so it will be like having my own personal library. I'm not going to lie –I *hate* special treatment, but sometimes there are perks that I cannot deny. I am not going to argue about a decision that got me a section in the library to myself.

I'm sure my sister has something to do with this, but she would never admit it. I want to check out the library during my free period. I figure that is where I can go every day since there isn't much else to do during that time and, if I am being honest, libraries are probably my most favorite places on earth. It doesn't seem like a bad way to kill time, even if there are only a handful of books.

"Mr. Pinkard," I say as class is dismissed. "Where is the library?"

"Oh, great! Is there something specific you're looking for? I can grab it for you and have it here tomorrow?"

I try to refrain from sighing because he is only being nice. It's habit for people to automatically assume I need help or assistance. I am sure most people are unaware of what ableism is, they are not trying to be malicious or belittling. It just comes with the territory.

"Actually," I say as I stand from my seat. "I want to check it out myself, thank you though."

"Oh, well it's all the way on the third floor. I'll send someone with you…"

"That isn't necessary…"

"Parks!" he interrupts and now, not only am I annoyed, but I am confused.

"What?" I say.

"Yes, Mr. Parks," he says again, but quieter. "Since you have a free period, would you please escort Miss Day to the library?"

"Absolutely," a somewhat deep voice answers immediately, coming from behind me.

"No, really it's fine…" I try to interject.

"Great," Mr. Pinkard says not acknowledging my polite protest. "I hope you enjoy, there are some great finds up there! You two have a good day."

I clench my jaw and sigh when I hear Mr. Pinkard shuffle some papers then walk away.

"You ready?" the voice –*Mr. Parks* asks. I turn and hope my frustration isn't blaring on my face because the way I feel it in my chest, I'm sure I am not doing a great job of hiding it.

"Actually, I don't need any help but thank you." I grab my cane, my bag, and my recorder and begin to walk. Clink left, clink right.

"Hmmm," Mr. Parks says and I can hear that he is following me out of the classroom. I ignore him. "Mr. Pinkard was pretty clear…" he says.

"Mr. Pinkard doesn't know my capabilities," I say. I can taste the shadow of an attitude in my tone. I am definitely worked up; I need to relax.

"…and what *are* your capabilities?" he asks and I am even more annoyed now because I truly don't feel like having a conversation with some random person.

"More than most would think," I say coldly.

"Hmmm," he says again. I continue to walk, searching for the stairs, once I found those it would be smooth sailing from there. I can hear Mr. Parks a few paces behind me.

After a minute or two, I stop abruptly and face his direction, "I don't need an escort, please stop following me," I try to keep my voice even and not saturated with the irritation I am feeling. I don't need caretakers, or babysitters, or *escorts*. Those things won't happen in the real world.

"I was actually already headed to the library," he says, and the way he says this lets me know he is clearly lying.

"*Really* now," I state placidly.

"I know, right? What a coincidence."

I inhale angrily then turn back around in search of the stairwell. I am trying with all of my might to not let my frustration and my annoyance take over my body completely. I am going to have a good first week without Maya. I am determined to.

After another two minutes go by of clinking the wall with my cane – searching for a hollow sound that isn't a classroom –it is clear that I am lost, but I refuse to ask Mr. Parks for help. Maya told me where the staircase was just in case, but I think I somehow got turned around dealing with Mr. Parks.

"Ezmerelda, can I suggest something?" Mr. Parks asks smoothly.

"It's Mazie," I say flatly as I keep walking. Great, everyone in the class did hear Mr. Pinkard say my name.

"May I suggest something?" he repeats. "I know that you are highly capable and don't need assistance, but we've passed the stairs three times." I can hear the humor in his voice. I'm embarrassed, irritated, and tired. I don't know what point I was trying to prove or to whom I was trying to prove it, but I do need help in this *particular* instance. I am well aware of how difficult I am being.

I stop walking and turn slowly in his direction. I just stand there defeated.

"It's back this way," he grabs my elbow and reflexively I yank my arm away.

"I can hear the direction you're walking," I state.

"Okay," he says and we begin to walk in silence. It's a loud silence, the kind of silence that demands to be heard. I don't know this boy well enough to try and fill this quiet with noise, so I continue clinking left and clinking right, listening intently to his footsteps.

"Barnaby..." He says out of the blue, cutting through the dead air abruptly.

"Excuse me?"

"You forgot to ask me my name. It's Barnaby."

Wow, *Barnaby*? I finally met someone my age with a name as odd and as outdated as mine.

"That's an interesting name," I say, but who am I to talk?

I hated elementary school, kids making mean nonsensical rhymes with my name, teasing me or just flat out mispronouncing it –which made no sense because it's pronounced exactly how it is spelled. Then in junior high school having nearly every teacher ask *why is it spelled with a Z and not an S?* I don't know. I didn't name myself. Maybe my great, great, great grandparents were illiterate.

"Family name –five generations," Barnaby says, snapping me out of my thought.

"Three generations for me," I say and I can tell my annoyance is seeping through. Ezmerelda is the name of a grandparent or a really old aunt. It isn't the name of an eighteen year old in the twenty first century.

"It's a beautiful name," Barnaby says. "It's very commanding. Anybody with a name like Ezmerelda is ready to take over the world. Agree?"

"Umm," I say. "I guess..." I don't know what the hell he is talking about, but I listen anyway.

"Ezmereldas don't *guess*, someone with a strong name like that knows there are no in betweens, she knows who she is. You should wear it proud, you should own it."

I laugh because I don't know if he is being serious or not because who just goes on a rant about the validity of someone's name? He's an odd egg.

"Make a left then there's about twelve steps each flight," he says and he grabs my elbow again to turn me. It throws me off because it's unexpected and sends a jolt of surprise right through me, causing me to jump slightly.

"Sorry," he says and let's go of my elbow immediately.

It's quiet as we walk up the stairs, *this school needs elevators*.

"So, are you?" Barnaby says.

"Am I what?"

"Going to own it? Your name?"

"I prefer Mazie." I answer flatly. What is his obsession with my name? Maybe he's just trying to keep small talk going; I'm not really contributing a lot.

"Hmmm," he says for the third time in the ten minutes I've known him.

"You say *hmmm* a lot," I state as we make it to the third floor landing, I'm almost a little embarrassed at how hard I am breathing.

"I do?" he answers quizzically. "*Hmmm*. I never noticed."

I sigh and shake my head trying not to laugh.

"We're here. Are you planning on staying the entire free period?"

"No, probably just fifteen minutes. It all depends on the selection."

"Okay, sounds good."

"You're not waiting for me," I say as I hear him open the doors to the library.

"I am not waiting for you. I'm going to read a magazine for no specific amount of time then leave. Everything isn't about you, Ezmerelda."

"Mazie," I correct him again and he laughs. I walk through the doors a little too quickly for not knowing anything about this library and realize I've already embarrassed myself, so I might as well ask for help.

"Barnaby?" I whisper, because after I walked in I am not sure where he is. He doesn't answer; I take a few more steps into the library then spin around walking back toward the door "Barnaby?" I whisper again.

"Yes?" and suddenly I sense that he is right in front of me, meaning that he heard me calling him.

"Were you ignoring me?" my frustration is blatant.

"I was lost in thought," he says easily. "That happens to me sometimes when I am observing."

And because he is so odd I don't know whether he is being serious or if he is having fun with the blind girl by playing some childish one sided version of Marco polo. I turn angrily and walk a few steps, immediately realizing that I *still* don't know where the front desk is and I don't know where the Braille reading is located.

For some reason when I convinced myself that I wanted to come to a public school and do everything on my own –I didn't truly consider the fact that I first needed to learn the environment in its fullness. I am having a more difficult time than I would like to admit. Maya was right. Of course, she always is.

"What did you need?" I hear Barnaby ask and now he is standing next to me. I sigh.

"Where is the front desk?" I ask, "I need to find the Braille section."

"I know where it is," he says and his voice seems softer as if he can tell his ignoring me stunt pissed me off.

"Thanks," I say.

"I'm going to grab your elbow, okay?" he says. I don't say anything and I let him. He trudges me along slowly for about forty five seconds. "There's a small staircase to go up, only five steps." He informs me. I nod and then we walk up, we walk for about twenty five more seconds turning two corners before we stop and he lets go of my elbow.

"There are about eight shelves of books," he says.

Eight! I think to myself in pure excitement, how much was that grant money check?!

"Thank you," I clink left and clink right until I hit one of the shelves. I balance my cane on the shelf and then run my fingers across the books. This is amazing, I loved reading and I'd been spoiled at my last high school because clearly everything in that place is Braille. I am realizing the many things I took for granted.

"For pain or pleasure?"

Barnaby's voice yanks me out of my reverie. I was completely zoned out.

"What?"

"Are you looking for school stuff to read or things to read in your free time?" he asks and I can sense that he is standing directly behind me now.

"For now, free time." I am still running my hands across the books. I truly appreciate literature. I think it is amazing that people have an ability to take simple and ordinary words then string them together to make extraordinary and life changing works of art.

Before I lost my sight, all I would do in my free time was write and read books. I would probably read two or three novels a week. After I lost my sight I went a year without the imaginary world of literature, I only had my world and nothing else to escape to. Braille had frustrated me at first and audio was not the same for me. I liked absorbing the words in my own tone and voice when I read.

"Are you looking for anything specific?"

Again, I'd zoned out forgetting that Barnaby is standing there.

"Ummm," I say grabbing my cane to move and navigate through another shelf. "Austen, Bronte sisters, Woolf…"

"I figured as much," he says and I want to question him. I want to ask him what about me gave it away that I would enjoy the classics, but I leave it alone. I am too wrapped up in this selection of literature.

"Do you read your favorite books over and over again?" he's followed me to the next shelf.

"You ask a lot of questions."

"I do, how else do you learn everything there is to learn in the world?"

"Well, you don't have to *learn* me." As soon as the words leave my lips I realize that my comment came across rude and dismissive. He doesn't say anything and I suddenly feel like I am being bitchy. "Yes," I clear my throat. "I read my favorite books over and over again. Do you?" I ask hoping that my rudeness hadn't offended him; it isn't solely his fault that I am kind of in a crap mood.

"Absolutely, you're guaranteed to find something you missed the first or second time or something you once loved may not give you the same emotion or something you once hated becomes your favorite part."

He answers in an upbeat tone and I am happy that it doesn't seem like he took my rudeness to heart.

"Good authors," he begins, "have layers to their work, things that they've actually written so anyone who reads it will see and then the things they have *not* written that only the true lovers of their work will understand. I think when we change and grow, the meanings in our favorite books start to morph into whatever we need them to morph into at that time. It's like a marker to show us where we are, how much we've grown or even how much we've digressed."

I stop and drop my hand from the shelf. "Did you make that up yourself?" I ask him and it's a stupid question to ask someone in hindsight, but I can't take the words back now.

He laughs, "I'm sure someone has said it somewhere in this world at some point. It isn't a big secret that some literature has hidden messages and hidden sub plots. No book means the same thing to different people."

I don't say anything for a moment as I lift my hand back up to the shelf, "Well, you're right. I agree." I say lowly.

I'd always thought something similar, that in my favorite novels the author has a story to tell, the main story for all of the critics and casual book readers to hear and read but they give the lovers, the fans, and the obsessed a little more behind the layers. They give us different emotions; different viewpoints that make you feel like you are in the novel. Makes you feel like the author is speaking directly to you and *only* you.

"Do you write?" I ask him. From this short time he totally seems like the type.

"It depends on what you consider writing," he says and I can hear him walk to the opposite side of me. His fragrance is very distinctive, it's like a woodsy smell but it's also sweet and very potent in a good way. I think I could pick him out in a crowd from his scent alone.

"Okay, do you put your thoughts to paper?" I correct.

"You ask *a lot* of questions, Ezmerelda," he says and the humor is blatant.

"Mazie," I correct him lazily, "…and I am sorry about how I've been acting. I'm not normally rude. I just hate …"

"People pitying you?" he interrupts and it takes me by surprise.

"Uhh," I say, shaking my head. "Yeah." *Is it that obvious?*

"I don't pity you," he says and then I hear him walk away. He and his distinctive scent are no longer right next to me. A few moments pass and he is standing next to me again, "I admire you, actually." he says casually. And that catches me completely off guard.

"Ummm, yeah, you don't know me," I finally say.

"I know that you don't take shit from people." He says and it sounds like he's about to rattle off a list. "I know that you pride yourself on your independence so it's difficult for you to ask for help. I know that you're smart because no teenager picks out classic English literature to read in their leisure time…"

I'm facing in his general direction, confused as to who this kid is and why is he still here talking to me? He'd done what Mr. Pinkard ordered but yet he is still here questioning me and dissecting me. I hear him flip through the pages of what sounds like a magazine.

"I know that one of the top schools for the blind is right here in this county and yet you're here at a public school…" The page turning stops and he doesn't say another word, but I can almost feel the question he is either intending to ask or has changed his mind about asking. I answer the unspoken question anyway.

"I wanted real life experiences," I say. "I wasn't going to learn about the real world by staying at a school where everyone is the same. I didn't want anything holding me back." And I cannot believe I am saying all of this to a complete stranger. Not that it's a big deal or some huge secret, but I am not one to have too many words for people I don't know.

"That's brave," he says and it is almost like I can hear the smile in his voice. "...and who could pity anyone who is that brave?"

I'm fighting a smile, but I lose that battle. This Barnaby character is *odd* because he doesn't seem his age, *annoying* because he won't go away, *talkative* because his words keep yanking me out of my library euphoria, *inquisitive* because he won't stop asking questions, and with all of that, he seems to be a genuinely nice person.

"Thank you," I say and my words fall from my lips lightly in a very weird way. "I mean, for helping me with everything today," I add for some reason.

"I feel like you're dismissing me," he laughs.

"No," I shake my head. "I mean, I *do* have it from here but I was just saying...I'm trying to be polite." I say exasperatedly.

"You're doing one hell of a job," he says sarcastically and though he can't see it because of my sunglasses, I roll my eyes, a habit that apparently blindness could not change.

"Well, if you're going to stay, help me find *Pride & Prejudice*," I say and turn back toward the shelf. That is as close to polite as I can get with him clearly. Barnaby Parks is like a double edged sword.

"Hmmm," he says as I hear him walk away.

I sigh, "Here you go with the *hmmm* again." I say it under my breath, not even sure if he can hear me, but then he laughs. He is back by my side.

"Here," he says handing me the book. "Why do you like *Pride & Prejudice*?"

"Why *wouldn't* I like *Pride & Prejudice*?"

"I guess the predictability of it all," he states and now I have the sudden urge to defend my favorite book.

"In what ways?" I nearly snap. "It's one of the most well written and beautifully told love stories of all time."

He doesn't say anything at first and I can hear something tapping, I think he is drumming his fingers on the bookshelf. "The buildup for Mr. Darcy and Elizabeth was so agonizing that you almost want to skip all of the pages just to get to the point. You read 300 pages just for two pages of the happily ever after and it was a little anticlimactic, if you ask me."

I want to bark *well no one asked you!* But I had actually asked him. I sigh in annoyance, "That's because it was realistic."

"It's realistic to deeply hate the person that you're eventually going to love and spend the rest of your life with?"

"Very," I say clipped, I can feel my cheeks getting hot. I take bashing my favorite book as a personal attack.

"Elaborate?" he asks and he is not letting up and that only annoys and fuels me more.

"The love of someone's life doesn't show up on your doorstep in a basket with a bow, ready and willing to be everything you've ever dreamed of," I say placing the book on the shelf. "It's not supposed to be perfect, it's not supposed to be all butterflies and happily ever afters. Austen wrote about the many sides of infatuation, how you can learn to tolerate someone, you can learn to like someone, you can learn to love them. Love at first sight, first impressions ... that's all make believe. It's *realistic* to know who you're getting and, once you've got them, it's important to *want* to keep them; you can't do that through rose colored goggles."

My rant is over and I hadn't spoken so passionately about something in quite some time. It felt good but also embarrassing. Maybe I am too worked up? But there are only a few things in my life I am passionate about. Literature is one of them.

"Hmmm," he says. After everything I said, after he purposely egged me on, his response is *hmmm*.

"Ugh!" I say and search my fingers along the shelf to pick the book back up. "You're so frustrating!" And I wasn't expecting to say that, but the words are out of my mouth before I even know what I am saying. Maybe I *am* overreacting?

"Is that your *first impression* of me?" he says. I don't say anything. I grab my cane and start walking until I found the stairs we'd come up.

"I'm grabbing your elbow," he says and before I can snap and say *I got it* he is gripped to my elbow and we are walking down the stairs. I don't object because I still don't know where the front desk is.

I check out my book and we head out the door, he holds on to my elbow all three flights of stairs. We don't say a word to each other the entire time. Once we make it to the landing he lets go. "Same time tomorrow," he says in a very friendly tone and, as I am preparing to tell him *no,* I can hear him already walking away, almost like he is jogging.

Barnaby Parks is by far the most odd and most annoying person I've ever met.

∼∼

I hear my bedroom door open and my sister plops down on my bed, nearly knocking my book over.

"Tell me everything," she says and she sounds so nervous. "How was it?"

"It was fine, how was *your* day?"

"Mazie, don't mess with me," she snaps and I force myself not to laugh. "You found everything okay? You didn't need help?"

My mind flits to Barnaby, the odd boy who didn't seem to have a filter or an off button, but he did help me.

"Mr. Pinkard sent someone with me to go to the library. They have a lot of Braille; I'm going to go every day during my free period."

"Who did he send with you?"

Of course she'd pick up on the part of that sentence I did not want to talk about. "Some kid in my class."

"Hmm," she says. What the hell is it with everyone today and their damn *hmmms!?*

"What's wrong?" Maya asks as she reads my facial expression.

"Nothing, I'm just tired. It's been a really long day."

"Oh, okay," she says slowly, and then she pauses for a moment before speaking again. "You sure you're alright?"

"Yes, Maya… just sleepy," I answer. I even offer a smile.

I feel her getting up from my bed, "Have you eaten? I'm ordering a pizza."

"I'm fine," I say.

"Okay, goodnight Mazie –My."

"Night Maya –Me."

I hear her leave and close my bedroom door and I sigh.

I close my book and lay back on my bed, just letting my mind wander. Today wasn't as bad as I thought it would be other than getting lost on my way to the library. My thoughts flit to Barnaby again, he is so weird and I am not quite sure if that is a good thing or a bad thing or if it's a thing that even matters at all.

I laugh and shake my head realizing that last week I was so angry that no one acknowledged me and then today I was so angry when Barnaby wouldn't leave me alone. It's clear I am not sure what exactly I want, but I am absolutely sure my stubbornness is playing a big role in this.

I got that from my mom; she was a strong woman, but so unbelievably stubborn. Maya always told me that my mother and I were the last two people in the world she would ever want to get into an argument with because, even if we were clearly wrong, we never budged from our stance. I think that's a good character trait to possess.

Maya is just like our father; he, for the most part, had a very calm and welcoming demeanor. He didn't take things too seriously and that's how Maya is. Very few things got her worked up so when she gets upset or frustrated you know it's something serious or something important to her.

I remember when we would have family game nights. It would be me and my mom versus Maya and our dad. My mother and I would always get frustrated and yell and lose our tempers when we lost. Maya and dad would laugh at us and say *it's just a game* and when they lost they didn't take it to heart. It's hilarious how polar opposite we all were, but blended together, we were perfect.

I missed my mother. I missed my father. I missed them every second of every day.

I sigh and decide it'll be better to go to sleep than to think about them right now.

The next day I walk into Mr. Pinkard's classroom, clinking left and clinking right, to find my desk.

"Good morning, Ezmerelda." I hear as I sit down.

"Barnaby?" I immediately recognize his voice.

"In the flesh," he answers.

"Are you sitting next to me?" I ask as I get settled into my seat. I hadn't noticed him at all last week, but Maya was sitting next to me and I was deliberately tuning out every single student in this school so I could focus on my school work.

"Yes."

"Have you always sat there?"

"Not always, I've sat in other chairs in my life but the last seven days since school started? Yes, I've been sitting here during this class," he says assuredly. I sigh at his stupid joke.

"...and it's Mazie, *just* Mazie," I say angrily and he chuckles.

Class starts and we don't say another word to one another. One hour and thirty minutes goes by quicker than I expect for a Tuesday. The bell rings and I hear students rushing out, chairs screeching, desks moving, and loud voices filling the room.

"Are you going to the library?" he asks.

I hesitate at first but I have a feeling that no matter what I say I am going to end up spending my free period with Barnaby.

"Ummm, yeah."

"Alright, let's go," he says and I sigh. I am still mad at him for his assault on *Pride & Prejudice,* but it doesn't matter at this point. I stand from my desk and he immediately places my cane in my hand.

"Oh, thanks," I say as we walk out of the classroom.

We are walking in the hallway silently. Since it is a free period, there aren't many students in the hallway. I can tell because it isn't as loud as it normally is throughout the day.

"On a scale of one to ten, how angry at me are you?" Barnaby asks, finally breaking the silence.

"Fifteen," I answer and he starts laughing a loud boisterous laugh. I try not to smile, but it's hard because he has one of those laughs that almost force you to join in. I am able to keep my composure.

"All because we share a difference of opinion?" he finally asks.

"No," I say. "Because I clearly think that book is important and you thought it was funny to egg me on and then not even say anything afterwards. It's irritating."

He's quiet for a moment and I almost think he's going to apologize, but I'm wrong.

"Learning every side of something is the only way we see things in a new light, even if it's what we don't want to hear. Me not liking that book isn't going to make you like it any less but you will realize that there are imperfections in things you once thought were perfect. That's life," he says "…I wasn't egging you on, I wanted to hear your point of view so that my view of the book could realize new light too."

I don't know what to say; he is so many different people in one. One second he's annoying and the next he's saying things like this. Things that make sense and could be deemed profound by some.

I exhale. "You're right, Barnaby," I say and it almost burns to admit.

"Doesn't mean that a healthy debate isn't always on the table. That's another way we learn," he laughs and I don't say anything as I silently eat crow. He grabs my elbow and we head up the stairs to the third floor library.

Three

Peace (n.): a state in which there is no war or fighting

It's been three weeks and this is my routine with Barnaby: we go to the library together, he bothers me, we argue about something, he tries to make me laugh, I force myself not to, we argue about something else and then do it all over again the next day.

Yesterday we got in a huge argument about American literature versus English literature and basically I've concluded that Barnaby Parks is the smartest *idiot* I have ever encountered in my entire life. He has absolutely no respect for the classics and I can hear it in his voice that he finds joy in pissing me off. All that crap he said about *realizing different views* of things means nothing because I am convinced he likes fighting with me and I am forever unable to be the bigger person, so I always fall into his trap.

I was so angry with him when I stormed off yesterday that I decided I would no longer need his assistance. I would have peaceful free periods from here on out, not ones filled with his Barnaby babble and our inevitable arguing.

"Are you ready?" Barnaby asks.

"For?" I ask as if I have no clue what he is talking about.

"Library field trip, of course," he answers cheerfully. He grabs my book out of my hand and hands me my cane. I sigh.

"I think I have a pretty good idea of where the library is, I don't need your help today. Thank you." I hope he detects my annoyance. He laughs and that just irritates me more.

"I haven't helped you in two weeks, I am very aware of the fact that you can find the library by yourself. I was planning on joining you," he says casually, clearly not paying my passive aggressive, silent, and invisible tantrum any mind. "You enlightened me," he adds as I stand up from the desk. I can hear the last of the students leaving the classroom.

"How is that?" I ask off of reflex and I am immediately kicking myself, because engaging him is the last thing I want to do. I clink left and clink right out of the classroom. Barnaby is close behind holding my copy of *Pride & Prejudice* and our English homework. I am realizing quickly that there is no point in trying to ignore Barnaby, his presence evoked acknowledgement. He is going to go to the library no matter what I do or say. I can always go somewhere else but where? And also, I have a feeling he'd just follow me there too.

"About *Pride & Prejudice*,"

"Oh God, I really don't want to debate this again. We clearly have different tastes, let's just leave it at that," I say dismissively.

"I think I see your point of view now," he says as if I hadn't spoken at all. "I went home last night and reread it."

"The *entire* book?"

"Yeah," he says quickly, "...I think I understand the allure of the buildup now."

"You do?" and I honestly can't tell if he is patronizing me or being completely serious. One thing I do know for sure is that Barnaby has a lot to say about a lot of things.

"Yes, two people who seem like the complete opposite. Two people who aren't particularly getting along somehow learn to appreciate the other person's flaws. I get it, I feel the symmetry."

"The symmetry in what?" I ask as we get to the steps. He grabs my elbow and we begin to walk up.

"Just real life."

"So it is realistic to you now?"

"You can't choose how you find love or how it finds you," he says. "Whether it's in a basket with a bow on it or not..."

I smile and say, "A very wise woman once said that."

Barnaby laughs and I keep my smile in place.

"Well, I am glad you have come to your senses," I add.

We walk up the last few steps to the third floor landing. "I'm always willing to learn and admit when I am wrong," he says easily.

"That's good to know," I agree. He lets go of my arm to open the library doors.

"It is?"

"I mean," I don't know why I suddenly feel cornered by his response. "In general …it's always good to admit when you're wrong."

"I have a feeling that's preaching you don't practice often?"

I stop walking and can sense him coming to stand in front of me inside of the library. "Are you implying that I am stubborn?" I question him accusingly. It is no secret that I *am*, but it is still offensive to be called out on it so casually from someone other than Maya.

"Yes, I am," he admits simply which catches me off guard. I wasn't expecting him to be blunt about it.

"Well, you're exasperating," I counter.

"That I am."

I just stand there not knowing what to do or say next when I hear a low gurgle coming from Barnaby. "You're laughing at me?" I question.

"Maybe a little, you're a very entertaining person, Ezmerelda."

"How many times do I have to tell you, my name is Mazie?"

He laughs and I sense him walk away. I sigh and turn slightly to the left and start to walk toward the Braille section. Once I get to the small set of steps I feel Barnaby grab my elbow. We walk in silence until we get to the books.

"What's on the agenda today?" he asks, his hand still holding onto my elbow.

"Silence," I say under my breath and he starts to laugh again.

"Am I really irritating you that much?" he asks. "You're still that mad about yesterday, even though I reread *Pride & Prejudice* as a peace offering?"

"Yes."

"Hmmm," he says and I sigh which makes him laugh even louder. All he does is laugh and annoy me. Those are his biggest character traits, his biggest character flaws. He finally let's go of my elbow.

"Can I start over?" he asks and I can feel that he is standing directly behind me. It doesn't matter what I say to him, he isn't going to go away. He might as well attempt to start over.

"Do whatever you want, Barnaby," I say as I continue to search for more classics.

"I have a non- annoying or irritating question to ask you," he states and the humor in his voice is too blatant to ignore. I hate that I am annoyed by him but at the same time still trying to stifle laughter. I do not want him to think I am enjoying his company because I would much rather be alone. "How are you doing your English paper?" he continues.

I shrug. "The same way you're going to do yours."

"That's what I was getting at; Pinkard said we could partner up with people…"

"I don't work well with others," I say and there is a hint of humor in my tone.

"I definitely believe that," he laughs and I flip my middle finger up at him, causing him to laugh even louder.

"You're going to get us kicked out of the library," I whisper forcefully, trying to keep my own laughter at bay.

"Be my partner on this paper," he demands.

"No," I answer. "Don't you have friends in that class you could ask?"

"Yeah, a couple," he admits. "But you're much more interesting than they are and, besides, I think *we* are friends at this point."

I don't respond because I really don't know how to, but he's right. He is the only person other than teachers that I really speak to in this school on a regular basis. I guess we are friends.

"Be my partner or I'll start yelling and singing so loudly that they permanently ban us."

I huff. "I thought you said you were starting over, that you were going to ask a non- annoying or irritating question?"

"I did ask a non- annoying or irritating question. Your answer is what is annoying and irritating."

I shake my head. "You're truly impossible," I say under my breath.

"Ten, nine, eight, seven…"

"What are you doing?" I interrupt.

"It's how many seconds you have left to agree to be my partner before I do my best rendition of "Single Ladies" by the great Beyoncé at the top of my lungs."

"Barnaby …"

"…six, five, four,"

The mixture of annoyance and amusement I am experiencing right now is off of the charts. I decide to call his bluff. I shrug and go back to trying to find some books to checkout.

"…three, two…" he whispers so lowly that if I weren't hyperaware of him standing right next to me I wouldn't have been able to hear him. "One."

I pay him no mind and then in a loud boom that causes me to jump, I hear, *"All the single ladies, all the single ladies!"*

He's yelling so loudly that I know every single person in this library can hear him.

"Barnaby!" I screech forcefully trying to focus on being angry and embarrassed, ignoring the urge I have to laugh. He is still going and doesn't seem like he is going to let up.

"Up in the club …something… something… something…" he mumbles. "I should've picked a different song," he says loudly, "I didn't realize I didn't know all of the words. To the chorus!" he exclaims, continuing to yell, *"If you like it then you should've put a ring on it!"*

"Okay!" I finally concede, "Okay, just shut up!" I say reaching out and grabbing his shirt as if this gesture is an off switch.

"*Okay*, what?" he asks and his voice is still loud.

"We can do the damn paper together, just shut up, please!" I practically beg.

"Okay, you can pick the topic," he whispers, and then he grabs my wrist from its grip on his shirt slipping his hand down over mine. I pause for an exaggerated moment as our hands are linked together before I pull away from his hold.

It's quiet and then I feel him move closer to me. "Something on your mind?" he asks and his voice is serious and soft. *What is happening right now?* My stomach feels warm all of a sudden, my heart picking up its pace just slightly. I swallow and shake my head.

"No," I manage to say. "I was waiting for security or a disgruntled librarian to storm up here." My tone is flatter than I intended it to be.

He doesn't say anything and I hear him walk away and sit down.

I exhale.

He's flipping through pages of what sounds like a magazine as I go back to navigating. I have five books so far. This is my favorite pastime; I could spend hours here if given the opportunity. I touch every single book in the third row, even though I know what I will choose. I have a bad habit of reading the same books over and over again.

"You're quiet," I say to Barnaby after about ten minutes and I don't know why I say it. His silence is all I've wanted for the last three weeks.

"Sorry, I'm just observing," he says. I hear another page turn.

"Observing what?"

"You."

I freeze momentarily then quickly regain my composure. *Observing* …my mind flits back to that first day when I thought he was ignoring me. He'd said he got lost in thought and that it happened to him sometimes when he was observing. At the time I didn't think to ask him what he was observing, but now I have an overwhelming feeling that I now know what –or should I say *who*.

"Me?" I finally say trying to play it off. "Are you just *staring* at me?" I accuse. "Staring at someone when they don't know is impolite. It's also a form of stalking." This is my attempt at keeping it friendly because I am beginning to sense a shift and a weird vibe forming between us and it's making me uncomfortable or at least confused.

He laughs, then I hear movement. He is standing next to me again.

"I could have you arrested," I state, my tone serious.

"You wouldn't have me arrested, who would make you laugh?" he counters.

"You don't make me laugh," I rebut. "Your horrible singing makes me laugh."

"I think I have the voice of an angel," he says and though his tone is serious, I know he is joking.

"Whatever helps you sleep at night, Barnaby," I laugh.

"Do you usually go to lunch after this?" he asks.

"Yeah…"

"In the cafeteria or…"

"Ummm, I usually eat in Miss Strauss' room, not a lot of noise."

"Could I join you?" he asks and now if it wasn't a tad obvious before, I think I know what he is doing. That weird feeling I had before is definitely a shift in the energy between us. The vibe changing by the second was and is something I am unfamiliar with.

"Barnaby, I…" I hesitate.

"Yeah?"

I have no experience in the boy department, so maybe I am completely off. But the little voice in the back of my head is getting louder and louder and I cannot shut her up. She won't stop pointing out that something is going on and I don't know exactly what that *something* is, but I know that I am not ready for it or even thinking about it and that's something I need to make very clear to Barnaby.

"Yeah," I say doubtfully. "You can join me."

∼∼

We are sitting in silence in Miss Strauss' room while I unpack last night's dinner.

"That smells delicious," Barnaby says.

"My sister made meatloaf last night," I say. "Strauss lets me use her microwave; the *pity* has its benefits sometimes."

He laughs. "I got it," he says and for a moment I am confused until I feel him take the Tupperware out of my hands. Four minutes later he is back from the back room, I can hear him place the food down in front of me.

"I could have done that, Barnaby." I say.

"I know you're capable of many things Ezmerelda, but I was just exercising my right to be chivalrous."

"Mazie," and I almost wonder why I am even correcting him at this point. "…and thank you."

"You're welcome," he says and then it is quiet. I can't be sure, but I can sense him staring at me and it's making me self-conscious as I ate. I clear my throat.

"What are you eating?" I say as I take a small bite of my food. "I smell peanut butter."

"A peanut butter and jelly sandwich because I'd rather eat like a five year old than eat whatever it is they serve in this school."

Now *that* I can fully agree with, after my first day here I knew I was not going to eat anything they served here. Maya and I make extra dinner so I can have the leftovers for lunch.

"I don't know the last time I've had a home cooked meal," he says and his voice sounds quizzical like he is trying to actually pinpoint the last time.

"You want half?" I offer.

"No, thank you," and again it's amazing how I am able to tell if someone is smiling.

"You know," I am saying the words before I really gave them much thought. "Since we will be working on the paper together you could come over for a home cooked meal. We try to cook every night as much as we can," I offer and then suddenly, I feel very stupid. "I mean, partnering for the paper saves me a lot of time and we will already be together. No, I mean, we always have extra food and if you're going to be there, you might as well have…"

"Yes, I would love that. When?" he interrupts my rambling and right now I kind of wish I could see how big his smile is.

Somewhere in the back of my mind I know this isn't a good idea, especially if the energy I am feeling from him is real. More time with him surely is not the answer nor a clear indication that I am not interested in him in any way beyond friends, but I am currently ignoring that part of my brain. I am currently drowning out that voice in the back of my head that hasn't stopped screaming since the library.

"Tomorrow night? Does that work for you?"

"It does," he says. "Thank you."

It's quiet again as we go back to eating and my thoughts are going a mile a minute. He's going to be in my house and meet my sister? I am overthinking, obviously. Right? Friends meet relatives, friends hangout at each other's houses. This isn't a big deal.

"You said we?" he asks, tearing me from my jumbled thoughts. "Your parents? Or your sister?"

I swallow and take a deep breath. "My sister, Maya, is my guardian. My parents died some time ago." I say and I quickly stuff some more food in my mouth. I hate having to tell people that. They always say things like *I am so sorry* or *what happened?* or *I'll pray for you.* I really hate when people say they are sorry, what's the point in saying that? I never know how to respond. Are you the reason they are dead? Did you take them from me? It's always so frustrating for me, even if it's irrational frustration.

"That's hard," he says. "I hope you have found peace, Mazie." He continues and I stop chewing. No one has ever said anything like that to me before; it takes me by complete surprise.

"I...I think I have in a way, or at least acceptance," I manage to say.

"Acceptance is another form of peace or it can be, I think. If you want it to be..."

"I do," I say quickly and a calming feeling fills my chest and I have to ignore it before certain emotions get the best of me. "Thank you, Barnaby." I add softly, not wanting to delve too much further into the topic of my parents.

He doesn't say anything as we continue eating and I realize that when I said Barnaby was a double edged sword, I was not giving his *many* sides the proper justice.

Four

Friendship (n.): a friendly feeling or attitude: kindness or help given to someone

"So…" my sister says as I hear her put a pot on the stove.

I don't respond and I start to set the table. I already know what she is going to say.

"He is a classmate of yours?" she questions.

"Yes." I've already been over this with her.

"Do you like him?"

I sigh and roll my eyes. "Like I told you before, he is coming over because we are writing an English paper together. Stop putting too much into this."

"Was dinner part of your English paper?"

I pause and then place another plate on the table before walking into the kitchen. "He was probably already going to be here because of the paper and he mentioned not having a home cooked meal in a long time. It's really not a big deal. Could you not be weird about it?"

"You never answered the question though..."

"What question?" I am beyond annoyed with her right now and she knows it, but she clearly doesn't care.

"Do you like him?" she asks again and then there is a knock at the door. I exhale, all my frustration is in that single breath. Maya yells *come in* as we both walk into the living room together.

"Hi," Maya says immediately. "I'm Maya."

"Hello," Barnaby says, "Barnaby, it's a pleasure to meet you."

"Good evening, *Ezmerelda*," the humor in his voice is blatant and I have the urge to kick him. He is so incredibly annoying and he hasn't even been here for a full minute yet.

"Hey," I say sourly.

"Dinner will be ready shortly," Maya says. "Have a seat on the couch."

I turn back into the kitchen to help with the final touches and then I hear Maya walking in. "Mazie, he's gorgeous!" she whispers in my ear excitedly. I don't respond. I open the fridge to get the pitcher of water.

"Oh, come on," she whispers expectantly.

"Come on, *what*?" I snap. "I *just* asked you to not be weird about this."

"Has anyone described him to you?" she asks ignoring me all together. "Don't you want to know?"

"No, I don't want to know." I lie because I did actually want to know. I know what I imagined, but I really didn't need to have a shallow bone in me trying to judge his looks and besides it didn't matter. He's my only friend at that school, who cares how he looked. He could have a third eye and one tooth. It wouldn't matter at this point. My sister is being ridiculous.

"He's at least 6 ft," she says still ignoring me.

"*Amaya*," I try to interject, but she is in her own world right now.

"His hair is super thick and brown; he is on the slender side, but he is not bony. His eyes are big and dark brown. He has a distinctive jaw line, and a little bit of facial hair, and his teeth are perfect. You should ask him if he had braces as a child. He really is gorgeous. His complexion is like a smooth …"

"Can you finish up in here?" I ignore her. "It's rude to have company waiting."

"You're right, go be with Barnaby." I don't like the smile in her tone when she says it, like there is a double meaning in her words. I walk into the living room and just stand there.

"Hey," Barnaby says and it sounds like he's patting the couch, "Sit down, you look stressed."

"Gee, thanks," I say as I take a seat next to him.

He laughs. "No, I mean –what's on your mind?"

"My sister is just being weird."

"How so?" he asks.

"She thinks…." I hesitate, because I don't want to tell him that my sister thinks we are more than just friends or will be more than just friends because we won't. "It's nothing, did you pick a topic?" I try and change the subject.

"*You* were going to pick, remember?" he says. "You seem really distracted, are you sure you don't want to talk about it?" he asks and I feel his warm hand on my knee. I stand up from the couch faster than I intended to and clear my throat.

"Mazie…" he begins to say.

"I have to help Maya with the last touches," I interrupt. "Just make yourself at home, turn the television on if you want," I say quickly, then I turn around to walk into the kitchen, slightly bumping my shoulder into the doorway which never happens.

"What's wrong?" Maya says once I make it past the door. I can hear that she's opened the stove.

"Is dinner almost ready?"

"Yeah, it's done. I just have to put the…"

"Dinner's ready!" I yell so Barnaby can hear me and then I turn around and walk out to sit at the dining room table.

I'm freaking out and it's my sister's fault for saying all of those stupid things and it's Barnaby's fault for trying to spend all this extra time with me and for saying sweet things and for touching my leg. I exhale.

I hear a chair being pulled out beside me and I know it's Barnaby. "Are you okay?" he leans over and whispers in my ear.

"Yeah, I'm great," I say and my voice overshoots the mark. I sound off, I sound like someone who is anything, but great.

I hear Maya walk into the dining room placing items on the table. "Okay, dig in!" she exclaims. We are having chicken, green beans, and mashed potatoes. It was my idea to make this; it seemed like a really *home cooked meal* type of thing to eat.

"Thank you so much for preparing this. I was telling Ezmerelda that I haven't had a home cooked meal in quite some time."

My nerves are so shot that I don't even attempt to correct him this time.

"It's no problem," Maya says to Barnaby. "...and you have an open invitation," she adds and I almost choke on my water.

"I will definitely take advantage of that offer."

I take a bite of chicken and just focus on chewing. Chew, chew, chew, chew, and swallow. Repeat.

I know I am being ridiculous and I am embarrassing myself. I need to shake this feeling. I decide in that moment that I need to just be who I've been with Barnaby. My sister's prying shouldn't change that and Barnaby just being a decent person shouldn't make me think he feels a certain way about me.

Maybe he isn't flirting or being weird; maybe it's all in my head because a boy has never made me laugh before, a boy has never been this patient and kind to me before, a boy has never wanted to be my friend. Maybe *I* am turning this into something it isn't.

I find my composure and try vigorously to bury any and all thoughts and assumptions that can cause me to freak out again.

"So," Maya says, "Tell me about yourself. Mazie only said you guys were doing a paper together. No other details."

I fight the urge to throw my drumstick at her. Why would there be any need to tell her anything more about him?

"What would you like to know?" he asks.

"Any siblings?"

"Yes, an older brother and a younger sister. My sister and I live with our father," he says. I didn't know Barnaby had siblings, and he only mentioned his father. I wonder what happened to his mother.

"And I'm assuming you're a senior since you're in Mazie's class?" she asks. I don't know what is with my sister, why is she asking him all of these questions? And as soon as I have that thought I realize, this is what *small talk* is. I take another bite of chicken.

We need to hurry up and eat so this can be over.

"I am actually graduating early, kind of. I skipped tenth grade, so technically I would be a junior this year. I'm taking some college courses now," he says and my jaw drops as I turn to his direction. I had absolutely no clue and in this moment I am realizing other than the fact that he annoys the living crap out of me and that he in equal parts makes me laugh –I don't know anything about him. For the last three weeks he's asked me so many questions, *too* many questions and other than a few trivial questions here and there, I've asked him nothing. Maya's gotten more from him in fifteen minutes than I did in nearly a month.

"You're a junior?" I question and I try to hide the astonishment in my voice.

"I'm a senior. I've taken enough credits to graduate this year…" he says.

"How old are you?" I ask.

"Seventeen," he says and his voice is a little lower, almost like he didn't want to admit his age. "I started kindergarten late so I'll still graduate at eighteen. I guess it wasn't so much as skipping a grade as it was getting caught up to one."

"Hmmm," I say and he laughs. I then realize that I'd used his *go to* response to most things, a response that I hate. I try to stifle my own laughter.

"Wow," Maya says. "That's amazing, what college are you taking your courses at now?"

Right now I am irrationally jealous of my sister. She knows all the right questions to ask. Am I bad at being a friend? Am I too unbelievably self-absorbed in my own world that I am incapable of holding a conversation if it didn't directly pertain to me? What else don't I know about Barnaby?

"The community college," he answers, "it's basically dual schooling. My freshmen year of college will actually be my sophomore year. I'm hoping to go to MSU next fall."

"MSU is on Mazie's short list of colleges," she offers and the excitement in her voice is a little too much. Again I have the urge to throw something at her.

"Oh, is it?" he asks and I can sense that he is staring at me. "I'll inquire about their Braille selection." he says and I smile.

"MSU is on the list," I say, "…but there is no way I'd be able to be that far away from Maya." I admit. Going away to college is fun to think about in theory, but I can't leave Maya, there is no way I will ever be ready for something like that. I can crave independence and still need Maya, right?

"Silly girl, I'd just follow you there!" she says and we all laugh and finally my nerves are completely calm.

As the evening moves along, we talk about random things. We talk about our favorite television shows, our favorite movies, and the kind of music we all like. My sister brings up literature and I immediately want to change the subject because Barnaby's opinion is practically *always* wrong when it comes to literature. It also doesn't help much that my sister is in her thirties and her favorite genre to read is Young Adult fiction books geared toward people half her age. *I* even judge her sometimes, so I just know Barnaby will have a mouthful about her fantasy reading choices.

Surprisingly, he is on his best behavior. He doesn't try to egg her on or get me worked up like he does so often. He doesn't dissect and discredit her favorite books like he's done with mine. I have a feeling it's intentional because what I do know about Barnaby is that he is never short of an opinion. Maybe he only holds such contempt toward things *I* like.

"I wish I could hang out longer," my sister says, "but I have to be up at 4 am for my shift. Think I'm going to turn in." I hear her stand and push her chair in. "It was so nice meeting you, Barnaby; I hope to see you around here often."

Sigh, why can't she just say goodnight and walk away like a normal person?

"You will, goodnight, Maya," Barnaby says and I furrow my eyebrows, not sure if anyone can see my reaction or not. He plans on being *around here often*? Well that is news to me, the English paper won't take longer than a week tops to complete.

"Goodnight, you two," she says. The smile is blatant in her voice as I hear her walk away.

"I'm going to clear the table and we can get started on the paper," I say while getting up.

"Hey, what's been going on with you?" Barnaby questions and he grabs my wrist lightly. I pause then tug my arm away. "That right there." He says and he sounds miffed. I stand completely up and feel around the table stacking cups and plates that are within arm's reach.

"Are you going to help me?" I finally ask, trying to deflect, which I know will not work.

"I can't touch you?"

And I am taken aback. I swallow because I know he is blunt, but *damn*. I don't answer and I walk into the kitchen. I hear him stacking items from the dining room table and then I hear him walk in and place what he's collected into the sink.

"Mazie," he says. He isn't going to let this go? He really wants to have this conversation now? I don't even know what this conversation is, but I know right now is not the time. We need to focus on this paper and nothing else. I thought I did well at dinner, I stopped being weird about the imaginary things Maya put into my head. I really wish he'd just drop it.

"No, you can't touch me!" I blurt out and I don't mean to snap at him, but that is how it came out. "And I don't have to explain why."

"I'm sorry," he says immediately, "I didn't mean it like that. I just…"

"I didn't mean it like that either…" I admit before pausing, trying to figure out my words. "I don't have a problem with you touching me." The words playback in my head, and, holy crap, that came out wrong! I quickly correct myself, "I mean, we're *friends*, Barnaby." There, I say it as clear as day. No grey areas, no confusion.

"I know that."

I exhale, "…and I don't think, I just think that…" I wish I wasn't so easily flustered by him. It would be a lot easier to get this sentence out.

"You just think what?" He asks and it almost sounds like he is pleading. I'm not exactly sure what's happening right now, but my chest feels hot and I can feel my heart beating in the tips of my fingers.

"I want us to stay friends," I nearly whisper, "I don't want to confuse things."

I am not even sure if what I am saying is making sense, but something shifted yesterday with Barnaby and me. Maybe I am completely off the mark and this could very well be the most embarrassing moment of my life *or* maybe I am right with what I am feeling and if so, I definitely need to stop it before it goes any further.

It's the truth though, I want to stay friends. He is my only friend at that school and I don't want him to think I am rejecting him. I don't want him to stop being my friend because he possibly wants more. It honestly doesn't make sense for him to feel that way about me, but I can't shake it.

"Okay, Ezmerelda," he says and his voice is calm and agreeable.

"Okay?" and I am unable to hide my shock. I am also unable to correct him for calling me Ezmerelda.

"Yes," he says. "Have you given anymore thought on what play we should choose for the paper?"

That's it? *King Asker of Questions* has nothing else to say? I should probably feel relief, but I don't. *Am* I off the mark? Have I been feeling the wrong vibes and concocted something that doesn't actually exist and he is showing me mercy by not embarrassing me about it? Or maybe I put too much thought into it and he just doesn't care that much to give it any real energy. I swallow and sigh. This is what I want so there is no need to harp over it. We are on the same page. We are moving on.

"I was thinking we could do *A Doll's House*?"

"Ibsen…" he says lowly, I can hear the hint of protest. "…hmmm."

I sigh again, but this time I sound drained. "*Please* don't tell me you have issues with Ibsen too?"

"Is that a rhetorical question?" he counters.

"What? No! How would that be a rhetorical question? It isn't obvious to *not* like Ibsen. I actually can't believe you're telling me you don't like him. I'm starting to think that you don't like anything."

My words are coming off a little condescending and I don't mean for them to, but seriously I am beginning to think he just enjoys arguing with me. He probably has a secret collection of Jane Austen, Charlotte Bronte, and Virginia Woolf writings hidden under his bed, writings that he probably has memorized. He probably has a secret obsession with Henrik Ibsen and has read every single play he'd ever written. I'm sure *A Doll's House* is even his favorite.

"I never said I didn't like him, it's just an interesting choice." I hear him walk away into the living room and I follow. "And actually, I like a lot of things and I doubt you'd be surprised at the things I liked," he says and I actively ignore what feels like a double meaning in his words. I am overanalyzing again. I am sure of it.

I exhale in one quick puff and stay on topic.

"You're kidding right?" I say. I sit down next to him on the couch. I hear him unzipping something then I hear a beeping sound, he's turning on his laptop. "How is it an *interesting* choice? What issues could you possibly have with Ibsen?"

"It's not an issue with him exactly, It's just…"

"It's just what?"

"You just have a type." He says under his breath as he starts typing.

"What is *that* supposed to mean?" I have no clue what he is talking about, but I know I am offended anyway.

"*A Doll's House* is fine, Ezmerelda."

"Mazie!" I snap, "...and what does that mean I *have a type*?" Now *he* is being the condescending one. He isn't going to try and placate me and act like my choice of play and playwright is beneath him.

"There's always some type of discontent with the stuff you like is all, it's not a bad thing. It's an interesting thing, but not bad."

"Discontent?" I snarl, "Because Nora is a strong woman? Because she realizes she deserves better, that she deserves happiness?" I dive right into the pages of the play figuratively. At this very moment, I feel like I am defending real people.

"I won't argue that," Barnaby agrees. "I think everyone deserves happiness, but she was immature and a liar and, in the end, look at her and her husband, an unhappily ever after..."

"Because it wasn't real!" I counter.

"What wasn't real, their marriage?"

"Well yeah, but more specifically their love. The whole point of this play wasn't just about Nora being one of the first well written feminist heroines, it was about learning that complacency isn't love, domination and submission aren't love. The play is trying to scream at us that real love can only exist between equals who would do anything for each other. An unhappily ever after? I think this play *does* have a happy ending because she was free. And that's the most important thing you can be, especially as a woman. She was going to love herself more than Torvald ever could. *Happily ever afters* don't always have to be the obvious ending. The ending where they float off into the sunset holding hands and the reader can imagine that their favorite characters never had another problem. That's not how life works and anyone who believes that is naïve. You can have a happily ever after standing alone. You can still be content and whole. What rule in writing says otherwise? What rule in life says otherwise?"

It's quiet for a moment and I can already hear him in my head saying *hmmm.* I can already feel the fury and I hope I can resist the urge to kick him out because we really need to start this paper.

"Do you think that's a cynical way of thinking?" he finally asks and his tone isn't as brisk as it had been.

"Yeah, maybe it is, but it's realistic and true either way."

"I agree," he says as he continues typing.

"You do?" I can't hide the surprise in my tone.

"Yes, I read it a long time ago and, maybe because I'm a male, I saw a different view of their relationship, but the way you explained it makes sense. She was still everything that I said, but in regards to their relationship, you're right. They weren't equals and her need to be heard and her need to be truly loved could never happen in that marriage. Nora grew a lot and Torvald was self-absorbed. I guess the wedge between them was too big for the marriage to be salvageable. I still think that we all are capable of having *happily ever afters.* I also think that we are all capable of sabotaging them too because of doubt and fear, but that's just my opinion."

I sit there not saying anything for an exaggerated moment. I refuse to find any symbolism in his words because I refuse to continue over analyzing every word out of his mouth. He talks too much; I'd drive myself mad if I did.

"I'm full of surprises, I know." He says cutting through the silence.

"I'm gathering that," I say and I'm still slightly shocked. "I think this may be the first time we agree on something."

"That's not true," he quickly refutes. "We both think it's hilarious that your sister reads YA religiously."

I laugh and shake my head, "You noticed that?"

"Yeah," he laughs. "You're a very easy read."

"How come you didn't berate her like you do me?" I ask.

"You think I berate you?" he asks and there is still humor in his voice. "We have friendly discussions and besides I didn't want to be rude or make your sister feel attacked."

"Oh, so it's okay to be rude to me?" I nearly bark. "I constantly feel attacked!"

"Again, friendly discussion between *friends*..." he emphasizes. "...and don't repeat this to Maya, but she is practically an elder, I didn't want to be disrespectful."

The laugh that escapes my mouth is so loud that I am hoping I don't wake or disturb Maya. He's laughing with me for a moment before we both calm at the same time.

"So," he speaks first, clearing his throat and changing the subject. "I typed most of what you said, we only need five pages. I think we should focus on the love theme –or lack thereof, not the feminist angle because that'd be too obvious. What do you think?"

"It's five to seven pages," I correct.

"Overachiever." He rebuts quickly and I shrug with a smile.

"Five to *seven* pages of the love angle?"

"Okay, sounds good to me," I agree.

"Look at us being two mature agreeable *friends.*" He emphasizes that word again and I swallow, are we not past this?

"Barnaby…"

"It's okay," he interrupts. "You were loud and clear."

I don't say anything and he goes back to typing. How is he managing to make it feel normal between us and different between us all at the same time? I am confused, but I ignore it. I don't have the energy to dissect anymore of his behavioral imbalances.

We spend the rest of the night discussing Ibsen as a playwright and *A Doll's House* as a whole. We even manage to not argue about anything else. It has to be a world record for us.

"What are you doing next Saturday?" he asks. My heart stops, and then picks back up at an accelerated speed. Where is this going?

"Umm, I don't know. I don't do much on the weekends," I answer honestly –timidly.

"Are you up for a little adventure?" he asks and I pause, my mouth goes dry that quickly. "Between *friends* of course…" he adds quickly, a hint of humor lingering.

I sigh and I have a feeling he is going to keep throwing that word in my face.

"What did you have in mind?" I ask, because curiosity killed the cat.

"Just be dressed and ready to go by 7 pm," he pauses, "…and wear black."

"Okay, maybe I am not up for some adventure."

"Live a little, you said you wanted real life experiences, right?"

"Yeah, but I have a feeling we aren't talking about the same kinds of experiences."

He laughs and puts his hand on my knee and squeezes. "Just trust me."

I nod, too hyperaware of the grip he has on my knee. He moves his hand quickly. "Sorry," he says lowly and starts typing again. I exhale and try to regroup my thoughts, *get it together Mazie.*

"What do you want to be when you grow up?" he asks and I always have to stop myself from laughing when he blurts out random questions to me that have nothing to do with anything we are talking about. It feels like he legitimately has a never ending sea of questions, ready, locked and loaded at any given time *or* he just truly likes the sound of his own voice. I'm thinking it's an even combination of both.

"Umm…"

"If you could be anything, just like that, what would you be?" he presses. "School didn't matter, money or experience. You could just snap your fingers and *boom* you're in your dream field."

"A writer," I answer honestly. Before I lost my sight, other than reading, all I did was write. It was my favorite pastime. I still have ideas and sometimes I let untold stories play around in my mind when I'm daydreaming, but I haven't written in five years. I can't imagine even trying to get back to that area of my life. It's too far away.

"Then write," he says. He says it like it's the most obvious concept in the world, like I'm an idiot for not having this revelation myself. "I was expecting an answer like an astronaut or president or a Bioinformatics Research Scientist…"

"*Bio* –what?" I interrupt.

"But, writing?" he continues as if I hadn't said anything. "If you want to write, then do it!"

"It isn't exactly that easy."

"Anything worth something isn't going to be easy," he states.

"I wasn't really in the market for a motivational speech tonight," I deadpan.

"You're telling me you want to write, yes?"

I sigh and nod because like so many things, I know he isn't going to drop this.

"…it's your dream?"

"Yes," I snap. My annoyance is deliberate.

"So, I am sorry. I'm failing to see an issue here…"

"Barnaby, it's just not realistic. Can we get back to the paper please?"

"Not realistic! Who the hell told you that?" he snaps.

"Barnaby …"

"You're really stuck on what's realistic and unrealistic to you and it's clearly holding you back! Anything and everything you want in life is realistic." And he's frustrated, but he has no right to be. I should be the frustrated one, hell I am the frustrated one. "Are you really going to give up on your dream without even trying?" he adds.

"It's not the same, okay?!" I snap at him, but my words come out much sadder than I intend them to be.

"What's the biggest thing holding you back?" he asks. He is much calmer now, his tone balancing out. "Are you a shitty writer?" he whispers.

He's trying to make me laugh, so I turn and shake my head so I can recover. "I had a routine," I finally say. "I would write a lot, just zone out and not think about anything else that didn't have to do with my characters and then I would go back and read the words over and over to fix mistakes and add dialogue and detail…it'll just be a hassle now. I don't like that robotic voice thing on my computer that reads my words back to me. There isn't any inflection and it takes away from the story. I don't know, it's just too different. "

"I'll do it," he says.

"Do what?"

"You write and I'll read it to you to help with editing, or you can tell me what you want to write and I type, whatever works for you. What do you say?"

"I say you're crazy and I can't ask you to do that."

"Good thing you didn't ask, I volunteered."

We sit silently for a moment; I'm tapping my foot because I know he isn't going to let this go. I should've just lied and said I wanted to be an astronaut.

"I didn't think you were that kind of person," he says out of the blue.

"*What* kind of person?"

"The kind of person who would rather find excuses instead of acknowledging solutions..."

I can feel it boiling inside of me, he hasn't known me even a month. He has no right to assume I am *any* kind of person.

"...and you're stubborn and you think your way is the only way!" I nearly bark.

"Pots calling kettles black?" he asks quizzically.

I huff, standing up from the couch. I don't know where I'm going to go, maybe my room? He can see himself out.

"Listen," he says, I hear him stand and then he grabs my hand so I cannot leave. "I wasn't trying to piss you off." I can't focus on his words because all of my neurotransmitters are focused on his hand engulfing mine.

"I'm not going to lie to you and say you should drop everything and become a writer because face it, you could be shitty," he says, "...but if by some chance you are talented, and I have this nagging feeling that you are, why waste it? Just give it a shot. What's the worst that could happen?"

"I'd have to spend even more time with you," I say under my breath and he immediately starts laughing. My hand is still in his and my anger towards him is faltering.

"So, am I your editor in chief?" he asks. "Human voice with inflection and all..."

My writing was so personal to me; I'd never shown it to anyone let alone have someone with me during the process of completing it. Just the thought of this is giving me anxiety. But Barnaby is right, I thought I was talented before and I've pretended like I didn't miss my passion. I miss it with all of me. What can it hurt? Am I afraid that he will criticize and tease me? He does that already anyway.

I sigh in defeat and I immediately feel him squeeze my hand.

"...and that won't be such a bad thing," he says.

"What? You being my editor?"

"You having to spend more time with me..." he says and his voice is lower and softer, I can feel the tenor in his voice vibrate through my chest. I move my hand from his and put my hands in my pockets. He laughs humorlessly. "Because *friends* often spend time together," he adds and I roll my eyes.

We go back to finishing the first outline of our paper for another hour or so when I yawn.

"Okay, I can take a hint," he says and I laugh.

"It is late, but I wasn't kicking you out."

"Are you begging me to stay?"

I don't say anything and he starts to laugh, "I'm leaving." I hear him stand from the couch gathering all of his belongings then I walk next to him to the door.

"You have a wonderful night, Ezmerelda. I'm leaning in to kiss your cheek." he says and before I can register his words, I feel his lips quickly press against my skin. It's like someone lit a match and placed it on my face. I am so taken aback that I don't even correct him for calling me Ezmerelda –*again*.

"I platonically peck all of my friends," he says quickly. The humor is there, it's blatant and annoying, "…see you Monday," he adds.

The screen door opens and shuts. I am still standing there and once again Barnaby is either leaving me angry, frustrated, awed, or surprised. I place my hand on my cheek and I can feel the warmth under my palm. I sigh. I feel like all I did tonight was sigh. It's my body's natural reaction to Barnaby because I rarely know what else to say or do.

F_{ive}

Heaven (n.) the place where God lives and where good people go after they die according to some religions (2) Something that is very pleasant or good (3) *the heavens:* **the sky**

For the last week I have been trying to figure out where the hell Barnaby is taking me on Saturday and why the hell do I have to wear all black? What kind of adventure has a dress code?

"Are you taking me to a funeral? Because that's morbid..." I say to him. We are eating leftovers in Strauss' room and he hasn't given me a single clue during my library time and lunch time interrogations.

"No funerals this week," he says.

"Are we going to a miming convention?"

He laughs loudly, "Eat your lunch before it gets cold."

"Are we robbing someone?" I whisper. "A bank robbery? A cat burglary? I won't do well in prison."

"You've waited practically a week, you'll find out tomorrow," he laughs. "It's not really a big deal. It's just something I think you'd enjoy."

I don't answer as I place a piece of broccoli in my mouth and start to chew it angrily.

"You're cute when you're pissed off," he says and I ignore him. "Tell Maya I said thank you for lunch."

I nod and we both go back to eating. I can hear him opening up two cans, placing one in front of me. "Thanks."

His phone buzzes, "Shit," he says and I can tell he has food in his mouth. "I won't be able to come over tonight, but I can come by Sunday to make up for it?"

He's been coming over every day after school to help with my writing. We'd decided to get our English paper out of the way so we could focus on my work, well actually, he decided. I've decided to pick and choose my battles with him.

"That's no problem," I say. "Is everything okay?"

He doesn't answer at first and I suddenly feel like I've stepped over a hidden line.

"Yeah," he finally answers. "Family stuff, it'll be okay," he says passively. I can hear him texting rapidly.

His tone is different than anything I have ever heard from him before, but I leave it alone. He clearly doesn't want to talk about it and I am not going to push it.

"Sunday morning's good..." I say lowly.

It's quiet and I can't put my finger on it, but something is definitely off and I want to ask him what is wrong, but it isn't my place.

"You checked out *Pride & Prejudice* again," he says. "Why?"

"I think we went over this already..."

"No, I mean if it's your favorite book why don't you just own a copy?"

"Oh, well, the version I want is entirely too expensive, so I just get it from a library every couple of weeks or renew it."

"There are different versions?" he asks.

"It's the same wording, just different kinds of Braille books."

"Oh," he says as if I were telling the most interesting story in the world. "What version did you want?"

"It's contracted Braille, but like I said, that ship has long sailed."

"Hmmm," he says and I sigh which makes him laugh.

"You know," he begins to say, "...you *sigh* just as much as I *hmmm*."

"I *sigh* because you are an exasperating person a lot of the time."

"And I *hmmm* because you are a captivating person who leaves me in wonderment all of the time…"

It's quiet and I can, once again, feel my face getting hot, I hope my cheeks aren't turning red right now. I press my chin closer to my chest.

He always manages to slip in flirting or a touch or a kiss on the cheek and it always leaves me stuck in cement unable to respond or react. I know how much he is enjoying this. After he left last week I thought about cancelling our Saturday plans because like a little school girl I kept replaying him kissing me on the cheek over and over again that night.

It was an innocent kiss, the kind you give your relatives over the holidays, but for some reason it sat with me. It was my last thought when I went to sleep that night and my first thought when I woke up in the morning. Then last night he kissed my cheek again but this time he lingered, cupping my jawline in his palm and I was pretty sure I felt my heart palpitate then pick back up rapidly. I heard him laugh as he walked away.

"What's on your mind?" Barnaby questions, snapping me right out of my memory of last night. The humor is blaring in his tone. His words are almost all knowing, like he is very aware that my thoughts are of him at this very moment.

"Just trying to remember where I put my black ski mask for tomorrow is all," I grunt sarcastically making sure to sound like I wasn't thinking about him kissing my cheek and how my entire body felt like it was on fire when he did. He laughs.

And of course, I sigh.

~~

I'm sitting on my porch, wearing all black, waiting for Barnaby to pick me up. I should actually be more nervous or a little more curious as to what is going on and where exactly is he taking me, but for some reason I know whatever we are about to do is going to be ridiculous and more than likely fun.

I hear a car pull up and park in front of my house and right at that moment my alarm goes off on my phone letting me know it's 7 pm. I stand up when I hear a car door open and close. Moments later I hear Barnaby saying *hi* and feel his warm hand wrapping around mine.

"I have my cane," I say quickly.

"Just platonically helping you to the car," he rebuts, like that's an acceptable response. I try so hard not to roll my eyes, but I fail, my sunglasses hiding my annoyance. He helps me in the car and drives off.

"Are you planning on telling me where we are going?" I ask even though I know the answer will be him *not* answering. "Or are you kidnapping me?"

He laughs. "I'm only committing one crime tonight."

"Wait, what?" I screech, as panic creeps up me.

"We are breaking into, or should I say onto, our schools football field," he states simply as if it weren't a big deal.

"What?" I screech again, but louder and in shock. "Why? I mean, no I am not!"

"Don't you trust me?" he laughs. He's laughing at my reaction and I am not finding the humor in this situation at all.

"Absolutely not!" I say and he continues to laugh. "For what reasons would you need to break into our high school and why the hell would you drag me along?"

"The reason? You will find out once we get there and I'm dragging you along because all you do is read classic literature that you've already read, do homework, and pick fights with me every day. You need some fun in your life –some adventure."

"I do not pick fights with you! You always start it!" I refute argumentatively and *still* he's laughing, acting like he does not see my near panic attack unfolding in front of his eyes.

"You're a minor," I add. "If we get caught you get a slap on the wrist. I'm eighteen, I'll be in jail – I already told you I won't do well in prison."

"No one is going to jail," he says unenthusiastically. Finally he isn't laughing. It is making my blood boil, him not taking me seriously right now. "When is your birthday?" he says lowly.

"What?" I heard the question, but it is so random and he is so random that it catches me off guard.

"Your birthday?" he repeats a little louder.

"August 20th," I say quickly, "what does that have to do with anything?"

"Mine is March 7th," he says as if I hadn't said anything. "That's only a few months, not really a big deal if that's what you're worried about," he nearly mumbles.

"What?" and I feel like that is all I've said during this car ride.

"We're here," he says. I feel the car come to a stop, apprehension creeping its way through my entire body, reaching my limbs like a fiery domino effect.

"I am *not* getting out of this car," I state, folding my arms over my chest. I am putting my foot down. I am standing my ground. I am *not* moving.

"*Yes*, you are getting out of this car."

"*No*, I'm not."

"You *are*."

"I'm …"

"We really aren't going to do this all night, are we?" he interrupts. "Please get out of the car I promise you we won't get caught and I promise you it'll be worth it." I hear his car door open and close and seconds later my car door is opening. I sense him reach over me to unbuckle me then he grabs my hand pulling it from my chest where I had it folded.

"If we get caught, *which we won't*, I'll tell them that I kidnapped you. No jail time for you." He adds and the humor is there again. I inhale and exhale. I don't know how much time goes by, but if I am being completely honest with myself, I knew what choice I was going to make as soon as he stopped the car.

Reluctantly, I get out of the car and for the first real time, I am truly trusting Barnaby. We walk for about two minutes hand in hand as he leads the way.

My nerves are getting the best of me and in all honesty I am not sure if my pounding heart is because of my fear or because of our connected hands. I do not want to send him any mixed signals. I was clear last week about where I believed we stood and should remain standing.

"I'm going to climb over the gate, then I'm going to let you in," he says. I nod, not caring if he saw me or not. This is stupid, so stupid. I really should have put my foot down. I really should have just ignored him and this invite. I could be home snuggled next to a book. Instead, I am here committing felonies.

A few moments go by and I hear movement and Barnaby say, "All set."

I hear the loud grinding and scraping of the gate opening. I begin to walk and he immediately grabs my free hand again.

"We are on the field right now. We're going to walk to the fifty yard line," he says. That means we are on the open field, no obstructions to get in the way, just a large flat surface for me to walk forward until he tells me to stop. So, we don't necessarily need to hold hands right now, but we are and I can't move my focus from that. I want to say *I got it from here*, I want to reiterate to him what I said last week, but instead, I continue to let him trudge me along.

"What's at the fifty yard line?" I ask.

"In due time," he says with a chuckle and I grunt.

Finally, after a bit, he stops us. "Okay, just stand here. I'll be right back."

"Where are you going?" I can't seem to hide the alarm in my voice.

"Be patient, I'll be back before you know it."

I grunt again and he laughs in the distance, he's already walked away.

I am just standing here awkwardly. I thought Barnaby was odd before but this put the icing on the cake and maybe I am just as odd as he is, because here I am going along with all of this. For some reason when everything in me is telling me to ignore him, there is something in me that is always interested in finding out what he will say next, what he will do next, how he will piss me off or confuse me next.

I shove my hand into the front pocket of my black hoodie and then out of nowhere I hear music blasting, guitars, drums, and bass are surrounding me completely. I turn as if I can pick from what direction the music is coming from, but it is clearly coming from everywhere. I stop and feel the bass vibrate in my chest, I feel like I am at a concert.

It's a band I'd never heard before but I like it. The music is bouncing throughout the entire football field. Surprisingly, it's nice, *very* nice but who would think of something like this? Break onto school property to listen to music loudly? I can't help but laugh. This is *so* Barnaby, I don't know why or how, it just is.

I sense him walking up to me. His distinctive smell not distorted by the open outdoors.

"This is insane," I say and I can't help the smile that brims across my face.

"Let loose!" he says.

"Ummm," I say confusingly. "What?"

"All your anxiety from the week, all the stress, just let loose. Dance with me!" he says and he sounds so excited, he sounds like he should be jumping up and down from this excitement. Knowing Barnaby, he probably is.

"Yeah, not gonna happen," I say flatly.

"Are you a shitty writer and a shitty dancer?"

I roll my eyes and shake my head.

"No one is watching," he adds.

"That's not true," I correct him immediately, "You would be watching…"

"I don't count," he says, "…and I would never judge you. I only judge your literary choices, you know that."

I can't help, but laugh.

"Come on, I love this song," he pleads. Whatever this song is, it has a fast tempo and a hard bass. It is full of energy and the lyrics are about living life to the fullest. I have a feeling that he chose this song deliberately. I sigh.

"…and you'll be dancing too?" I ask and I can't believe I am even considering this. I don't dance, ever.

"…but of course," he answers assuredly.

I take a deep breath, then let it out slowly. "Okay…" I say and as soon as I say the word I feel his hands grab both of mine. I let my cane fall to the field and suddenly he is spinning me around. My hair blowing wildly against and with the wind, my feet are matching his spins and I am laughing, mouth open, guttural laughs. I can feel him pulling and pushing and jumping and, before I know it, I am pulling and pushing and jumping too.

He lets go of my hands and I spread my arms out as I spin around and around feeling freer than I have felt in years. I can hear Barnaby laughing too and I know he is laughing with me and not at me. He is singing along to some of the lyrics and he has a very nice voice, but I will never tell him that. I take deep breaths and let the cool fall breeze touch every inch of my visible skin as I aim my face upward toward the sky.

We dance and dance and dance. Every new song a new wave of energy conquers me. My heart is racing, the blood in my veins pulsating, my breathing uneven and exhausted but *God*, I am actually having fun! I don't have a single thought, my brain is clear. I just let the music envelope me. My body moves the way it wants with each drop of the bass in its own unique pattern. I am relaxed, letting myself be temporarily unrestricted from anything that'd been weighing me down.

I feel Barnaby grab my hands again and I smile as we twist and spin. We are both laughing like dorks, but it doesn't matter because no one can see us and no one can hear us. I lean forward to push like we'd done before, but instead of pulling, he leans forward too and then I feel his arms wrap around me. He is hugging me and, as the song changes and our feet slow, I am hugging him too.

I have him tightly embraced, just as tightly as he is embracing me and for a moment I don't hear the song and I forget where we are and who we are.

It takes a while for me to remove myself from this moment. Slowly, I can feel the heat in my cheeks, the fluttering in my stomach, and the tightness in my chest. We are folded into one another and I can't muster up the energy I need in order to let go, to back away, to ignore everything that is happening.

I inhale, letting my hands gently fall to my sides.

I dislodge myself from his hold and lay down on the cold grass of the football field, it pricks the back of my neck. I inhale deeply to catch my breath. For a brief moment I pretend that I am looking at the sky, that it's a clear night and I decide to name the stars. The first two are named after my parents. The next two are named Mazie and Maya and the last one is named Barnaby. I pretend that if I just reach my hand straight up, I can touch one of them and bring it down to earth with me.

In my imagination, the star doesn't burn, it just glows and illuminates around me. I pretend that I can *see* all of this, not just feel, not just sense. I can describe it in great detail because I *saw* it with my own eyes.

I hear Barnaby lay down next to me. He doesn't speak and neither do I; it's just our heavy breathing and a new song filling the open space. Then, gently and unexpectedly, I feel his warm hand latch with mine. I think about pulling away, but I don't. He is holding my hand and I am holding his hand too.

"You understand what I'm saying?" he asks out of the blue after about five minutes and I can't help but laugh.

"How often do you do this?" I've finally caught my breath. If there is one thing I learned tonight it would be that I am way more out of shape than I thought I was.

"A couple times a month…" he admits. "I played my freshman year and I ran the scoreboards last year, so I know what nights they don't have security scheduled."

"You played football?" I ask, "Why did you stop?"

He doesn't answer right away and again I am getting that vibe that I've asked a question he does not want to answer, that there is some imaginary line I keep crossing.

"Scheduling issue, missed too many practices," he says quickly, "but yeah, like I was saying I come here a couple times a month. I don't usually dance. I usually just lay here at the fifty yard line and zone out or sometimes I get some homework done. I know it's silly but…"

"No, I would never imagine something this random being so much fun…being so peaceful," I say and he squeezes my hand and it's quiet for a moment as another song comes on.

"It is peaceful; it helps me clear my mind," he says softly. "Somewhere to escape to when I don't want to be home. You don't feel so small here."

"What do you mean?" I ask. His voice had an off note. I can tell he is thinking about something, but I can't be sure.

"I don't know if I can explain it right," he finally says.

"Try me," I reply, squeezing his hand in return – reflexively.

He exhales and then says, "This football field is big in retrospect," he begins, "but compared to let's say the entire high school, or this city, or country… this entire universe –this field is really insignificant. Being here when it is empty puts it all in perspective for me," he pauses. "We have a small presence in the world, but sometimes we want to feel like we are a big chunk of everything that is important, everything that is real and significant, we want to be a part of it all. We want to be felt."

His words are resonating with me. At first, I wasn't sure what he was getting at, but wanting to be felt and truly exist are some of the reasons why I transferred schools. I didn't want to be another faceless blind student in a sea of others who were going through the same experiences.

I want a chance at being me and not being just my handicap. Like he said, I want to be a part of it all too, no matter how terrifying it can be.

"So the football field is the universe in this analogy?"

"The football field is insignificant in this analogy," he corrects. "We are titans on this football field; we are immeasurable on this football field. If someone were to walk in right now they'd see us. They'd know we existed. Our presence wouldn't go unnoticed in this small corner of the world. We are real, living, breathing people. But, in the universe we are trivial, barely specs."

I understand exactly what he is saying and now I am convinced he did write in his free time. These are the kinds of thoughts writers have, I would know.

I cannot see, but I can *feel* the enormity of this field all around me, but when we were dancing, when my mind was free of any conscious thoughts, I felt like he and I were the only people in the world, the only people in the world who had ever danced before. I *felt*.

"So, tonight, we are immeasurable," I exhale, letting him know that I understand.

"We are." I can hear the smile and I can't help but smile too.

"You're a very interesting character, Barnaby Parks," I add, he chuckles but he doesn't respond. It is silent for a few minutes when something dawns on me. "Wait, why'd I have to wear all black, if you knew no one would be here?"

He starts laughing, "No reason, I just wanted to see you freak out for a week. I enjoyed myself."

"Barnaby!" I go to snatch my hand away from his, but he just holds it tighter.

"Forgive me sooner rather than later," he says. "You have to admit that was funny!"

I'm pouting exaggeratedly, but it *is* funny and all I can manage to do is shake my head. He's rubbing his thumb up and down the back of my hand and suddenly my throat has gone dry, now that I am focused on the movement and feeling.

It isn't like an electric charge or that shock you read about in books, but whatever I am feeling whatever this something is, is different and strange. I wonder if he feels it too.

"What do you think is up there?" he says snapping me from my thought.

"In the sky?" I clarify.

"Yeah."

I hadn't really thought about it, but I would like to think there is a heaven up there or at least something close to it. I would like to think that both of my parents are up there

–together and happy watching their daughters figure out life without their presence. I feel like that is a bit much to say to Barnaby, so I flip the question to him.

"I don't know," I finally say. "I'd have to give it some thought. What do you think is up there?"

"Everything," he answers immediately.

"You're very philosophical tonight," I say with a smile. "What do you mean?"

He squeezes my hand again and I continue to ignore the buzzing feeling traveling through my body as our hands stay connected. I am starting to think he knows exactly what he is doing.

"It's you and this football field; it just brings all these thoughts to mind," he chuckles humorlessly. "…and I mean everything. We are all just thoughts and emotions clumped into these different sized and different colored bags of flesh. Then we die."

I burst into laughter. "That's a little dark coming from you," I interrupt.

"I don't think that's dark, I think it's the truth. All of our days are numbered. We all just hope that the number we get is a *really* big one."

He doesn't know how prevalent that has been in my life.

"Who's being the cynical one now?" I question him, trying to stop my thoughts from travelling to a darker place.

He doesn't answer, but he intertwines our fingers, clasping our palms together and my heart is beating so loudly that I am convinced he can hear it too.

I swallow, "You were saying?" trying to distract myself from the buzzing and the loud beating.

"Don't you ever wonder if we are all that we are supposed to be?"

He pauses, waiting for me to answer but I don't. I enjoy hearing him speak. I enjoy navigating through his words, even if they are all over the place and random sometimes, even if I don't always agree. I meant it when I said he was an *interesting character*. I give his hand a light squeeze.

"I don't think I am explaining this right," he continues. "Maybe there really is a deeper meaning to everything, but we won't know now; we aren't supposed to know now. We don't find out until *after*."

I can't ignore the fact that I'm still not pulling my hand away, the fact that I don't necessarily want to pull my hand away.

"Deeper meaning?" I repeat, clearing my throat. "Like, God and the pearly white gates and stuff?" I ask.

"I don't know, maybe, maybe not. Everything has to have a reason or a why though."

Going back and forth is what Barnaby and I do the most. I actually think arguing is the foundation of our friendship. He sounds so passionate about what he is saying just like how passionate I am when I speak about literature. I can't help wanting to give him a taste of his own medicine.

"Maybe there's no deeper meaning," I finally say. "Maybe there isn't some existential reason for everything that is or isn't in this world. Maybe we just *are* until we *aren't...*"

I'm trying not to smirk as I feel him squeeze my hand again. He knows what I am doing, I can tell by the silence hovering.

He makes a sound that sounds like a light chuckle. "*Or* maybe there's rhyme and reason for every little thing that's ever happened and will ever happen. From natural disasters to a small ant being stepped on at a cookout… *maybe* we have less of a choice in this life than we would like to believe. Maybe it's already written? We are given multiple roads to travel, multiple maps to follow but inevitably they all lead to the same place."

I can feel it, our battle of wits tackling each other in a merry-go-round of words. The *what if* game. The game of *hypotheticals* and *maybes*. I want my maybes to outweigh his. He wants his maybes to overpower mine.

"Or *maybe,*" I begin to say and he starts to laugh lowly, "…every single choice is just that. A choice. We choose up when down would have been the better option, the *right* option. The world doesn't end; the moon doesn't vanish taking the tides away with it. We just accept it and move on. If we both died right now, time wouldn't stop. Everything would go on without us."

"And that's the point," he says almost urgently. "Whether superficial or not we are going to do things we hope will leave our print here. It may not mean anything to millions of people but it may mean everything to one person and don't you think that's worth it? We think we have a choice of how our lives will be lived and, in that believing, we hope that when we are no longer breathing, we'd done something meaningful. Even if all of our efforts are for nothing, we still do it because maybe, just *maybe,* it will change everything in what we've left behind."

I don't say anything.

The merry-go-round stops. I am really listening to him. Sometimes these *Barnaby babbles* were full of gems. I exhale softly before speaking.

"So free will is just an illusion?"

Our fingers are still intertwined.

"*Maybe,"* he says. "We are just throwing a bunch of maybes up in the air right now hoping that one lands and sticks, hoping we can make sense of it all." He pauses for a moment before continuing, "maybe –is the safest and most honest answer for most things. Definitive answers stop us in our tracks, the yeses and the noes, but maybe? Maybe leaves the door wide open for anything."

I want to feign ignorance just so he can keep speaking. Just so I can ask him more questions and listen to where his mind travels. Listening to him is like reading a good book, I get lost in the words and the layers, I find myself swimming in the information and meaning unable to detach myself from the plot.

I am holding onto every word he is saying. Of course I won't tell him this, because I don't want him to get the wrong impression and I know he won't let me live it down either.

"Are we done with this?" he asks and the humor is fully back.

"Whatever do you mean?" I reply quizzically and I am smiling. Still, in the back of my mind I am picturing the sky as I look up toward it. That is something I miss, staring at the stars for hours wondering if they knew something we all didn't know, pretty much answering all of Barnaby's *maybes*.

He undoes our fingers and just grabs my hand the way he was holding it before. I feel like he has been holding my hand too long for me to pull it away now.

"The point I was trying to make before you sidetracked me," he says in a low playful tone, "What if we are not at full capacity? What if this is just a placeholder until we are *up there* and then we go from being, I don't know, let's say 40% all of our lives to being 100%? Every single thing you've ever wanted is now accessible. All the answers to our *maybes* are right there." He pauses and squeezes my hand again. "You're probably at 60% already though." he adds.

I ignore his weird compliment, but I think about what he is saying. He and I have never had a conversation like this and I am having a hard time deciphering whether we are joking and being ironic or really shedding new lawyers of our beliefs and personalities to one another.

"Are you talking about heaven again? Or is the *up there* just the up there?" I finally ask, I want to be clear. I don't know where any of this conversation is going but I know I am at least enjoying the ride.

I feel his arm move and I'm assuming he shrugged, "A little of both. They meet somewhere in the middle, one probably more than the other. Who knows, the universe has it all figured out. I don't have all of the answers." There's a hint of humor in his last sentence.

"*Now*, I feel like you're just speaking in riddles to spite me," I say. "You either want to confuse me, impress me, or every single thing you're saying is brilliant and my mind is just too simple to comprehend it." I was trying to make a joke but my words came out much more somber than I intended.

"There isn't a single thing simple about you, Ezmerelda."

"Mazie," I say and I don't even put my back into it when I correct him.

He laughs and then he lets go of my hand. And, surprisingly, I don't like how empty and cold my hand is now that it is no longer in his.

Suddenly, I get a quick and up close whiff of Barnaby's distinctive fragrance. He is hovering over me, I can feel his body heat. I feel and smell his fresh breath on my face.

"I'm going to kiss you," he says softly, but confidently.

"What –" I am unable to finish my sentence because his lips are now on mine. And for a split moment I am going to push him off, close my fists and punch him in his chest until he is not hovering over me, but I accidently allow myself to *feel*, to feel the warmth of his body pressed to mine, the soft plumpness of his lips laying on mine, his warm hand cradling my face in place and in this moment I am lost and I am confused and I am now kissing him too.

I open my mouth, allowing entry and I taste the sweet intoxicating flavor of his tongue. My hands are on both sides of his face as if I am trying to pull him closer to me than he already is. I no longer have a single thought. It is just like when we were dancing, it's just us two in the whole wide world and all I can do is *feel*, not think.

This kiss is passionate; there is a hunger and need behind it, a pull that is trying to entangle us closer and closer together. He'd just said that we were thoughts and emotions and right now I am flesh and emotions and thoughts and skin on skin and feelings on top of feelings I'd never experienced before.

One, two, three, kiss, kiss, kiss, moan, bite, pant, kiss and I push him off of me with all of my strength. I dart up from the grass breathlessly. "What the hell!" I yell at him, not exactly sure where he is because my senses are all out of whack now.

"Stop it, Ezmerelda," he says placidly, as if he is speaking to a misbehaving child.

"Don't call me that!" I yell, and I am mad. I am fuming.

"It's your name."

"No shit." I go to stand up ignoring that I am slightly dizzy. He grabs my elbow and places my cane in my hand. "I got it!" I snap, angrily yanking my arm from his hold.

"Where are you going?" he asks, still, he seems so unfazed by my outburst and it only infuriates me more.

"Home," I bark. I am trying to find my center. I am trying to find my place back in this moment because I am disoriented.

"I'm driving you."

"No."

"Ezmer –" he pauses, then corrects himself. "Mazie, don't be stupid."

"*You're* stupid!" I yell at him.

"Wow, should I pull your hair and break your crayons now?"

I will admit that wasn't one of my brighter moments when arguing but I am too annoyed to care. I keep walking. I know I'll find the gate sooner or later, then I'll call Maya to pick me up. I hear him walking next to me for a few minutes before he grabs my arm and faces me toward him.

"How long are we going to act like we don't have feelings for each other?" he asks. "It gets a little old after a while, don't you think?"

"I don't have feelings for you," I state.

"You kissed me back."

"I'm stupid, remember?"

He sighs and deep down in that part of my being that tells me when I'm right or wrong, tells me when and how to fix my moral compass – deep down *in there* I know I am overreacting. I did kiss him back and I enjoyed it, but I wasn't supposed to. He shouldn't have kissed me, it didn't make sense for him to like me. Now I am confused and the confusion has turned into anger.

"I'm sorry I kissed you, but I am *not* sorry I kissed you," he finally says.

"Again, with the riddles."

He grabs my hand and I pull it away.

"I held your hand pretty much all night. You *let* me, that didn't raise any flags for you?"

I don't know why I let him hold my hand, or maybe I do know why, but I am not willing or ready to admit it to him or myself. I sigh. "Fine, Barnaby. What do you want me to say?"

He's quiet and grabs my hand again, this time I let him, but I'm rigid. I'm too flustered to acknowledge that buzzing feeling, whatever that *something* is that I can't put my finger on.

"In the unlikely event that the world is indeed flat, or that there are aliens out there or that God is fake or that God is real, I think you would like me either way. I believe you actually like me the way I like you, but you're afraid so you're fighting it. Tell me what you're afraid of, tell me something –*anything*..."

I feel warm all over, my heart is racing and my hands are sweating I'm sure he feels that right now. My mouth has gone dry because I don't know how to respond to him. I don't want to respond to him. I just want to go home and forget he ever kissed me.

"Tell me what it is," he repeats. "Is it because I am seven months younger than you? Is it because I cannot sing? You shouldn't hold that against me, plus I never heard *you* sing. You're probably a shitty singer, right along with being a shitty writer and a shitty dancer. You really shouldn't be so hypocritical and judgmental."

"You're so weird," I say and my voice is way lighter than I intend it to be. This is a pretty serious moment and he has somehow managed to make me *almost* smile. I do not want to smile, I want to be angry. I want to scowl and storm off. I want to have a reaction that my brain and heart are not comfortable with. My temper is by herself, left to her own defenses as Barnaby weasels his way in with his annoying charm.

"You're weird too." His words pulling me from my self-berating. "We could be perfectly weird together…" he says with a trace of hope in his voice.

"You just called a blind girl weird. That's in poor taste."

"I called a smart, hilarious, and beautiful girl, who *happens* to be blind, weird," he corrects easily.

And that's it, *that's* why I've been drawn to him. He got on my nerves like no other, but deep down I know I enjoy our banter and aside from the fact that he makes me laugh, that he is helpful, interesting, full of life –aside from that impressive list, the most important thing to me is the fact he doesn't see my handicap first like everyone else and he doesn't treat me as my handicap.

He truly sees me; he doesn't classify me, or categorize me or *pity* me. He likes me because he likes me, even if it doesn't make sense to me. And I don't know why I am fighting this. I don't know why this is a problem and suddenly my hand is climbing up his chest to his chin so I can locate his mouth and I reach up and he meets me *somewhere in the middle like heaven and the up there* and we kiss for the second time tonight.

~~

It's Sunday morning and Barnaby and I are sitting in my room. I am on my bed and he is sitting on the floor by the side of my bed. I'm nervously waiting for him to give me feedback on the chapter I wrote Friday, but he's been quiet for going on twenty minutes. That can't be a good sign.

I kicked him off of my bed because every time I went to type something I felt his hand on my leg or on my back. He would sneak kisses here and there and, as much as I enjoy it, we need to get this chapter edited and squared away.

"Hmmm," he finally says.

"Barnaby Parks, so help me God I will kick you out of my house!" I threaten and he immediately starts laughing. I hear and feel movement and I know he is back sitting on my bed.

"It's a great chapter," he says.

"What *aren't* you saying to me?" I accuse. "Don't tell me what I want to hear just because I let you put your tongue in my mouth a couple of times," I say.

He laughs, "Do we have an ETA on when I can do that again?" he says placing his warm hand on the side of my face. For a moment I almost melt in his hands and succumb to what he's been trying to do all morning, but I need to be the responsible one and the mature one. I swat his hand away and he laughs again.

"What's wrong with this chapter?" I ask, trying to keep us on track.

"Nothing, I swear to you," he says. "The book is taking a turn and it's just darker than I thought it would be."

"Oh," is all I say.

"What's that about?" he questions.

"What do you mean? It's just fiction."

"I don't know about that," he rebuts incredulously. "I have a feeling you're trying to convey something. I don't know what but…" he trails off.

I sigh. I know exactly what he is talking about. "I've had a lot of *dark* in my life Barnaby so it's easier for me to write these themes," I admit.

My thoughts flit back to the conversation we had the first day we met, about how writers will tell the blanketed story but hidden in between the lines is another story for the real avid fans to decipher. It makes me smile because Barnaby is reading in between the lines. He is finding more in my writing; things that only I should know are there at this point.

He doesn't say anything and maybe he isn't quite sure what to say. I don't blame him.

"Thank you for taking my writing seriously," I say and I feel his palm on my cheek again and then his lips softly touch mine. It is a gentle and quick kiss, but it is still enough to make my entire body hot and my thoughts jumble. He pulls away, but leaves his hand on the side of my face.

"I'm taking you on a date next Saturday," he says.

"A date?" I repeat and for some reason that four letter word made me nervous.

"Yes, we're going to do this right," he says. I inhale and exhale slowly.

"We hang out a lot, already. It can't be too much different than that," I say. I am basically calming my irrational nerves down, *out loud*.

"No," he answers immediately. "Those weren't dates. I want it to be special."

"Okay," I smile nervously and my smile feels forced. I am praying he can't tell. After we kissed last night and he came over today, nothing really felt too different. He is still flirting with me like he always did; we are still joking around and teasing each other except now when he flirts I reciprocate. I didn't think about the fact that we would start dating. *Duh,* of course we would, but I am so new to this, that it didn't cross my mind.

For some reason the thought of him and I together as *more* than just friends, in a different atmosphere outside of going to the library, Strauss' classroom or my home, is very overwhelming. I know I am being crazy, but I can't help how I feel.

His phone ringing snaps me out of my thought. "Hold on, sorry," he says to me.

"What's wrong?" he questions the person he is speaking to and his voice sounds angry and serious, a complete and total departure from how he was just moments ago. "Damn it," he snaps angrily. "Okay, okay I know. Amelia …calm down, just stay in your room, okay? I'll be there in ten minutes. Okay."

"I'm so sorry, but I have to go." I hear him hurriedly packing his things and I realize he is off the phone and talking to me.

"Is everything okay?"

"Yeah, family emergency," he says. He pecks my lips quickly and then I hear him nearly run out of my room. The front door opens and then slams closed. This is the second time he's said something about his family.

Amelia? This must be his younger sister. He sounded so mad, frustrated, and a little panicked. I wonder what is going on and I want to ask him, but I also don't want to be intrusive or step over any boundaries. Everything with us is still so new.

I lie back on my bed and think about how interesting the last month of my life has been and it is because of Barnaby. This odd boy, *who liked me for reasons that were beyond me*, is dominating my thoughts as I imagine how our first real date will be.

Six

Fear (v.): to be afraid of something or someone (2) to expect or worry about something bad or unpleasant

Saturday has arrived and I am sitting in my room anxiety ridden and annoyed before I can even say a word to Maya. I know she is going to blow this whole thing out of proportion and ask me a million questions that I in *no way* want to answer, but I need her help.

I exhale, "Maya?" I call out and in less than a minute I hear her walking into my room.

"What's up?" she asks.

"I'm going somewhere tonight and need you to pick an outfit for me," I say quickly.

We'd finally organized my closet for school clothes so I would know what colors and style of shirts were where, but we didn't organize my nicer clothes because in my head if we had a special event to go to she would pick my outfit. I never considered the fact that I'd be dating.

"Where are you going?" she asks casually. I hear her opening my closet door. "Did you forget the color order? We can go over it again if you want?"

I sigh, "I don't know where, maybe dinner…" I say under my breath. I hear her stop moving the clothing.

"Dinner? With whom?" she inquiries and now her voice has gone from casual to suspicious.

"Barnaby," I just say it. There is no point in trying to hide it at this point.

"Like a date?"

I clear my throat, "yeah…"

She doesn't say anything. She goes back to looking through my clothes. I hear the hangers gliding back and forth, "Is it a nice restaurant?" I know she's smiling. "I don't want to underdress you."

"He didn't say."

"Okay," she is still rummaging through my closet and my heart is pounding uncomfortably because I am waiting for the onslaught of questions I know she has for me.

"Okay," she says again after a few minutes. "That light blue top you like with the V-neck, black leggings with the gold zipper and those dark brown boots. I figure it could pass for elegant or casual." I hear her put the outfit on the bed next to me. "It's all set."

Wow, is she actually going to leave it at that? I almost exhale, but then I feel her sit on the bed next to me. We both sit in silence for a moment and the silence is screaming.

"Change of heart?"

I inhale, "I guess." I say, when I know that is a lie. It was never really a change of heart. I'm sure I liked Barnaby this entire time, but I couldn't make sense of what was happening, so I pushed those feelings down. "He's a great friend. I like his company," I add and that is the truth.

I don't have many friends. Of course I have buddies from my old high school and a few people who speak to me about classwork at my current high school, but not people I can imagine having serious conversations with about life or the fact that I probably won't even speak to half of them ever again once we all graduate.

For some reason Barnaby's friendship doesn't seem so fleeting, whether we are going on our first date or had we stayed exactly the way we were. Other than Maya, I think I consider him to be my best friend in this short time if I were to hold him to those standards. I wonder if he knows that.

"I think this is good for you," Maya says. "Barnaby is…" I'm nervous to hear what she truly thinks of him. I know he can be *a lot* at times, but that's what makes him special. "…he's refreshing."

I smile because that much is very true.

"You know, I knew he liked you the second I saw the way he looks at you," she continues. "His eyes were always on you, and when you spoke, even something as trivial as what seasonings we used on the chicken, his whole face would light up." I'm warm all over and trying not to show how much her words are affecting me right now.

"It was kind of clear you liked him too. It was all in the body language and the way you smiled and laughed at his stories. I've never seen you like that before. I was waiting for you to come to your senses and realize what was going on," she laughs.

"Me too," I admit lowly and suddenly I wish I could see how he looks at me or more so I wish I could see what he sees when he is looking at me. Maya puts her hand on my leg, then lets out a sigh.

"With that being said, this is your first boyfriend and I just want you to be safe, okay?"

Boyfriend? I don't know why I hadn't considered that. Is Barnaby my boyfriend? Can he even be my boyfriend if we haven't gone on a single date yet? I mean, we do spend a lot of our free time together and we've held hands and we've kissed. But does that constitute a relationship? I feel my palms beginning to sweat.

"Mazie?" Maya says once she realizes I've drifted off into some other thought.

"Sorry," I say, "yeah, I'll be safe."

"I'll need his cellphone number and license plate number before you leave," she says and her entire soft spoken demeanor is out of the window. She is every bit of a *mother* right now and I can't decide whether to smile or be annoyed.

She is acting as if she doesn't already know him, as if he wasn't here practically every day for the last two weeks. Going to the football field could've been a date for all she knows, how would my being with him *this* Saturday differ from when I was with him last Saturday? "Is the license plate info really necessary?"

"If it weren't I wouldn't ask," she states flatly and that comment made my decision. I am annoyed.

"I have to get dressed," I say under my breath. She gets up, but then I feel her lean down and place her lips quickly on my forehead.

"No curfew, but be respectful of my anxiety, okay?"

I smile and *there* is my sister. I've never really had a curfew for the most part because I don't go to too many places without my sister. Secondly, it was awkward having certain ground rules when I was fourteen and fifteen because our whole lives we were sisters and then our dynamic changed and she was my guardian. We both had a difficult time trying to figure out the ins and outs of the power struggle. Cool sister vs. want -to -be strict mom. It's a thin line that we have somehow figured out over the years.

I am sitting on my couch nervously. Barnaby will be here any minute. I am with him pretty much every day but yet, I am sitting here like I don't know who he is, like we don't already have a comfortable history.

I hear the door and I jump.

"Come in!" Maya yells from what sounds like the back hallway. I hear the door open and I freeze, I don't stand or welcome him. I just sit there face aimed straight ahead, like I am a mannequin.

"Wow," I hear Barnaby nearly whisper, I turn in his direction. "You're beautiful."

I am not used to this whole blushing thing, but I've blushed more times in the last week than I have my entire life. Maya insisted on putting some lipstick and blush on me, ignoring my initial protest. She also tricked me into letting her put three small French braids in the side of my hair. I am wearing a shirt that shows a little cleavage and though I am sitting down I know that the leggings I am wearing are hugging every single curve of my hips and legs. Maya made sure to tell me that.

He's only ever seen me in ripped jeans, t-shirts and hoodies. I am completely and utterly self-conscious and out of my element. "Thank you," I say and my voice is not my voice. My voice is this shaky shadow of what it's supposed to sound like. I clear my throat then turn away from him.

"What's wrong?" he asks, but before I can try to come up with a response, my sister comes in. *Thank God.*

"Hey, Barnaby," she says as I hear her entering the living room. "I got your number from Mazie, but I'll need your license plate number before you head out."

"Maya!" I almost snap.

"It's fine!" Barnaby quickly interrupts, "I'll write it down, no big deal, precious cargo. I get it."

And though he is probably just joking and making small talk with my sister, I blush again. Ugh, is this ever going to end? How can I possibly go on this date when everything that comes out of his mouth makes me feel warm and fuzzy inside? I don't think I like feeling like this or behaving like this.

"Okay," Barnaby says. "You ready?"

"Yeah," I stand up and immediately feel him grab my hand; I love the feeling of my hand inside his. I wish it were enough to calm my nerves.

"Wait," Maya says, "I'll grab your cane…"

"It's okay," I say. "I'm not going to take it tonight."

"Oh," she says and I am not sure how to interpret her response. I've gone without my cane on occasion, but only with Maya guiding me because I trust her explicitly. Barnaby squeezes my hand and I squeeze his back. We are just going to dinner. I can go a couple of hours without it.

"What time should I bring her home?" Barnaby directs towards Maya, cutting through that beat of silence.

"Please, no crazy hours, just have fun and be safe," she says. Being eighteen finally had some benefits.

We are finally all settled in his car and I haven't said a word. I hear him start the engine and we're off.

We've been driving for ten minutes in complete silence. There has never been a time when either one of us didn't have something to say or argue or laugh about, but here we are. Maybe we are better fit as friends. Maybe the energies we were giving each other got crossed and this relationship is supposed to remain platonic...

I know as soon as I think the words that there is no truth to them because just the thought of his hand holding mine, his lips touching mine... There is no way *those* kinds of feelings could ever be for a platonic friend.

"You're acting very strange," Barnaby finally breaks the silence; the words yank me out of my thought. It's as if he can sense what I am thinking.

"Sorry," I say.

"What's wrong?"

I don't say anything at first because I don't know how to word it without sounding idiotic. "I'm nervous. Is this…"

"Is this what?"

"Is this weird for you?" I finally reply.

"That you're acting like I'm a complete stranger? Yes, that is a little weird," he laughs and I sigh.

"I'm sorry," I say again, "I've never dated before. I don't know how I am supposed to be …I don't know how I am supposed to act..." I say honestly.

He sighs and then grabs my hand holding it on top of the armrest. "We don't have to change our dynamic because we've decided to start dating," he says. "I know why I like you and though I don't know exactly why you like me –you have your reasons. Remember those things and let's just have fun, okay? Don't think about it, just be you."

I smile and nod, "You're right." Because he is, I am overthinking this. Barnaby is still Barnaby and I am still Mazie. That is something that isn't going to change. The atmosphere doesn't feel so intense now as he holds my hand and continues to drive.

"Have you ever been out of the country?" he asks out of the blue.

And I stifle my laughter, "When I was three, my family and I went to Mexico to visit extended family members on my dad's side. I'd seen the pictures when I was younger, but I don't remember a single thing about it," I answer. "You?"

"Unfortunately, no," he sighs and I can tell this bothers him.

"You know you're still practically an infant, you have plenty of time to leave the country,"

He laughs, "I can't wait until I am elderly like you so I can share all of my wisdom with the youths."

I laugh and he squeezes my hand. "If you could go anywhere right now, where would you go?" I ask him.

"Right now, in this very moment?" he clarifies.

"Yes."

"Nowhere."

"What?" I question, slightly shocked because I feel like over the time I've known Barnaby I can pick up on his tone and demeanor pretty easily. He was truly disappointed when he said he hadn't been out of the country. "Why wouldn't you want to go anywhere? There has to be some place you want to go."

"Well, yeah, there are plenty of places I want to visit, but you said right now in this very moment and right now in this very moment I am here with you and there is no place in the world I'd rather be than sitting here holding your hand."

I feel the butterflies fluttering and my cheeks reddening and I can't keep the smile from spreading across my face.

"You are beautiful," he states out of the blue for the second time tonight and the way he says the words are as if he is astonished or mesmerized. He is saying the words as if it's the first time he's ever looked at anything *beautiful* in his whole life.

I can't handle this.

"You have to stop." I say, the smile falling from my face as my heart continues to pound against my rib cage.

"Stop what?"

"I…" how am I going to word this without sounding completely crazy? "I can't handle all of the sweet crap you say to me." I pause, "I mean, not that it's crap. I just…"

I'm cut off by his bark of a laugh. It is so guttural that it causes me to jump. His laugh really does force you to laugh along with him, but I am being serious.

"Barnaby, it isn't funny," I finally say, but he is still laughing, my hand still in his.

"I'm sorry," he says between near snorts, and then finally calms down. "I had to filter myself around you a lot and now that we're dating, I feel like I don't have to think about what I say to you."

That takes me by surprise because Barnaby is the least filtered person I have ever met. I am actually convinced that whatever thought pops into his head he assumes he has to say or fears he will combust.

"Filter?" I mock incredulously.

"Yeah, if I said stuff like this the first day I met you, we probably wouldn't be friends right now let alone going on a date."

"The first day you met me?" I repeat because that too catches me by surprise. The question sits in the air for a moment before I continue, "Did you... I mean, you liked ..."

"Yes, I liked you," he says interrupting my stammering. "I knew I wanted to ask you out the moment you yelled at me in the hallway and told me not to follow you."

I smile and shake my head, "I didn't yell at you." That's not how I recall that memory.

"I thought you were beautiful. Well, honestly, I thought you were sexy the second I saw you on the first day of school," he says as if I hadn't said anything. "When you walked in with your sister I couldn't stop staring at you."

"Everyone was staring at me."

"I doubt they were staring for the same reasons I was," he laughs lightly. "Well, like I said, you're sexy as hell, maybe they were."

"Shut up," I face out the window imagining the trees and the night sky whipping past the car before it stops at what I am assuming is a red light.

"I'm serious; I liked your whole look –the vintage shirt, ratty converses, your big hair, your complexion, and your lips," he pauses for a moment. "Your lips were the first thing I noticed." His voice is a little lower and suddenly the energy in the car feels intense, the memory of kissing him is fresh in my thoughts. Reflexively and embarrassingly, I lick my lips.

"And your curves…" he says huskily, and I feel my core constrict. He tightens his hold on my hand and I can tell he is looking at me, I can sense it. I face his direction trying to wordlessly *will* his lips to mine. I am hot all over, I am flustered, and I want him to kiss me. It is hard to think about anything else in this moment. "We're here," he says lowly.

I exhale; I'd been holding my breath that entire time. We both reluctantly let go of each other's hands. I hear him open his door, I go to open mine, but I am interrupted. "Don't. Chivalry is *not* dead, Ezmerelda," he says.

"It's Mazie, damn it!"

"Let it go," he says with humor. I sigh and, that quickly, it is like how it's always been between us. Is this how it will be? Our friendship will be at the core of it all, with occasional kissing and tension? I can live with that.

Once inside, we are seated and all I can hear are the low murmurs of people talking and silverware and plates clinking.

"Where are we?" I ask. The first thing I noticed when we walked in was the overbearing smell of fish.

"Leo Bells," he says and I am stunned.

"What do you mean *Leo Bells?*" I say in utter shock. "This is too expensive!" I whisper forcefully because I am not quite sure who all can hear me. Leo Bells is an expensive seafood restaurant. My sister had a part time job here a few years ago and I remember how she would talk about all the high rollers and big spenders who would come in here. They would leave hefty tips. It was *not* the place for a couple of teens.

"It's fine. I just hope you like seafood. Come to think of it, I probably should've asked before I made the reservation. I'm sorry, do you like…"

I interrupt him and shake my head, "We can't stay here, I can't let you pay for this, it's too much. We can get pizza and hang out at my house or something. I …"

"Stop," he interrupts me. "I can afford this, it is not a problem. Please, don't make it a big deal," he says calmly as if he is speaking to a misbehaving child. I hate when he does that.

"*How* can you afford this?" the question leaves my lips before I realize what I am asking. That is entirely too personal and inappropriate but God, I want to know. Barnaby doesn't have a job, not that I know of anyway. When would he ever have time to work? He's always with me in his free time. Regardless, it's still inappropriate of me to ask. "I'm sorry. You don't have to answer that."

"My mother isn't in the picture so she set up an account for me and my siblings," he says as if it were uninteresting.

"She's not in the picture?" I ask, but then I hear the waitress asking if we are ready to order. I remember him telling my sister that he and his sister lived with his father. I didn't know it meant that his mother was completely out of the picture.

"Do you want what I am having or do you want me to read the menu to you?" he asks and I can tell he is happy for the subject change.

"What you're having," I say. I listen to him order the wild salmon with lemon, shrimp, brown rice and mixed veggies. I am starving, I was so unnecessarily nervous about this date that I didn't eat much today.

"Okay, where were we," he ponders and I can hear the smile in his voice. "No my mom is not in the picture. Now, about you…"

"What about me?"

"All of it, please."

"Huh?" I ask.

"I want to know as much about you as you're willing to tell," he clarifies and I can feel my cheeks redden at the imaginary spotlight.

"There really isn't much to know," I say lowly patting the table until my fingertips meet the ice cold glass of water. I take a sip.

"I don't believe that," he counters. "What's your favorite food?"

I laugh then sigh. "Pizza…and tacos…and potatoes in any and every form," I admit.

"The holy trinity," he states and I nod, still smiling.

"What's your favorite food?" I ask and there is a long pause.

"I have a sweet tooth," he says. "…so anything that falls under that category is a favorite of mine."

"That doesn't count," I say before taking another sip of water.

"Why not?"

"Because everyone loves dessert, what's your favorite meal?"

"Who is to say I can't have dessert as my meal?" he counters. "Who is to say I haven't?"

I sigh.

"I never thought of you as the *play by the rules* kind of girl," he laughs.

"I'm not even going to pretend I know what you are talking about." I have a feeling that is a sentence I am sure I will use more than once in regards to Barnaby.

"Society has taught you to believe dessert can't be a meal,"

"Actually, society didn't teach me that. Common sense and trips to the dentist taught me that."

He laughs and then I hear our waitress placing our food in front of us. It smells so good. It's taking everything in me not to just nose dive into the plate.

We are eating silently for a few minutes and it's comfortable. I don't feel the need to fill the air with chatter.

"Do you like it?" he asks.

"Yes, it's delicious," I say. "Thank you for all of this, even though I think it's too much. I really appreciate it."

It's quiet again and I go back to eating and I am finally able to come back down from the cloud I have been on. "Do you see your mom at all?" I ask, realizing that this is kind of left field, but he'd distracted me before and he isn't the only one who can ask random off topic questions out of the blue.

"No, I do not," he says and there is finality in his voice. I take the hint and continue eating.

"I want to know the story, if you don't mind," he says.

"What story?"

"How long have you been blind?"

I inhale and take another bite of my salmon and I chew slowly. A lot happened when I was thirteen, I think over the years I'd kind of blocked out most of the details. People are usually too scared to ask me questions about my blindness, afraid they will offend or upset me, but of course, Barnaby doesn't have a single hesitation.

"I got sick when I was thirteen," I say lowly, "had to have surgery and lost my sight as a result. There really isn't a story."

"Sick?"

"Cancer."

It's quiet and my cheeks are hot because I am praying that Barnaby isn't pitying me. One of the reasons why I like him is he doesn't treat me any differently than he would treat anyone else. Knowing that I had cancer as a child may change his view of me and right now I can't think of too many things that would hurt me more than him seeing me for my illness and not seeing me for who I am.

"Damn," he says. "That's heavy."

"It was."

"Can it come back? I mean, is…" he stops as if he is trying to gather his words, which is odd to hear because Barnaby never has trouble finding the right words, "Shit, I'm not trying to be insensitive. I'm sorry, I just wanted to…"

"Yes," I interrupt, "There is always a chance of it coming back for anyone who has ever had cancer, but in my case it isn't likely. I've been healthy for five years, that's a major milestone." I clear my throat and take a sip of water. It's quiet and I don't know what else to say and for the first time, I don't think Barnaby knows what to say either. My chin is to my chest, I feel like I am recoiling.

"Hey," he says and I feel him grab my hand when I put the glass down. "What's wrong? I'm sorry I asked you about…"

"No," I interrupt. "It's not that, I just don't want you to look at me differently or treat me differently because you know I am a cancer survivor."

"Why would I treat you differently?" he asks and he is truly confused by my comment. "You told me what happened because I wanted to know. It's shitty, but it doesn't change how I feel about you."

I exhale and I squeeze his hand. "Thank you," I say lowly. It's quiet and it's starting to feel like it's *our* quiet, the kind of quiet only he and I can enjoy together.

It feels like a weight has been lifted off of my shoulders. It isn't like I was keeping a secret from him, but it was always in the back of my mind. I knew one day he'd ask, I just didn't think I expected that day to be our first date. It's very *Barnaby* of him.

"Okay, what is your biggest fear?" he asks; *King Asker of Questions*, snapping me out of my thought. He isn't kidding when he says he wants to know *everything*.

"My irrational fear or my real fear?" I counter because there is a difference.

"Humor me. Both," he says.

"My irrational fear is being on the water, boats or anything like that. I don't like it at all."

"Why?"

I don't answer, but I do know exactly why I fear it, in a way. Being on a boat was something I did with my family a lot growing up. The last happy memory I have before I got sick and before I lost my parents was on a boat. That's why this fear is irrational, I just can't stomach being back on the water. The thought sends a nauseating feeling through me that I can't explain.

"I just don't like it," I say because I feel like delving into the full story would be a little too much for a first date, even if the first date is with Barnaby.

"Hmmm," he says and then he laughs because he knows how annoyed I get when he does that "…and your real fear?"

I inhale, "My biggest fear already happened, losing my parents. So now that fear has morphed into just never wanting to lose anyone ever again. I don't have many people in my world so I need to keep what I have well and alive." And my words come out much more somber than I intend them to be. I didn't want to delve too much in my boat story, but then I lay that all on Barnaby? I am beginning to think my filter is just as bad as Barnaby's at this point.

"You're afraid of losing your sister?" he asks. I told him before that the only blood related family I have are out of the country and I don't know them. Then there is Maya's mother, but she lives on the other side of the country and she and I are not close at all. Hell, Maya considers my mother her mom, more so than she did her biological mother. He knows that since my parents died all I've had is Maya. I've had no one else in my life that I can talk to, trust, relate to in any way, just her… and then when that thought flits across my mind, my words are leaving my lips effortlessly …

"...and I'm afraid of losing you, too, Barnaby," I say and I cannot believe I've said that. I can't believe my brain allowed those words to leave my mouth without a second thought. "You're like a best friend at this point," I add trying to recover, trying to sound less crazy than I already seem. "I mean, I just...at that school I don't really..."

"Ezmerelda," he stops my stammering by grabbing my hand. He squeezes it tightly and I snap my mouth shut. "I don't want to lose you either," he says lowly, *softly,* as if he is trying to calm my nerves with his tone.

I exhale and feel warm all over. I can feel my heartbeat pulsating at my fingertips. "Mazie," I correct him lowly and he laughs softly then sighs before letting go of my hand.

It's quiet; our words are still heavy in the air. We just told each other how important we are to one another. This is a moment and I am having a very hard time getting rid of these butterflies in my stomach.

"What's yours?" I finally ask.

"My what? My biggest fear?"

I nod because I know he is looking at me.

"I already told you."

"When?"

"On the football field."

I pause and think back to that night. I remember every single second about that night. Everything is still so fresh, so new, so vivid in my mind. I do not remember him once telling me what his biggest fear is.

"No you didn't …" I say trailing off still trying to place the conversation.

"*Insignificance*," he says plainly and, immediately, I realize what he means. He talked about how it felt to just be swallowed up by the universe, to feel small, maybe even invisible.

"You're afraid of being insignificant?" I ask and it's hard to hide my surprise.

He doesn't answer right away and I am a little overwhelmed at how sad this is making me. He is such a strong force, well, in *my* life at least. I can't imagine him ever feeling less than. He did an amazing job of hiding it. I can feel his huge energy and his positive vibes every time I am in a room with him. He is many things, but insignificant isn't one.

"Yes," he finally says as if he didn't want to admit it.

I'm quiet for a moment trying to figure out how to respond. I am trying to figure out how to let him know that though I didn't agree with his assessment of himself, I still understood that it is a true feeling.

I slowly slide my hand across the table turning my palm facing upwards. After a second he realizes what I am trying to do and he grabs my hand again. I intertwine our fingers together, squeezing my palm to his.

"You're not insignificant, Barnaby. You could never be." I say softly. "*You* are immeasurable, remember that."

He doesn't respond, but he squeezes my hand tighter. "You're significant in my small world if that counts for anything," I add after a moment and again my filter does not exist. My brain doesn't alert my mouth to shut up.

"It counts for much more than you think," he says and, like so many times before, I can hear the smile in his voice.

Over the last five years I've had plenty of times when I wished I had my sight, but it was always fleeting because I accepted that this was my life. But right at this moment, I don't think there have been too many times when I've wished I could see more than I wish it right now.

I want to look Barnaby right in his eyes. I want to not only feel this powerful energy that has been floating between us but I want to *see* it. I want to brand it into my thoughts. I want him to be able to look in my eyes and see it too.

"Now, your irrational fear?" I ask.

"Hmmm," he says and I roll my eyes. "Okay, this irrational fear is something that just started for me." He stops as if he is waiting for me to say something, but I don't. I'm just listening, enjoying every second of this time I am spending with him.

"My irrational fear is finding the perfect girl of my dreams and her breaking my heart or, worse, I find some way to screw the whole thing up."

I feel his other hand wrap around our already connected hands and my stomach gets warm and I know my face is flushing red.

I swallow and inhale. "I don't think that's irrational."

"You're right," he agrees immediately. "It's a very real fear."

"I don't think she'd break your heart. I think she'd be more afraid of you breaking hers." I say this so lowly that for a moment I don't think he will be able to hear me with all of the noise going on around us.

"More water?" I hear the waitress ask and I almost jump. I am so focused on this conversation and our connected hands that I'd tuned everything else out around me. All the background noise, the classical music, chairs scooting and scratching. I was zeroed in on Barnaby.

"Yes, please. Thank you," Barnaby says as we both reluctantly let go of each other's hands.

We go back to eating as if we hadn't just had another *moment*. I want to bring it up again, but I also just want to go with the flow of things. I'm less anxiety ridden when he and I are just normal with one another. I am too new to everything, every emotion is heightened, and every thought is swimming around like a tsunami. I want to embrace these moments when I am not blushing and when my heart isn't pounding against my rib cage.

I am done eating and drinking my second glass of water when Barnaby finally says something. We haven't said a word to one another since the waitress left and it isn't uncomfortable or awkward. It's just *our* quiet.

"Are you ready for our next adventure or do you want dessert? I know how important dental hygiene is to you."

I roll my eyes again. "Next adventure?" I ask. I did love this balance we had, being honest and serious with one another, but also, at the core, still being the friends we were a month ago. That's something I didn't want to lose no matter where this goes.

"I want to take advantage of the fact you do not have a set curfew."

"Don't you have a curfew?"

"Nope!" he says triumphantly. "Do you know the havoc we could cause in this town? The adventures we could embark on?"

I laugh as I hear the waitress coming back, I assume he took care of the check already because I hear him stand up and then he grabs my hand and leads me out of Leo Bells.

We drive for about thirty minutes before we get to wherever it is he is taking me. He helps me out of the car and in the distance I can vaguely hear music playing. "Where are we?" I ask. He has my hand gripped tightly, our fingers intertwined.

"Hold on to me because we have quite the walk and the ground is rocky and uneven."

"Where are we?" I repeat as we begin to walk and he is not lying. I can feel the rocks under my feet, we are stepping over and around things. I must truly trust Barnaby, because in any other scenario I would be freaked out right now.

"Almost there," he says after five minutes of trekking through wherever we are trekking.

"Almost *where*?"

"Tisk, tisk Ezmerelda. Patience is a virtue."

"Mazie," I sigh and continue to let him lead the way. The music I'd heard in the distance is now louder and clearer. It sounds like a live band is playing.

"Okay, we are here," he says and I can hear the excitement in his voice.

"Not to sound like an annoyed broken record, but *where* are we, Barnaby?"

He laughs and quickly kisses my lips; I wasn't expecting it so it throws me off. My lips are suddenly tingling and my cheeks are hot and I want him to kiss me again, but this time I don't want him to pull away.

"It's like this outdoor underground poetry/live music thing," he says and I am having a hard time following his words because I am still reeling from the kiss. "It goes on for twenty four hours and they only happen a few times a year. It's super secretive. You only get a day's notice if you want to attend or be a part of it. It's all word of mouth. No paper trail."

"That's amazing," I say because it is. Again, leave it to Barnaby to know about some super-secret random underground concert thingy.

"Let's go find a spot," he says and he grabs my hand. We end up walking down a slope for a few minutes then stopping. "I have a blanket for us to sit on," he says and I smile.

He helps me sit as we listen to some woman singing what sounds like an almost heavy metal version of the blues. It's something I've never heard before and her voice is like wind chimes. It is beautiful in such a weird and eclectic way.

"This really is amazing," I nearly whisper in astonishment because I didn't know things like this existed. "How did you find out about this?"

"You know me. I know a little bit about everything," he laughs and I can't help but laugh too because it's true. The woman finishes singing and there are a few people clapping.

"How many people are here?"

"Not too many, less than seventy five I would say. Most of the performers are basically performing for other performers." He says quietly into my ear. "We aren't near anyone on this side of the hill; there are a few couples on the other side."

"Oh, okay." It's quiet for a moment when I hear the screech of a microphone being adjusted, a few more seconds pass and one guitar is being strummed. It's just two chords being played in a slow repetitive pattern, and then a deep voice begins to speak in a very soft tenor.

He is reciting a poem, but only repeating the same four words *And then we were.* It is hard to describe but it is beautiful. It's as if this poem, these words could mean any and everything you wanted them to mean. I don't need to hear more of the guitar; I don't need him to add more words. *And then we were* is enough.

"I'm glad you're enjoying yourself," Barnaby says, pulling me out of the zone I'd slipped into. I realize that I'd been smiling while listening to this man's soft growl.

"I really am," I say gently. "Thank you for bringing me here, it's very…peaceful."

He doesn't say anything, but then I feel him grab my hand and reflexively my smile gets bigger. Any and all contact with Barnaby always awakened every cell in my body; all wishing to be touched by him.

I focus back on the deep voice coming from the stage and the guitar stops, then he says firmly and angrily *And so it goes –until we weren't.*

The pain in the words vibrates through the microphone and, suddenly, I feel sad. Barely any words were spoken, but I know that this poem is about a relationship or about love. Whatever it is made my chest feel hot and, embarrassingly, I had the urge to cry because I know that in my life I never want to go through that level of pain ever again. I've experienced enough loss in my life to know that it is a permanent reminder that nothing in this world is promised. I've experienced enough loss to know that whether you do everything wrong or everything right, some things happen that you cannot change.

"You okay?" Barnaby asks as he squeezes my hand.

I clear my throat and force a smile. "Yeah, I'm fine that was beautiful."

"It was," he agrees and I feel his lips gently kiss my cheek, the sadness I was feeling evaporates that quickly. I wonder if Barnaby knows he has this type of *power* over me. The type of power that is able to wipe my memory clean of any negative thoughts even if it's only temporarily.

"Can you wait right here for a second?" he asks, letting go of my hand.

"Oh, sure," I say a little caught off guard.

I hear Barnaby get up and I sit with my legs crossed on the blanket. I can hear people taking stuff apart or putting stuff together where I believe the stage to be. I really like the two acts I've heard so far; I hope there is more music and poetry like that throughout the night.

For my first date, I'd have to say that this is going better than I could've ever expected. I feel so comfortable with Barnaby even if I was overthinking it in the beginning. I like our conversations; I like our energy together... I like *him* –a lot.

It's been about five minutes, but Barnaby still isn't back and a part of me is a little nervous because I have no clue where we are. I expected him to be back by now, but I'd let overthinking almost ruin tonight once, so I am not going to do it for a second time. I force my brain to be patient and just wait like he asked me to.

I start tapping my foot to pass the time, but that just turns into me tapping my foot impatiently as more minutes tick by. The little bit of nervousness I was experiencing before is now full blown anxiety and there is no more *will* in me to force my brain to relax.

I pull out my phone and say, "Call Barnaby," and wait for it to ring. It starts ringing and then I hear a buzz go off next to me. He left his phone with me. *Crap.*

I stand up and I don't know what I am going to do at this point, maybe try to get to the other side of the hill and ask someone if they'd seen Barnaby, but how would I describe him? I don't know what the hell he looks like aside from what Maya told me and now I am in full panic mode.

Where could he be that would take this long? Surely he hadn't forgotten about me –that would be absurd. Maybe he is lost and can't find me? That's absurd too. Maybe I am being classic Mazie and freaking out unnecessarily? That didn't seem too absurd at all.

I hear that annoying piercing sound from a mic as if someone is adjusting it.

"This is short and personal, so bear with me," the voice says and my heart drops.

It's Barnaby and he is on stage. I stand frozen as he continues. "This is called 'Somewhere in the Middle'," he adds as he clears his throat and my stomach starts fluttering.

Somewhere in the middle of need and want is where I live.

In this haze, it's just your light. And mine.

Somewhere in the middle of fear and hope is where you live.

In this dark, it's just my heart beating. And yours.

Somewhere in the middle like heaven and the up there is where we live.

Together in all of these moments, we are everything; we are every bit of it all.

Somewhere in the middle, we are Titans, we are immeasurable.

We are, we are, we are...

"Thank you," he says and I hear a few claps and *still* I am standing here frozen. He wrote this? He wrote this for me? This strange feeling wraps itself around my chest in the most indescribable way. Those words were...

"Hey," I hear Barnaby say from a distance, ripping me from my thought. "Leaving?" There is slight humor in his voice, but I can't pay attention to that. Without a second thought, I reach out for him, moving forward until I can feel him. I wrap my arms around his neck and pull his face to mine and crash my lips against his. I kiss him passionately; my hands are in his hair, the side of his face. His hands are all over my body and I never want to disconnect from this moment.

Breathlessly, he pulls away but his nose is touching mine, his body still pressed to me. "I should write you poetry more often," he says and I smile, pressing my lips back to his.

"Thank you," I say softly.

"Do you want to stay or maybe go to the car?" he says huskily and I detect the meaning of his words. He isn't asking me if I want to *leave*.

"Car," I say breathlessly. He pecks my lips quickly then grabs my hand as we trek back to where he parked.

Once we are in the car, our lips don't disconnect and his hands never leave my body. This is my first time making out with someone. I've never felt these feelings before and I want to feel these feelings all of the time.

He pulls away slightly, "I don't want to go too far," he says as his hand lies on the skin of my lower stomach just above the zipper of my leggings. I can't believe how much I want him to *go too far*. Who am I? What am I thinking? Though we have hung out almost every day for the last month, this is our first date. I am not even sure if he is my boyfriend and I definitely never imagined my first time being in the back of a car in the middle of nowhere.

"You're right," I whisper, as I lay my hand on top of his. He intertwines our fingers together and starts kissing my neck and I wonder, just for a split second, if I made the right decision.

After about thirty minutes, Barnaby decides it's time to leave; he doesn't want to take *too* much advantage of the fact I did not have a curfew. We drive holding hands and talking about the most random things because of course *King asker of Questions* has one million questions ready in his arsenal, from wanting to know my favorite color – didn't have one –to wanting to know what was my least favorite subject in school when I was in the fourth grade –math. I admire his need to know everything, this same need that just weeks ago would've annoyed me to no end.

"We're here," he says once we get to my house and I hear him open his car door. Moments later he is opening my door and helping me out. He's holding my hand as we head up my walkway.

"You know, you don't have to walk me to the door, I've made it up here by myself before I even knew you," I say jokingly because I did need his help since I decided to leave my cane behind.

"Before you knew me? You mean those sad and depressing days before I put a spark into your life?"

I laugh and answer sarcastically, "Yes, those would be the days…"

"...and like I said," he continues, "Chivalry is not dead. It's not that you're incapable of walking to the door by yourself, it's the question of why would I waste an opportunity to have more time with you, even if it's just seconds?"

"God," I say shaking my head, feeling the flush and heat devour my entire face and chest.

"What?"

"I told you. I don't know how to respond."

He laughs loudly again, then stops walking once we make it to the top of my steps. It's quiet for a moment as we just stand here. I am sure he is facing me and, with that thought alone, I start blushing even more than I already know I was.

"Tonight was wonderful," I say breaking the silence. "Thank you."

"You're very welcome, Ezmerelda."

And just like that, he is capable of pulling me out of my nearly euphoric moment. I go to growl and correct him per usual, but his lips are unexpectedly on mine, his hand at the back of my neck under my hair. He kisses me with an eagerness that I can feel in my chest, passion and need always are the focal points of our kisses and it is dizzying every single time.

His lips leave mine and I am breathless, caught off guard from the kiss, but also feeling high from it too. Just like how I felt for most of the car ride home.

"Can I see you tomorrow?" he asks lowly, his forehead touching mine, his hand still resting on the back of my neck. I nod, unable to speak at the moment.

"Okay," he pecks my lips quickly and I hear him walking away. "You have a restful night," he shouts as he sounds like he is already back to his car. I stood there for a moment trying to regroup and find a normal breathing pattern. I lick and bite my bottom lip and I can still taste him. I smile and touch my lips with the tips of my fingers and exhale, shaking my head at the whirlwind I am feeling in my thoughts and body.

Once I open my door I hear a car drive off and realize he must've been sitting there watching me. The euphoric feeling I was just experiencing, again, has now turned into embarrassment.

I go into the house and head straight to my room. I pull out my phone and tell it to call Barnaby. He answers on the first ring.

"Ezmerelda," he says and the joy is present in his voice, "want me to come back and sneak into your window?" he offers jokingly.

"Mazie," I snap at him *almost* playfully. Why did he insist on calling me by a name I despised?! "I called to tell you it is impolite to stare at people when they don't know you're staring. That's basically stalking."

He's laughing, I'm sure remembering that this isn't the first time I have said these words to him.

"I could have you arrested," I state firmly, not letting his laughter make me laugh.

"You wouldn't call the police on me," he says confidently. "Who would leave you breathless and *needing* on your porch if I were in jail?"

"Wow, *that* was intentional?" I accuse and now there is humor in my voice. "That's not very gentlemanly of you, Barnaby."

"I never said I was a gentleman. I said I was chivalrous, two different things."

And though we are joking, my face feels flushed because already he knows the effect he has on me. I wonder what effect, if any, I have on him.

"I'm learning a lot about you," I say.

"Ditto," he says back. It's quiet on the line for a moment. It's as if we are enjoying each other's silent company. Just like in the restaurant, it's *our* quiet.

"Well, I'll let you go," I finally say, not really wanting to hang up.

"Are you going to sleep?" he asks.

"Umm, I don't think so. Not yet."

"I wouldn't mind staying on the phone a little longer," he says and I cannot help the smile that spreads across my face.

"I wouldn't mind that either," I say.

Ten minutes later, he is home. I put him on speaker as I stack my Braille books on the floor next to my bed and organize my school work for the next couple of weeks. He has me on speaker as he cleans his kitchen. He has loud and obnoxious music playing in the background and I tell him how horrible it is and that he needs to turn it off. He tells me it's his band and I spend the next ten minutes apologizing to him only for him to say, "Just kidding, I don't know who the hell this band is or what they're saying."

Jerk.

More time goes by and his phone starts to die, so he goes upstairs to his room to put it on the charger. My smartphone still has a lot of life left in it because I am never on it much, not until I met Barnaby.

Now I am lying on my bed as we laugh uncontrollably about childhood stories, like him tripping and knocking his tooth out in front of his third grade crush or how in the first grade I was in a play and got so nervous that I threw up on stage and instead of walking off the stage I just stood there still trying to recite my lines. That wasn't one of my prized moments in life.

"Wow," he says out of the blue. "It's almost 6 am."

"What?" I am shocked. How could it be six in the morning?

"It's 5:54 am," he says and starts laughing. "I'm not even sleepy."

"Me either," I say. "What time did you drop me off?" I ask.

"Around midnight," he says.

"We've been on the phone for six hours?"

He laughs at my astonishment, which makes me laugh because I am sure the sound he makes is contagious.

"So you're not sleepy?" he asks.

"No," I say honestly. "I'm not at all."

"Are you still dressed?"

"Ummm, yeah. Why?"

"Good, I'll be there in fifteen minutes," he says.

"What?" I question, but there is no answer. "Barnaby? Hello?" he hangs up on me. I sit up in my bed for a moment and shake my head. I sigh and head to the bathroom to quickly brush my teeth and then wait in the living room.

"Hey," Maya says, I can smell the coffee. "Why are you up so early? I didn't hear you come in last night. And you're dressed?" her voice goes from normal to incredulous.

"I got home around midnight, but didn't exactly go to sleep,"

"Why?"

"I was on the phone with Barnaby."

"Right after a date you were on the phone with him?" I wonder just about how big her smile is right now. "And you're still dressed because..."

"Time slipped by when we were on the phone and he asked if I were still dressed. I said yes and then he said he'd be here in fifteen minutes."

"What? I mean, okay... where are you going?" she questions, there's no hiding the surprise in her tone.

"I have no clue," I say and my voice sounds exasperated. "Barnaby is an *in the moment* kind of person," I say and shake my head, unable to mask the smile that pops up on my face when I say the words.

"I see," she says. "I don't know the rules for morning dates, so umm, just have fun and be safe I guess."

I laugh and then my phone rings. "Hello?"

"Hey, I don't want to come to the door in case your sister is asleep, but I am here," Barnaby says.

"She's awake, but here I come," I hang up the phone. I walk over to Maya and kiss her cheek and when I walk over to the door to grab my cane, I hear two light knocks. I open the door and I immediately feel Barnaby grab my hand.

"Where's your sister?" he asks.

"In the dining room, why?"

He kisses me and then I hear him walk by. "Barnaby?" I ask, but he is already in the house.

"Hi Maya," he says and his voice is so cheery.

"Good morning, Barnaby," she says happily, matching his exuberance.

"I'm taking Ezmerelda to breakfast, is there anything you would like me to bring you back?"

"Oh wow, that's very thoughtful of you, but I just ate. I really appreciate that."

"No problem," Barnaby grabs my hand and pulls me towards the door. "Have a good day," he yells out and she says it back.

Once we are settled in the car, I smile brightly, "Long time *no see,*" hoping he will find the humor in my using those particular words. He laughs and I laugh along with him. "You are a gentleman by the way, Barnaby," I say as I place my hand on the armrest, seconds later his hand is in mine and he drives off.

We drove for fifteen minutes before he parks. "Okay, we're here." I hear him open his door, seconds later he is opening mine and holding my hand.

"Please tell me we are at Denny's or something and not some high end $50 a plate breakfast café that only you know exists because it's exclusive." I lift our connected hands and air quote.

The sound of his laughter is easily becoming one of my favorite things in the entire world.

"No," he says in between his chuckles. "It's just a diner. We could order every item on the menu and I'm sure it wouldn't add up to $50."

"Okay," I say squeezing his hand, "just making sure."

We walk right in and he leads us to a table. He tells me it's a booth and he sits right next to me instead of across from me. His arm is around my shoulders and it's indescribable how I feel being this snuggled and hugged up against him.

"Are you a pancake or waffle kind of girl?" he asks. I can hear him flipping over what I believe is the menu with his free hand.

"French toast actually," I say.

"Wow," he says. "That was very left field of you. I knew you could live on the edge."

"Shut up," I laugh as he holds me closer to him. The waitress comes and I order French toast, scrambled eggs and two pieces of turkey bacon. He orders a stack of chocolate chip pancakes, with chocolate drizzle, whipped cream, extra cherries, extra chocolate chips on the side, and nothing else.

"I told you I could have dessert as a meal," he whispers in my ear when I hear our waitress walk away.

"All of your teeth are going to fall out," I whisper back and then his lips are gently on mine without any warning. I wish I could just kiss him all day.

"I have something for you," he says against my lips. He pulls away and then I hear something being placed on the table in front of me. He takes my hand and places it on the item that is now sitting there.

"*Pride and Prejudice*?" I say. I run my fingers over it and it is a contracted Braille copy of my favorite book, a book that I always get from the library because I refuse to spend one hundred plus dollars on a copy for myself. I'd told Barnaby this. "Are you giving this to me?" I ask in shock.

"Well, as much as I like to know a little bit about everything, I do not know how to read Braille. So, yes, I am giving this to you. There are three books in that volume."

"No," I say as I push the book in front of him on the table. "I can't accept this."

He sighs and I hear him push the book back in front of me. I put my hand back on the book to push it right back to him, but he leaves his hand on it firmly so I am unable to move it.

"Along with beautiful, smart, and hilarious," he says lightly, "…you are stubborn, difficult, and frustrating."

I huff. "It's funny, I could say the same thing about you," I snap.

"Aww, I've never been called beautiful before. Thank you," he says cheerfully.

I scowl at him and I know he is either silently laughing or trying not to laugh, either way he is enjoying this too much.

"You're taking the book," he says as if it were written in stone.

"I am *not* taking the book," I say. I fold my arms across my chest.

"You are."

"I'm not."

"Ezmer –" he stops and exhales. "Mazie, why can't you take the book? It's your favorite. You said you wanted to own your own copy and it's right there..." and finally his lighthearted tone is gone. He's annoyed with me. Well, the feeling is mutual.

"I'm beginning to think you get your kicks off from arguing." He continues, "Is this really an argument you even want to put energy into?" The humor is back, though very slightly. "There are so many other things we could fight about."

And because I have become so accustomed to Barnaby's babble I, without even realizing it, take the bait and indulge him. "Like what? Because I am really confident about winning this particular fight."

"We could argue about the fact that you don't like the bands I listen to."

"They're all garbage," I state with a shrug.

"Or the fact that you always tap your foot."

"It's to drown you out."

"We could argue about the fact that you chose plain French toast over chocolate covered pancakes. It's inhuman."

"I *like* my teeth," I state and it's quiet for a moment.

"Why can't you take the book?" his tone serious again. "I really want you to have it."

"It's too expensive," I answer honestly. "And when did you even get it?"

"It really wasn't expensive and I got it the day you told me you wanted it."

"Why are you just giving it to me now?"

"Because I thought giving it to you when we were just friends would freak you out. I was going to wait a little longer, but then our date went so well I figured why not …but clearly you are still freaking out."

"You were that confident that we would eventually start dating?"

"Yes," he answers immediately, assuredly.

"…and why was that? I was very clear about wanting to remain friends," I say undoubtedly; his admission momentarily sidetracking me from the book itself.

"Because the way you reacted around me, if I said something nice to you or something interesting you'd start blushing. The way you laugh at my stupid comments and jokes…" he lists. "If I touched you, you would hold your breath. It was little things; I knew that eventually you would feel what was happening," he says easily with no humor. I didn't know all of that was so noticeable to him.

"Like right now," he continues, "you're blushing because you're embarrassed, but you shouldn't be. I was and am the same way around you."

"You are?" I question and then my thoughts drift back to what Maya said about how she knew he liked me the second she saw the way he looked at me, how his face lit up every time I spoke. I smile.

"Yes, Mazie," he says.

It's quiet before he speaks again.

"Listen, I wanted to do something nice for you because I like you and because everyone should own a copy of their favorite book. Your refusal of it is kind of an ego crusher, if I'm being honest."

I sigh and brush my fingers over the book again. This is such a sweet thing for him to do and I am ruining it, but I just don't feel comfortable with him spending that kind of money on me. Between dinner, breakfast, and this book he's probably spent over $300. The thought made me queasy. But his words are replaying in my head and I did feel badly, he probably expected me to be happy and excited and we ended up arguing.

I pick the book up and hold it to my chest, "Thank you, Barnaby." I exhale, "I really do appreciate this. I'm just not good at this dating thing and the money spending thing…"

"Well, we will practice because you need to get used to it," he says quickly. I start to object, but I hear the waitress coming with our food. He kisses my cheek and then we dive in.

We eat quietly for a few minutes then Barnaby says, "I think we could be in the Guinness Book of World Records."

"For what?"

"Longest first date in the history of mankind," he says and I can't help but laugh.

"This is like a fourteen hour date," I continue to laugh, "Are you sick of me yet?"

"Impossible."

I smile because I feel the exact same way. I love the newness of it all, but also the comfortability of it all. I just enjoy being near him and I am not embarrassed or scared to admit that.

I am almost done eating when I yawn.

"I could drop you off at your house," Barnaby says, "…or we could go to my house and take a nap before we get the rest of our day started," he adds, an unspoken question lingers.

I smile again, "I could use a nap."

~~

Our lips haven't disconnected in the last twenty-five minutes. I am in his room on his bed for the first time. I can say that when he picked me up at 6:45 pm last night, I never imagined that at 8:30 am the next morning I'd still be with him doing this. He moves his lips to my neck and I am able to come up for air. "We have to work on what your definition of a nap is," I say breathlessly.

His lips are back on mine. "I'm sorry," he says against them. "Did you want to sleep?" Before I can answer, his tongue is in my mouth, how easily he is able to distract me. This house could be on fire, armed masked men could run in, or a tornado could hit and I don't think I would be able to dislodge myself from him. I don't even think I would notice.

"Did you?" he asks as he lifts his lips from mine.

"Did I what?" I am finding it hard to breathe evenly.

"Want to sleep?"

"No," I say, grabbing his face and pulling it back to mine, "No sleep."

I don't know how long we make out on his bed, but eventually we manage to fall asleep.

Slipping deeper into my unconscious thoughts, reality starts to fade away. Bright colors and familiar sounds take over my senses. I am sitting on a beach. It is the middle of the summer and the sun is beaming brightly; its rays reflecting off of the clear water. It's hot, *so* hot I can feel the sweat moistening on my exposed skin. I am wearing a bright yellow two piece bathing suit that compliments my complexion and curves perfectly.

I am watching the waves ripple in an uneven pattern. It's relaxing. To my left, Barnaby is sitting there holding my hand. I can't exactly see his face, but I *know* it's him, I can feel it. Maya is at the shore kicking the water and sloshing her feet in the muddied sand. To my right, my parents are sitting there. My mom is holding a little girl; she looks like she is about four years old; she looks like me when I was that age. My dad is playing with the little girl's feet as she giggles uncontrollably.

I feel so happy, but this aching feeling of *loss* is in the shadows. It's lingering, trying desperately to get my attention. I fight against it because I have everything I want: I have my sight, I have my family and I have my Barnaby. I feel free and blissful. I am with everyone whom I care about and everyone who cares about me.

I don't want to move from this fragment of my life, ever. I don't want the *loss* to take over.

"Ezmerelda," I hear a faded voice say to me and I scowl. Even in my dreams I can't escape that name.

"Mazie," I hear the voice say and the voice sounds familiar. It sounds like Barnaby –I smile fleetingly or at least I think I try to smile, and then I feel a finger brush my cheek. "Wake up, I think you're having a bad dream." That is definitely Barnaby's voice. Then I feel something tug at my sunglasses.

"No!" I practically yell, grabbing my sunglasses with both hands to keep them in place. *I'm not in my bed. This is not my bed?*

"I'm sorry," Barnaby says quickly, "Are you okay?"

My heart is pounding and my mind is slowly sifting through the fog. It takes a second for me to realize where I am and, when the realization washes over me, soon follows the embarrassment. Also, waking up so abruptly is not fun and I *never* take my sunglasses off around people. Barnaby would be the *last* person I would want to see me without them on.

"I'm fine," I say as I catch my breath. "I like to keep my sunglasses on because I…"

"No," he interrupts, "I meant, you were crying and you kept saying *stay, don't leave me* I thought you were having a nightmare."

Now I am even more embarrassed. I was unaware that I spoke in my sleep. I exhale, "I had a dream, it wasn't a nightmare. I don't know why I was crying." I say honestly as I lift my hand back to my face and feel the wetness on my cheek.

"Can you talk to me about it?" he asks as I feel the palm of his hand rest on my cheek to wipe the rest of the tears from it.

"It's silly and doesn't mean anything," I say wishing that my brain had waited until I was home to have this dream and not when I was sleeping in a bed with a boy for the first time.

"Could I be the judge of that?" he asks softly. "It's difficult seeing you cry."

I don't know what to make of his words, but the warmth I've only experienced when in his presence, cascades through my body.

"I had my sight and I was on a beach on a perfect summer's day. Maya was there and…" I pause and swallow before continuing, "And you were there next to me holding my hand and my parents were there and my mom was holding my little sister."

"You have another sister?" he asks.

I sigh and can feel my eyes starting to water again as the details of the dream groggily come back to me.

"My mom was almost five months pregnant when she died," I say and for some reason the emotions I thought would overwhelm me, don't come. It actually feels good to say these open and honest words to someone other than Maya or the childhood therapist I met with for a year when I was fourteen.

"Mazie…"

"No," I say lightly interrupting him, "It was a dream, it was a *beautiful* dream and I am fine. I promise you. It's okay."

I feel his warm arms wrap around me and I turn so that my front is facing his front.

"Okay," he finally says and I hear him exhale as he pulls me closer. It's quiet and we lay comfortably in the welcomed silence. I am having a hard time believing this is real, that I could like someone so much and that they could like me, *in this way*, too.

"I wouldn't break your heart," he says lowly, yanking me from my wonderment and placing me back into real time.

"What?" I mumble into his chest.

"Mazie, I'm not going to break your heart," he says assuredly.

"Okay," I say. My voice is barely a whisper.

"I promise," he adds. Then he kisses my forehead, lingering before pulling away.

I inhale. "Okay," I repeat and the word is almost stuck in my throat. I'm warm all over and I know he can feel how quickly my heart is beating. We don't say another word to one another and after a few minutes I hear him snoring lightly. I smile as I nuzzle myself even closer to his chest, my head resting underneath his chin.

I don't know if I fell or if I am still falling, but right here in Barnaby's arms feels like the only place I ever want to be. If I can't stay in that dream, *right here* in this moment feels like the next best thing. *Right here in his arms*, is real, not a figment of my imagination.

And the thought of such permanence is more comforting than it is scary.

~~

"Have you thought of a title yet?" Barnaby asks. He's typing while I sit with my legs crossed on my couch next to him. We'd planned on going to the football field, but I woke up this morning with a migraine after staying awake pretty much all night writing. I hated that I would have had to cancel our plans but, Barnaby being Barnaby, decided he would just come over and sit with me. I'm feeling better. It was nothing a couple of pain pills couldn't solve, but I feel like him being here with me helps too.

"Kind of…" I answer hesitantly. "I mean, I know what I'm looking for."

"And what's that?"

"I want something that says, we spend our whole lives chasing something, searching for something, moving through these moments that are seemingly unattainable, just to end up…"

"Dying?" he finishes my sentence and I nod.

"Yeah, I want that vibe but less morbid."

That's my life, summed up. Something is out there that I want and I don't know exactly what it is, but I know I'll die before I ever reach it. It's a haunting reality and a discouraging thought, but it won't stop me from trying to find out what it is. If I can't find it I will just write about it, which is the next best thing.

He laughs at my words, "Well, what are some contenders?"

"If I tell you, will you laugh at me?"

"Probably," he answers immediately. Clenching my jaw, my face slips into an immediate scowl. "What? Honesty is the cornerstone of all healthy relationships," he adds.

I roll my eyes. The click of his laptop closing lets me know that he's putting it away for now. His hands are immediately pulling both of my legs from up under me and turning them so that my calves and feet are on his lap. "*Fine*, I won't laugh," he mutters, while taking off my socks.

"Okay…" taking a deep breath, I finally tell him my ideas, "*Obtaining Forever*… or *Looking For Forever*…"

He doesn't say anything right away and it feels like I've just bared my soul. This book is close to my heart and I'm still adjusting to the fact that I am sharing every little piece of it with Barnaby.

"Hmmm,"

"Barnaby…"

"I mean I get what you're going for, but does that feel a little cliché to you?" he asks and his voice is honest.

Repeating the titles in my head in a constant loop, it is clear that he is right, but what other options do I have?

"You're right," I say lowly, still not liking to admit when he is right, "but I need something that is unobtainable, something that exists but we can never grasp it in our lifetime." I sigh. "We can't achieve forever; forever doesn't exist but we chase it anyway."

"Infinite," Barnaby says softly, and he doesn't say anything else.

"What?"

"Infinite," he repeats. "You want *forever*, you want to keep going, you want to reach the hypothetical other side and grasp something that has never been grasped before. *Infinite,* you can chase it, you can set your life goals to attaining it, but you never will. It keeps going –it keeps moving even when you can't. It'll always be ahead of you, but it doesn't change the fact that it's what you want, maybe it's even what you think you need."

His words make my eyes prickle and I am so happy he cannot see my eyes behind my sunglasses; I am praying a tear doesn't fall. He's managed to convey what I am trying to say with one simple word. He quickly captured the essence of what I've been trying to relay and it makes me fall for him even more.

"*The Improbable Infinite*," I say lowly and that is it. That is the title of my novel and it is perfect in every way and it is everything that I want. Sitting up, I reach out to Barnaby so I can place my lips on his. "Thank you," I say against them. He's slowly pushing me back onto the couch, so that he is completely over me. It is clear that our writing and brainstorming session is over.

Seven

Boyfriend (n.): a man with whom someone is having a romantic or sexual relationship

I'm at school early today because Maya was called into work and had to drop me off before my usual time. The classroom is empty and I'm wishing I would've called Barnaby and told him I would be early. This wasted time could've been spent with him, spent making out with him. At the thought of his lips on mine, I pull out my phone and call him. It will be about an hour before class starts. The phone rings and rings then goes to voicemail. This is odd because any time I have ever called him he has answered on the first ring.

I call again and it doesn't even ring this time, it goes straight to voicemail. He deliberately turned his phone off. I have an uneasy feeling. Is he ignoring me? Have I done something? We've been dating for a little over a month now and everything seems okay. I'm nervously tapping my foot on the ground wondering if I should call again and leave a voicemail. Calling three times, that would make me one of those stalker girls. I don't want to be like those girls but knots are forming in my stomach.

I call him again and it goes straight to voicemail, "Hey," I say, "It's me. I was just calling to tell you I'm at school already because Maya had to go to work early and if you weren't busy maybe you could come up here. Umm, I hope everything is okay and talk to you later." I hang up and that feeling of unease is not gone. That feeling won't go away until I speak to him directly.

I imagine scenarios as to why he is ignoring me. Maybe he decided that dating the blind girl was too much work or maybe I was too clingy? We did hang out every day and talked on the phone every night. I usually called him. What if my argumentative nature was just too much and he has realized he doesn't want to deal with me anymore?

The knots in my stomach are now boulders. I am panicking and I haven't even spoken to him. I take a deep breath, trying desperately to calm my nerves and then my phone rings. I answer hastily on the first ring.

"Hello?" embarrassed at how breathless and how quickly I say it.

"Are you okay?" Barnaby asks immediately, once he hears my panic.

"Yeah, sorry I'm fine. Are you? I couldn't reach you." And I don't want to come across as crazy but I am pretty sure that's exactly what he is thinking. It is early, maybe he was sleeping, maybe he was just busy, or his phone wasn't charged.

A few seconds goes by before he responds, "I don't think I'm going to school today, some family issues, but I will call you, okay?" he's nearly whispering.

"Oh umm sure," I stutter, "Is everything alright?"

"I have to go, but I will call you."

"Okay, I just…" he hangs up before I can say anything else. Why is he missing school? Family issues, *again*? He sounds so different than the Barnaby I am accustomed to. If I were able, I would leave right now and go to his house to figure out if there was any way I could help. That would definitely put me in the stalker girlfriend category.

Girlfriend –I sigh.

I am still not sure if I am even his girlfriend. It's as if we talk about everything under the sun *except* that and I feel too foolish at this point to even mention it. I *feel* like his girlfriend, but what is that supposed to actually feel like?

The next hour goes by slowly, just like my entire school day. I don't think I realized how empty and dragged out my days are without Barnaby. Our schedules and lives have become so intertwined. We had our routine down to an exact art, but right now I am wandering the hallways somberly, knowing that I am just going to go home and wait for him to call. I sigh.

Once I get home, I go straight to my room and start on my homework. The hours continue to tick by and still no call.

A little later, I join Maya for dinner. We talk about our days, she asks if I am *okay* an annoying number of times and each time I lie and say that I am. I help with the dishes and sit on the couch with her for a bit while she watches a movie. I am too focused on my cellphone to actually listen to whatever is happening in this movie. I am too focused on the fact that it is getting late and my phone has yet to ring.

I take a shower and try to put two braids in my hair. I quit halfway through the first braid. My hair is too thick; I will ask Maya to put braids in this weekend.

My alarm beeps, letting me know that it is 11:15 pm which is usually when I go to sleep and *still* no call from Barnaby.

My anxiety won't let me fall asleep until closer to 1:00 am. I contemplate calling him, but he was very clear that he had a family issue. An issue so important that he had to miss school. An issue so important that he was unable to call me back like he said he would. I breathe a slow and steady breath and tell myself that whatever is going on with him and his family is under control.

The next day, I get to school at my normal time and, usually when I walk into the classroom, if we aren't already together, Barnaby speaks or I can smell his distinctive scent as he is walking up to me. But as I sit, no one says anything to me and I don't smell him.

The nerves that I was able to extinguish last night are back, but this time in full force. What if something is wrong? What if he is hurt? I stand up from my seat and leave the classroom to go to the first floor bathroom. I pull out my phone and call him. It rings six times before the voicemail picks up. "Hey, are you okay? You didn't call and you're not here. Just let me know you're okay." There is no way he won't hear the nervousness in my voice.

He doesn't call back and ends up missing another day of school. When I get home I debate whether I should have Maya drive me to his house but first, I don't have the address memorized and second, maybe I am overreacting. Maybe I am too needy, thinking that I need to talk to him every single day. He has a life outside of me and I need to respect that. I say the words to myself, but they don't make my nerves go away, the words actually make me feel worse.

At the thought of our everyday routine, I realize that no matter what is going on, he should be able to carve out at least one minute of twenty -four hours to let me know he is okay or that he isn't going to school. I think I deserve that much.

I don't know if I should keep worrying or be upset at this point. The more I allow myself to think he is ignoring me, the more pissed off I get and I would rather be mad that he is ignoring me than to be afraid and anxiety ridden thinking he is hurt.

I decide to call him again, girlfriend or not, I deserve an explanation. If he doesn't answer, I'm going to tell Maya that I am worried and go from there. As soon as I pick up my phone, it rings. I exhale and answer on the second ring.

"You're home?" Barnaby asks as soon as I answer, not even giving me a chance to say hello.

"Yes." Though I am relieved that not only did he call, but the fact that he is alright, I still have some residual anger towards him and it's evident in my voice. It's been practically two days and he didn't say anything to me at all. Maybe I am not his girlfriend; maybe that type of info is only privy to actual labeled girls in his life. The thought makes me sick.

"I'm on my way over," he says then he hangs up.

I can't tell what kind of mood he is in but he doesn't sound as down as he sounded yesterday morning. He sounds more like the Barnaby I know and though I am mad at him, I can't help the happy feeling that encircles me.

When he gets here he knocks and I yell, "Come in." Before I can even speak to him, his lips are on mine and we are shuffling backward. He is guiding me to my room and I smile against his lips. My anger toward him is now forgotten.

I hear my bedroom door close behind me, our lips never disconnecting, then my back hits my bed. His lips are on my neck when I am finally able to find some clarity and string together a few words. "What happened? Where were you?"

He kisses the right side of my neck, the left side of my neck, and then his lips are back on mine. We are done talking now.

I don't know how far we'd go, but ever since our very first date we'd been testing the water, nearing the deep end nearly every time. His hand is hovering around my zipper and I stiffen, like I always do. It isn't *me* that stiffens; my body does it on its own. He stops and then I no longer feel the heat of his skin on my chest. I am wearing only a bra and jeans. My shirt didn't last long in the bed. He kisses my neck and cheek softly as he is now on the side of me.

"I'm sorry," I say and I sit up interrupting his soft sweet kisses.

"Sorry for what?" and he sounds genuinely confused.

"I want to be ready," is all I say and he doesn't say anything. "I want to be ready with you." My voice is shaky and low, not at all me.

"Mazie, there's no pressure."

"…but I do want this with you." And I can't believe I am saying these words.

"I want this with you too, but when you're ready. You'll know when it's right. Either way I'm here."

"Am I your girlfriend?" I blurt out. The words leaving my lips before I even realize what I am saying.

"What?" and he almost sounds like he wants to laugh and I immediately feel gutted. I've never done this whole dating thing so I don't know the rules. I'd just embarrassed myself thoroughly. He's just been having fun and I am sitting here wanting to put labels on it.

My face is red; I can feel the heat in my cheeks. I can feel my eyes start to prickle with tears, could this moment be anymore humiliating?

"Wait," he says as I feel him sit up. He lifts my chin up. "You're serious?"

And the answer is *yes*, this moment *could* be more humiliating. It is like he is taking the knife that is in my chest and twisting it.

"Ezmerelda, of course you're my girlfriend!" he sounds like he is in shock. "It's not obvious? You don't consider me your boyfriend?"

My words are caught in my throat and now I am embarrassed for a completely different reason.

"I do, I just…" I trail off.

"You just, what?"

"I told you, I've never dated or had a boyfriend I didn't know, we never said…"

He laughs lightly then pecks my lips softly. "I'm not big on huge proclamations… not when it comes to things you just feel. I'm sorry if that's what you like. I should've been clearer. Will you be my girlfriend?" he asks and though his tone is serious I know he is being lighthearted.

"You're not into proclamations?" I mock incredulously. "Everything out of your mouth is a proclamation."

He laughs, "In the grand scheme of things, I guess so, but I'd rather feel something than hear it... than to see it," he pauses, "it's realer that way. I feel with you, I honestly didn't think it needed to be said. I am with you and only you. I really am sorry if you thought otherwise."

I pause and let his words spin around in my thoughts for a while and the compulsion to say *now or never* creeps up on me and the words are leaving my lips before I am even sure of what I am saying. "I'm ready, now." And I think I am, or I want this so badly that I will force myself to be.

"Ready?" he questions confusingly, then comprehension slowly settles in. "Oh, ready for..." he trails off. I don't say a word. I just nod.

"You're not," he says as a matter of fact with no inflection. I am stunned by the response. It's not what I expect. "Ten seconds ago you didn't know if you were my girlfriend. You're not ready for sex, Ezmerelda."

I am frustrated that he just blew me off like I don't know what I want. I am a young adult and extremely capable of making these kinds of decisions. I ignore him and reach out to where I sense he is and touch his bare back. "Shut up, I want to." I grab his arm and pull him to me as I lay back on the bed. "And it's Mazie," I mumble angrily against his lips.

And I am woman, I am brave, and I am a ball of flesh and lust and I want my first time to be with Barnaby. Hell, I want my last time and all the times in between to be with him too. I shake that heavy thought out of my mind as he finally kisses me back, his body on top of mine. Our kiss, like most of our kisses, is passionate and stimulating, but Barnaby is making no other moves than putting his hands on my face and in my hair.

He thinks I'm bluffing, it is clear.

Just to show him how serious I am, I muster up the confidence to unbutton and unzip my own jeans, sliding them off as I lay underneath him. Shakily and clumsily I manage to get them off.

"Mazie..." he says, and his voice is husky, the words are nearly caught in his throat. Now I have his attention.

"I want to," I say again and my voice betrays me. It trembles and quakes, no confidence or validity whatsoever. It actually sounds like I am crying or about to.

"You want to?" and the huskiness in his voice is now gone. He sounds incredulous, my shaky hands and wavering voice negate all of my efforts and Barnaby has picked up on it.

To regain some ground I take a deep breath and tell myself that this is eventually going to happen and it is going to happen with Barnaby, that much I've known since we started dating. So what would be the point of waiting? I swallow the large lump that is lodged in my throat and, with my heart pounding like it's going to rip itself from my chest, I reach down to take off my underwear.

He grabs my wrist immediately. My hands are shaking even harder. My heart is now pounding in almost a zig zag of a rhythm and I am breathing like I just ran a full marathon.

I am fully aware of how embarrassing this is. But nerves are normal, right? Nerves are a part of this whole thing. It's my first time. *It will be my first time*; I am allowed to feel like I am drowning in quicksand, burning at the stake, about to die any second.

"If you're actually ready for this, I would like to do that," he whispers against my lips and I shiver. I know what he is doing, he's teasing me but I want this to happen, I think.

I am eighteen. I am probably the only senior in my school who hasn't had sex before. I wanted life experiences and this is something that I feel I need to check off my list, not that it was ever on my list of things to do when I transferred schools. Meeting my first boyfriend, meeting someone like Barnaby, was also not on my list, but I am more than happy about the new additions.

He traces his index finger across my panty line right and left then back again and again and it is torture. He isn't taking me seriously, but then suddenly he snakes his hand into the side of my panties, his warm hand resting on my hip and I swallow. My heart starts hammering against my rib cage more erratically than the zig zags just moments ago.

Then I hear a car door slam. He and I both freeze, that could just be the neighbors. His lips are back on mine and then a few moments later I hear the living room door open and keys hit the coffee table.

"Shit!" I hiss. Barnaby is off of me in an instant. It isn't like Barnaby and I aren't allowed to be in the house together alone, but I am sure Maya will have an issue finding me sprawled out half naked under him. Eighteen or not, I know there are limits.

"Here!" he whispers forcefully and then I feel something hit my face. It's my shirt.

"I'm home!" Maya calls out.

I've never moved so quickly in my life. "Pants," I hiss at Barnaby and then I feel jeans hit me roughly in the face. "Hey, could you please refrain from throwing things fifty miles an hour into the face of a blind girl?" I add whispering forcefully too.

"I'm just going to go out there," he says ignoring my comment. "Why are we freaking out? She knows I'm here. My car is parked out front. Not responding looks suspicious."

"What? No! I'm not ready." And then I hear my bedroom door open. "Barnaby!"

"Hi, Amaya," I hear his voice in the distance. "She's using her bathroom, we were just doing homework. How was your day? Do you always work twelve hour shifts? I couldn't imagine." He prattles on and on.

I hear Maya speaking but she is speaking so lowly that I can't decipher what exactly she is saying. I exhale and realize that for a first boyfriend I picked such an odd human or maybe he picked me, either way we are each other's. I walk out of my bedroom timidly, not knowing exactly where Maya is.

I wonder what I look like; did I look like a girl who'd almost had sex for the first time just moments ago? Oh shit, was I really going to have sex with him, in my bed? Did he even have protection? I can feel my pulse in my palms as I realize that unbeknownst to my sister, she'd just saved me or maybe not. I don't know.

Of course Barnaby is right, he said I wasn't ready and maybe because I am stubborn or maybe because I don't like people telling me what to do or what not to do, especially him, I somehow made myself believe I was ready. I want to, that is the truth. I just can't get the rest of me to go along with it. Whoever truly knows when they're ready though? That's a tricky slope, but I know if I am going to do this one day it will be with him. I won't want to share that part of myself with anyone else. He and I are going to need to talk.

"Hey," I hear Maya walk up to me and kiss my cheek.

"You're home early," I say and I don't mean for my voice to sound so accusatory.

"Umm," she says as she picks up on my tone. "Alexis switched shifts with me. Was I interrupting something?" To me, her voice sounds knowing and it makes my heart skip a couple of beats.

"No," I say a little too hastily and then I hear Barnaby clear his throat from across the room, clearly trying to stifle laughing at me. I want to shoot a scowl at him, but Maya will see.

I don't know why I am acting this way, my sister is my best friend. I tell her everything, but boys have never been in the picture. That area of our sisterhood and friendship hasn't been explored yet. I don't know how she will react if she knows I am contemplating sex. On my first date with Barnaby she said to be safe, could she have been referring to sex? In the last month I've told her about the dates and the conversations he and I have had, but the extracurricular activities I leave out.

"Barnaby," my sister says, she's walked away from me. "Would you like to stay for dinner? It's Mazie's turn to cook. Has she told you what a wonderful chef she is without my help?"

"No, I didn't know that," he says and I can hear the smile in his voice. "I'm always learning something new about Ezmerelda." And I know he is staring at me because he likes to get a rise out of me.

"There isn't enough to go around," I say angrily as I turn and walk into the kitchen.

"I'd love to stay for dinner, thank you so much for the invite, Amaya." I hear him say and I huff, slamming open a cabinet door grabbing a box of noodles. I guess I'll make pasta. It's one of Barnaby's favorite foods that does not categorize as a dessert, even though he disgustingly puts sugar on his pasta. Yuck.

"You know you can just continue to call me Maya." I hear her say.

Good luck with that. I made the mistake of telling him her real name and he clearly doesn't have the best track record with calling people by the names they prefer.

"Mazie," Maya says, I feel her behind me. "Pasta? Okay." I hear her opening cabinets and turning on the sink. "I'm going to run out, I forgot to pick up my dry cleaning. I should be back before the food is on the table. All the timers are set and pots are already on the stove." Moments later I hear the front door close.

I am at the sink washing the lettuce for our salads with cool water when I feel Barnaby's hands snake around my stomach, his face nuzzles under my wild hair while his lips and tongue suck and nip at my neck. "There isn't enough food for me to stay?" he whispers on my skin. It's as if my entire body is set on fire. I am tingling from the pads of my feet all the way up to the hair follicles on the very top of my head.

I spin around and, like a magnet, his lips are on mine and this kiss is eager and hungry and encompassing. My wet hands are wrapped around his neck, the water dripping down his back. I have this urge to wrap my legs around him, squeeze around his neck tighter, have him as close as humanly and physically possible. Maya will be gone for at least a half hour. That's enough time to do this, right?

I stop questioning myself and let my body do what she sees fit. Her emotions and needs are much louder than my questions and doubts. I pull up on the tips of my toes and, as if he can read my mind, he moves his hands to the back of my thighs, bends his knees slightly, and hoists my legs around his waist.

This kiss, his body pressed this close to mine, all of it has me dizzy and wanting, dizzy and panting. It feels like every live cell in my body is calling his name specifically.

He moves his lips from mine then places them gently and lazily on my neck, all the passion and fire gone, just like that. It's now sweet and innocent. "Mazie," he says softly and I can hear something off in his voice. I don't know what, but the flat note gives me a moment of clarity. We are in my kitchen. My sister could walk in on us. Is this how I imagined my first time being?

"You're not ready," he murmurs softly interrupting my thoughts. How does he do that?!

He is still kissing my neck gently. I am sitting on the edge of the counter and my legs are still tightly wrapped around him.

"I haven't done anything to indicate I'm not ready," is all I can say. How he knows this is beyond me. Being nervous isn't such a bad thing.

"You didn't have to do or say anything," he says and he finally moves his lips from my neck. He's only inches from my face, I want to kiss him again but things get foggy when I kiss him and I think we need to have this talk now. "Remember? We are all just thoughts and emotions. Your body might want this, but the rest of you? Not yet, and I don't want you cheated out of your first time because you rushed it. I don't plan on going anywhere."

My heart is racing because his words are what every single girl in the world wants to hear. But I am stubborn and it is in my nature to argue, to debate; it's what *we* do. And plus, I don't like it when he is right. "I took my pants off," I say.

And he chuckles.

"You thought I was ready twenty five minutes ago," I add, "and now I'm not?"

"Taking your pants off wasn't sex, and I didn't think you were ready twenty five minutes ago. I was just indulging you. I got to enjoy myself in the process though. Also, you were practically having a seizure and an asthma attack, never really good signs of someone being *ready* for something," he says and he's laughing at me. One, because that's his favorite thing to do and two, because he knows this is going to be one of those frivolous and pointless arguments. So I decide to give him the full show.

"You were about to take my panties off," I state solidly. "I was going to *let* you take my panties off before Maya interrupted."

"Maybe you were, maybe you weren't." I can feel him shrug because my legs and arms are still wrapped around him. "We wouldn't have gone too far either way."

"My laying almost completely naked under you is already too far."

"So you admit it!" he says quickly. "Things went too far because you're not ready?!"

Damn it. I don't say anything because in the rarity that it happens, a point has been proven against me.

"Listen," he says and his lips are back on my neck, "I mean what I said, when you're ready. I'm not going anywhere unless you want me to. And that will suck and hurt, but if it's what you want and you decide you don't want me around any…"

"Oh God, shut up." I cut him off and grab the sides of his face and pull his lips to mine. "Thank you for understanding."

We spend the next fifteen minutes making out. We do not disconnect until we hear Maya closing her car door. I then realize I never started cooking. Maya isn't particularly enthused with me about this.

Once we finally sit down for dinner, it's the *Barnaby Show*, and I enjoy every second of it. He has a story for everything, an opinion on everything, an idea about everything. He's a tornado, *all consuming*, larger than life and brilliant. All the things that once annoyed me when we first met are all the things that I now cherish and admire.

He's sitting next to me and Maya is sitting across from us, this is the usual seating arrangement.

"So, what I was asking earlier," Maya says, "what exactly happened to your eye? That's a pretty bad bruise."

My head immediately snaps to his direction as if I could see what she's talking about. Bruise?

"Me and my brother were rough housing and I slammed right into the edge of a door."

He is lying.

I know he is lying because his brother is away at college and Barnaby is not the *rough housing* type, but I can't exactly call him out on it in front of Maya.

"Oh, well, if you want me to look at it I can. Looking at the redness I think you may have a few popped blood vessels. How's your vision?"

A few popped blood vessels! What the hell happened!? I am now eager and ready for dinner to be over. I need to be alone with Barnaby *now*.

"I can see perfectly. It's okay, thank you though," he says and I can tell that *he* can tell that I know he is lying and that I have one hundred questions for him.

Twenty minutes goes by and dinner should have wrapped up ten minutes ago, but Barnaby keeps on babbling about nonsense. I'd tuned him out because I know exactly what he's doing. He's stalling; he is buying time. Does he think he can keep my sister at this table long enough that I'd magically forget the questions I have for him? Has he forgotten who I am?

"It's getting late, I'll clear the table," I say interrupting his story about a trip he took to Orlando when he was eight. I stand and grab my plate and I hear him clear his throat.

"I should be turning in," Maya says. "It's always great talking with you, Barnaby," she says.

"You too, Maya," he says, and I almost pour ice water on him for agreeing to call her by her shortened name and not calling me by mine 90% of the time.

I hear Maya's chair move, then I feel her kiss my cheek. "Goodnight, Mazie- My," she whispers.

"Goodnight, Maya- Me."

A few seconds pass and I hear her bedroom door close down the hall.

"I guess I should be going," he says.

"You're not going to offer to help your girlfriend clear the table? Very chivalrous of you, Barnaby."

"You're a capable woman, Ezmerelda."

"And you're a liar!" I snap and he sighs. "Why did you tell my sister that story? I know that's not what happened and why didn't you tell me about your eye at all? And why were you gone for two days? You didn't call me like you said you would and you didn't show up at school today! I was worried and pissed off and..."

"Shit, can you give me a second to answer at least one of the seventeen questions you just threw at me?"

I slam down the plate onto the table, a little harder than I intended to, but I think it made a solid point of how angry I am. I sit back down with my arms folded over my chest. He knew I was mad the second he came over, that's why he distracted me with kisses so we wouldn't talk, so I wouldn't question him. He made me foggy and forgetful. I'd forgotten that I was furious with him, but above all worried about him.

He needs to give me answers to every single question I have.

"Me and my dad got into an argument," he finally says. "It's not a big deal."

"Your dad hit you?" I respond immediately, the shock in my voice is evident.

"It's not a big deal," he states again but much more firmly and I want to be agitated with him but something is missing in his voice. That tornado, that energy that annoys me sometimes, but also pulls me in like a moth to a flame, is gone and suddenly my stomach feels warm and I can feel my eyes start to prickle.

"This isn't the first time." My voice is shaky. It's supposed to be a question, but it comes out as a statement.

"I want to share everything with you," he says and he pauses for a very long time. So long that I am about to say something, but then he finally speaks. "...but this is something that I don't want to talk about right now and I don't want you to be mad or to think I don't trust you because I do. You're actually one of the only people in my life that I trust explicitly, but right now I just want to kiss all over my beautiful, caring girlfriend and forget everything else in the world for a little while."

I just sit there, stuck between wanting to force him to tell me what happened or what *happens*. But also wanting him to know he can rely on me, that I won't pressure him into anything, just like he doesn't pressure me into anything...

What's going on in Barnaby's world apart from me? I want to know, I need to know, but I also don't want to push him away.

"Please, Mazie?" he begs softly and his voice turns me into liquid. I go against my better judgement and let it go, for now. It won't be far from my thoughts and Barnaby knows that. All I want to know is that he is safe and that he is okay.

I sigh and before I can speak, I feel his warm hand encircle mine. I stand and he walks us to the couch and as soon as our bodies hit the cushion, his lips are on mine.

~~

I'm sitting on Barnaby's living room couch. It smells like floral air freshener has been sprayed to cover up the strong fragrance of cigarette smoke –it isn't working. I hear music playing loudly upstairs, some boyband and I giggle. I've jokingly judged his taste in music, and secretly I like the odd stuff he has me listening to, but if he is listening to boyband music I will have an entire new world of jokes to tease him with.

I hear the music cut off and then someone jogs down the steps and into the living room. I assume it's Barnaby, but he sounds a little too light on his feet.

"Oh my God, are you Ezmerelda?" a high pitched female voice asks enthusiastically.

"Uh, yeah, I go by Mazie," I correct.

"You're so pretty. What are you doing with Barnaby?" she says in mock shock and I blush, and immediately know that this has to be his younger sister.

"You must be Amelia," I say with a smile.

"Yep, but seriously did you lose a bet? Did he drug you or something?" she laughs and I can't help but laugh too.

"Sometimes I wonder," I shrug. I *am* always abnormally intoxicated after making out with him. Amelia and I are both laughing like we'd known each other for years, laughing at the expense of Barnaby seems to be a common ground for us.

The couch moves and I know she is sitting down next to me. "Your hair is amazing," she says genuinely. I am used to people being fascinated by my big hair. Besides being blind, I think it's the first thing most people see when they see me.

"Thank you," I say.

"So where is that brother of mine?" she asks.

"Outside, something is going on with his car," I say. "He told me to wait here."

"There's *always* something going on with that death trap."

I laugh and slowly the sound of my voice fades into the quiet room. I feel the urge to fill this space with questions and conversation, but Barnaby tells so little of his family to me. I wouldn't know what to talk about other than Barnaby himself.

A few moments later I hear the television. Each channel she turns to, the voices are blaring. It's too loud for my liking, but this is her home. I wouldn't dare say anything.

"When exactly did you guys start dating? September? October? That's around the time he stopped being around here," she says out of the blue. She is laughing, but it doesn't seem like a humorous laugh. I suddenly feel guilty. Does she miss her brother? Have I been taking time away from her? He and I did spend a lot of time together.

"September," I answer and my voice is small. It's filled with guilt.

"Hmmm," she says and suddenly the guilt is in the back of my mind because I want to burst into laughter. The *hmmms* must run in the family.

"He's never had a girlfriend longer than a couple weeks and he has *never* brought them here. You clearly have him wrapped around your fingers, so, good job!"

I am sure I am beet red right now. Also, it's weird thinking about Barnaby having girlfriends before me. Of course he did, he's wonderful and hilarious and according to my sister, he's gorgeous. I am the one who hasn't dated, kissed or anything of that nature, but still I feel like this universe doesn't make sense if the names Barnaby and Mazie aren't linked together.

Barnaby and Angela? Barnaby and Jennifer? Barnaby and Tisha? Barnaby and Lisa? Any of those faceless names beside Barnaby's just doesn't make sense. At that thought I realize that this feeling I'm experiencing is jealousy. It's irrational and stupid, but prevalent nonetheless.

"I'm going to tell you something he doesn't know that I know," she begins to say.

I am nervous, but also more curious than I've ever been about anything in my entire life. I feel like I know Barnaby in a way others don't, but there is still this restricted area that I am not allowed near, a part of him that I don't have access to. Amelia may be the only chance I have to at least crack the door open that Barnaby has bolted shut.

I don't respond to her and I just wait for her to continue. A whisper in the back of my mind is telling me that this could possibly be an invasion of privacy and that I should respect my boyfriend by declining any information his little sister may have, but I am actively drowning that voice out.

"He has this notebook that he always carries around and usually there's just a bunch of nonsense in it. Lists, things to remember, poems," she says, "I've looked at it a few times in the past, but the last couple of months he's been super protective of it, so that only made me want to look in it more." She starts laughing. I smile, unable to laugh because I have no clue where she is going with this.

"A couple weeks ago, I went into his computer bag and got it out while he was in the back fixing his death trap and it was a completely new notebook with a bunch of stuff in there about you. That's how I figured you were Ezmerelda. Page after page…" she adds.

And I feel my face blush. I want to ask her where the notebook is right now, I want her to tell me every single word he'd written in it and when.

"Oh." Is all I actually say, because I am not really sure how to respond to this, it's definitely not where I thought this conversation was going.

It's quiet again while she continues to surf through the channels.

"I think they are all poems and just random things about you. I can't tell because none of them rhyme and he writes like a damn five year old." We both laugh. "Seriously, you should see how tiny he writes. It's worse than chicken scratch!" We continue to laugh and then abruptly, she stops.

"I'm sorry," she says immediately. It takes me a second to even figure out what she is apologizing for before it hits me, she's apologizing for saying I should *see* Barnaby's handwriting.

"I didn't mean to say…"

"Amelia," I interrupt, "there's no need to apologize or walk on eggshells around me." I say, with a bright smile,

"Your brother doesn't." I laugh and then finally she joins in.

"Okay." And I think it's safe to say, she is smiling too.

"So, this notebook," she continues, "There's this thing he wrote about giving you the sunset, and it was so sweet and as much as I like to tease my brother, I think it's pretty cool that he likes you this much. He's nicer since knowing you."

And this is too much to take in at once. First, I can't imagine Barnaby not being nice, is there a mean side to him that only his family knows that I don't? I honestly hope I never meet that side, if one exists. Is this mean side bolted away in that restricted area?

And he wrote a poem about *giving me the sunset*? I need to know what it says; I need to know what he means by that.

"Ugh," Amelia says and it snaps me out of my thought. "There is never anything on, 200 channels and nothing!" Her words are saturated with frustration.

I want to bring up the poem again, but decide I'd rather hear it when he's ready for me to hear it, it will be more meaningful that way. She and I are sitting there quietly when my thoughts are suddenly flooded with the urge to ask about their father.

In this short time, I feel like I can get more out of Amelia in ten minutes than I've gotten out of her brother in months.

I know it isn't my place and I know that I could offend her and if Barnaby finds out he won't be too happy with me, but it has been a while and he hasn't given me any answers. He hasn't given me *anything.*

I try to figure out how I can word this, how can I discreetly broach the subject without sounding like I'm fishing for information?

"What grade are you in?" I ask. Barnaby very rarely spoke about his family. The fact that I even know his siblings' names is because I asked. He never offers up anything further.

"I'm a freshman," she says. "I don't go to your high school," she adds as if she knows that's going to be my next question, and she's right.

"Where do you go?" I ask, truly curious. It really didn't make sense for her to attend a different high school than her brother.

"I go to an all girls' school," and the way she says this, I can tell she is pissed about it. "My dad is an asshole," she says regretfully and I cannot believe the door she has just opened for me. My heart is pounding because I have anxiety about walking through this theoretical door. I will be deliberately walking over one of Barnaby's boundaries, his only boundary. I am jiggling the handle to the restricted area.

"He is? How so?" I try to sound casual. I try to sound like I won't care if she doesn't answer, that I am just being conversational. She doesn't say anything at first and I can't help but feel like running away from this door and standing on the other side of the line where I cannot disturb her or Barnaby.

"All dads are assholes." She says this blanketed statement lowly as if it were common knowledge and though I don't know her at all, I know she is holding something back. I wonder if he hits her too… I feel my cheeks get hot and I am actively forcing my tears to stay put. Just like her big brother, all of the rapid talking and multiple questions are out of the window when the topic of their father is brought up.

"Have you been blind your entire life?" she asks randomly changing the topic completely. Before I can even process the question I hear Barnaby's voice.

"Amelia!" he barks in surprise. "What the hell are you doing?" he questions angrily. "You're not even supposed to be here!"

"Barnaby, it's okay…" I say, but I know it is falling on deaf ears.

"God, calm down. Tiana is running late and besides, Maze and I are friends," she says, as I feel her get off of the couch. "It was nice meeting you!" She touches my shoulder and though she doesn't call me Mazie, I'd take Maze over Ezmerelda any day.

"It was nice meeting you too, Amelia." I smile brightly.

"You can call me Mel," she says and I sense her walk away. "She's too cute for you," I hear her whisper, obviously speaking to Barnaby. I stifle a giggle. Seconds later I feel the couch move and Barnaby's hand on my leg.

"I'm sorry about that," he says. "I got the car running again…"

"Sorry about what?" I cut in confused. "I like her, she reminds me of you a little bit."

"I'm not going to take that as a compliment," he says flatly and I laugh.

"Well, you should. You both are very curious and not afraid to ask questions." I shrug.

"You used to hate my questions."

"I've never hated anything about you, Barnaby," I say honestly. "Annoyed? Yes, but never hate."

He kisses my cheek and grabs my hand, intertwining our fingers together. I rest my head on his shoulder. "How's your headache now?" he asks me for the second time today while he massages the back of my hand with his thumb. Last night I had a horrible migraine and had to go to sleep early. I feel fine now, but last night the only thing that could make me feel comfortable was lying down.

"I feel good, thank you for staying on the phone until I fell asleep," I say with a smile. He wanted to come over but I told him not to, and plus I was so tired I knew that if we were in the same room together there would be no way I would get any real sleep. I blush slightly at the thought.

"Of course," he says. "I still think you should take some more Tylenol just to be safe." It's cute that he's worried. I nod in agreement because he's right I guess. I won't actually tell him that though. We sit in silence, our breathing being the only sounds I hear in the room.

"So what all did she tell you?" he asks all-knowing and out of the blue. He's clearly talking about his sister.

I laugh, "Why? Are you nervous that she told me about all the other girls you bring here throughout the week?"

He laughs too, dislodging our hands and putting his arm around my shoulders. "Seriously, I know my sister, she doesn't know how or when to shut up."

"Ah, genetics?" I inquire and his laugh is so loud that I can't help but follow and laugh too. It's unbelievable how infectious that sound is. "She told me that you're nicer since meeting me," I offer. "Do you have a mean streak that I don't know about?"

He sighs and at first I can't tell if he is relieved or frustrated. "I have a bit of a temper, but it's usually reserved for nosey and annoying fourteen year old sisters."

"She also says that you've never dated anyone longer than two weeks."

"That's not true," he says immediately and that aching feeling of jealousy comes roaring back. I don't want to hear about the girls who held his attention before me. "You and I have been together for almost three months," he says and I sigh in relief.

"Besides me," I say lowly.

"Oh, yeah, then that's true." I feel him shrug. "Seems like I was just passing time when I look back at it. I think I was just waiting for you and didn't know it."

I don't even think he knows what his words do to me. I am sure he doesn't even realize how beautiful his words are. They fall from his lips so effortlessly as if he doesn't have to think before he says them.

I reach my hand up to place it on his cheek, I feel him nuzzle his face into my palm and then turn to kiss it.

"She said that I was the first girl you've brought home," I say lowly, barely audible.

"Also true," his voice is husky and I know what that means, the energy in the room is changing. "That's because you're important," he says and I can feel his face move closer to mine and without a second thought I close the gap between us.

Eight

Love (n.): a feeling of strong or constant affection for a person

"Okay, close your eyes!" Barnaby says, while helping me out of his car. I scowl in his general direction.

"Very funny," I deadpan.

He chuckles then grabs my hand before we start walking. "There are six steps coming up." We walk up slowly, and then I hear a door open. We walk for a few more minutes then I hear another door open and a cool breeze hits my face. My big curly hair, that I decided to let roam freely, whips and spreads across my face wildly. We are back outside.

Barnaby called me last night and said he had a surprise for me. He told me to wear a dress, which ended up being a ten minute argument because I don't wear dresses and he knows this. Eventually I conceded and had Maya pick one out for me. It has white spaghetti straps with lilac flowers on the hem. He told me we were being fancy today. I'm excited, but also nervous because I am never quite sure what Barnaby has up his sleeve.

When I told Maya about this fancy date he was taking me on, she wanted to straighten my hair but I didn't like the fact that my curly hair couldn't be synonymous with attire for a fancy event. It's how it grows out of my head; that's how I should be able to wear it, regardless of how some may view it.

I did, however, put a little lipstick on and wore a small heel. I have to trust that Barnaby won't let me fall. Anything other than boots and converses are new and uncharted territory for me.

I hear birds chirping, and I feel the sun beaming on my face which is odd because the weather should be much colder this time of year, but it's not and I am not complaining. I smell and hear water, the water crashing softly against something.

I freeze.

"Barnaby..."

"What?" he asks as he tugs on my hand trying to pull me forward, but I am cemented in place.

"I told you that I don't like the water," I nearly whisper, the fear gripping the words in my throat.

"I know, that's why we are here. We have a boat for the whole day. Come lunch time you'll want a boat of your own."

"No," I say and now I am angry. "I told you it was one of my fears." My thoughts flashing back to the last time I was on a boat, the last of the happy days in my life.

"You admitted yourself that it was an irrational fear. What kind of life do you want to live, Mazie?"

I'm so frustrated with him that I'm counting backward from 100.

"You said you wanted life experiences; you didn't want anything to hold you back! Well don't let a little fear hold you back from having a fun and relaxing day with your boyfriend."

I don't say anything…seventy -eight, seventy -seven, seventy -six…

"What is it that you are afraid of the most?"

I inhale and I wish I knew where we were because I would storm away from him and ignore him for a few days. I manage to calm myself and somewhere deep, deep down I tell myself that he is trying to help me, though I didn't ask for help. "I can't find my bearings," I say quickly and angrily.

"So, like what? It messes with your senses?"

"Yes, I can't move the way I want, I don't know what direction I am coming or going. I can't hear against the crashing water, everything is off balance. It's overwhelming." *Also my parents used to take me and Maya on a two week boating trip every summer. The last time I was on a boat I didn't know I had cancer yet, I still had my sight and both of my parents were still alive.*

"Do you trust me?" he asks sincerely and it cuts through my memory and throws me off.

"What?"

"Do you trust me?" he repeats emphasizing each word. "Do you trust me not to lead you wrong in any way? You can do this, you know you can."

I inhale deeply and let out a shaky breath. Of course I trust him. *Ugh.*

"If you're really scared," he begins to say, "we don't have to do this. I just think you'll feel better if you do, to not hold on to this fear anymore, to have one less thing nagging at you. But if going home is what you …"

"Fine," I interrupt irritably. I am not in the mood for one of his motivational speeches. I am still angry with him, but we are here and I did admit that my fear was irrational. I wish I hadn't told him.

He leads me onto the boat and I am a walking sweat bucket. I am on the verge of shaking.

"The hardest part is the doing, but once you get to the done part, it's smooth sailing. No pun intended."

I don't have time for his Barnaby babble either. He can't distract me from the fact that I am on a boat for the first time in five years. Fear is hugging me so tightly that I am almost unable to breathe. What I said to Barnaby is true, it just wasn't the full truth. It's like somewhere in the back of my mind I felt like all the good things were left on the water. Five years ago I walked onto that boat with everything and when we finally got back to land everything changed; all the happy days were gone for a very long time. I inhale.

"Hello," I hear a woman's bell- like voice coming from behind me. It startles me and I jump embarrassingly, Barnaby holds my hand tighter. My nerves are haywire and it is all Barnaby's fault.

"You must be Mr. and Mrs. Franklin. I'm Alania," she says and I immediately turn toward Barnaby. He squeezes my hand in one quick squeeze as if to say shut up and go with it. Who the hell are Mr. and Mrs. Franklin? God, what did he get us into?

"Yes, my wife and I are scheduled for the entire day," he says in a voice and tone that is so odd and such a departure from the loud and fun Barnaby I know. He sounds like a businessman, like he's gone to graduate school and has a well-paying job. He sounds like the type of person who sniffs wine and sends it back immediately if it's corked and then asks for a better year. I try not to laugh at the thought of this alternate Barnaby.

"Right this way, Mr. Franklin," she says and he starts to pull me forward. I am taking small careful steps. I don't feel like we are on the water which is a good thing but also we are docked. Who knows what that could mean once we aren't?

"Have a seat and your server will bring you your breakfast and then you can be on your way. The weather is just lovely, a perfect day for yachting," Alania says happily. When I hear a door close I realize we are inside the boat. *This* I can handle, up on the deck will be an entirely different issue.

"We are on a yacht?" I can't hide the astonishment in my voice.

"What would you like to drink, *Mrs. Franklin?*" Barnaby asks smoothly.

"Barnaby, did you steal a yacht?" I accuse and one would think I would have more shock in my tone but this is Barnaby, so nothing really shocks me anymore.

"You should actually say it a little louder so the police can hear," he says in an even tone. "And no…" he continues whispering, "I borrowed one. My cousin does the scheduling here and I was owed a favor."

"What if the Franklins show up looking for a yacht?" I question, but this time I am whispering.

"They are in France." He grabs my hand across the table. "Relax and enjoy. Hey, you're on a fancy yacht about to eat fancy food with your fancy boyfriend. How do you feel?"

"Fancy," I say flatly and he starts to laugh which nine times out of ten makes me smile or laugh because the sound is that infectious. "Thank you, Barnaby," I say lowly. "This is very special."

"You're very special to me, Ezmerelda." His voice is serious and his grip on my hand is tighter and even though he uses my full name and that makes me hate him, I realize in this exact moment, I love him.

I love Barnaby Parks.

Everything I've been feeling, every thought I've had, every moment I've shared with Barnaby has been adding up to this realization. I wonder if he loves me too.

"So…" he says, letting go of my hand. "We are of age according to that file, so are we getting shit faced or would you like to remain fancy and high class?"

"Somewhere in the middle?" I offer.

"Like heaven and the up there." he states. And I smile wanting to close the space between us and rest my lips on his.

He orders us mimosas and they are delicious. I want to just drink mimosas and do nothing else but Barnaby reminds me that it's important to eat before and while drinking especially on the water because I could throw up. That is enough reason to put the champagne flute down.

"You seem relaxed now," he says as we eat our breakfast. It's pancakes, sausage, and scrambled eggs with melon and pineapples on the side. I am pretty sure these are the fluffiest and most delicious pancakes I've ever eaten.

"I think the three mimosas have something to do with that."

He laughs, "We have a long day ahead of us and two more meals to go, so I'm cutting you off until our romantic dinner."

"Romantic dinner?" I smile, because he really planned everything out. "What's the special occasion, Mr. Franklin?"

"We are alive, we are together, and we are happy," he says, "That's *always* a special occasion."

And it takes every ounce of willpower I have not to stand up and lunge myself at him. He always knows the right thing to say, even when he is speaking in his riddles or his words go over my head and I don't realize what he means until days later, even then it's always something that sticks, it's always something important.

He's important.

"Thank you," I say lowly. "You didn't have to do all of this…"

"Yes I did," he answers.

"Why?"

"Because I…" he says, then he kind of fumbles over the sentence, and in that split second I think he is going to say it. I think he is going to utter the words that I am too cowardly to utter first.

"…I think you need more adventure in your life and it was an excuse to spend the entire day with you outside of your house." He clears his throat, his words falling off at the end as if he knows what I am thinking.

My chest feels hot in an uncomfortable way and I am so close to just saying it, to ripping the band aid off. He's told me he isn't big on proclamations, that if he felt it, it meant more than saying it. What is he feeling now? Because I know exactly what I am feeling.

"Barnaby," I begin to say, but then our waitress comes, and I hear the clinks of silverware and plates being stacked. Barnaby exhales softly. He's nervous? So am I.

We are having a very serious conversation without words right now and it is intense. There is no way he doesn't feel the energy that I am feeling at this moment. I hear the waitress walk away.

"You were saying something?" he asks immediately and his voice sounds almost impatient and unsure. Here is my chance, right now is the perfect time. What's the worst that can happen? He knows what I want to say and he knows what I want him to say and vice versa.

"I am really glad you planned this, you have to introduce me to your cousin so I can thank him."

I swallow and feel like a punk, but so should he. We are both cowards. We are both trying to swim, but drowning in these immense emotions traveling between us in a powerful electrical charge. Those three words are tormenting us, looming in the air like a puff of smoke –so delicate and fragile.

It's quiet and I wish I knew exactly what he was feeling. I wish I could stare into his eyes and figure out what his thought process is right now. What emotion is he exuding?

"*Her*," he finally says. I am so lost in my thoughts that his voice almost makes me jump for the second time today.

"What?"

"My cousin has a vagina."

I sigh, "My Barnaby, the weird and the blunt." I laugh feeling the tension that was stacked up between us slowly slipping away.

"My dear sweet Ezmerelda, the beautiful and the brave."

I smile and bite my lip; I can feel the blush spreading all over me. I don't correct him, "Now I wish I'd said something nicer."

"Weird and blunt are compliments to me," he says and I hear his chair move and seconds later his hand is under my chin and our lips are touching. Softly, gently – *lovingly*.

Later, he managed to convince me to stand in the front deck of the yacht. He promised he would hold on to my hips so that I wouldn't fall. He told me that we were facing north, that I didn't need my bearings because I was with him and everything would be okay, nothing would happen. And he was right. I put my trust in Barnaby. When the yacht started moving I felt nauseated and I wanted to put my foot down and tell him *no this was too much* but I didn't. I let him lead me to the front, I held on tightly to the railing and his hands never left me.

He kissed and nibbled on my ear and neck, I knew what he was doing; he was trying to relax me –distract me from my thoughts and fears. And after a few minutes, it worked. I enjoyed his touch and his kisses. I enjoyed the fresh air as I took deep breaths letting the cool air massage my lungs. I loved the light sprinkle of the water splashing my face. My hair was soaring, no doubt it was blowing in Barnaby's face. I was enjoying myself, I was conquering a fear, *a very real fear*, of mine when I think about it and it was all because of this weird and blunt boy whom I loved.

Tonight, the yacht will dock so we can have dinner at the harbor. We are still out on the water when Barnaby grabs my hand and walks me back up the steps to the deck. It is much colder now, so moments later he wraps a jacket around me. Instead of standing in the front of the yacht again he sits us down.

"So the sun is setting," he says, "I don't want you to miss it."

And for a moment I think he is ruining this sweet moment to make a stupid joke, but then he continues.

"It's mostly a burnt orange; there are some soft pinks and yellows at the top,"

"What are you doing?" I interrupt.

"I'm giving you the sunset."

I inhale, feeling butterflies flutter in my chest and stomach. The poem Amelia told me about. This is what he meant. He wanted to literally *give* me the sunset.

"You don't have to do this," my voice is low and full of emotion.

"You don't have to *see* beautiful things to know that they are there, to know that they are beautiful," he says. "You can experience the world the same way I do or the same way anybody does. You *deserve* it."

"You think I deserve this beautiful sunset?" I ask and I don't know why I do, but being told you are *deserving* of something you did not even know you wanted, being deserving of *anything* beautiful and pure is an unmatched feeling.

"I think you deserve this beautiful world, Ezmerelda."

I am quiet and I love him.

He continues to describe the sunset to me in great detail, in so much detail that I am actually picturing it. I feel like I am looking right at it. The oranges and the soft pinks are blending with the yellow. Closer to the water, there is a purple hue that bounces with the rippling of the waves. The sky is clear and a few stars are already glowing. I imagine grabbing one again; I imagine holding it close to my heart. I imagine that it is Barnaby.

"What's wrong?" he asks, one of his fingers wiping a tear that manages to fall. "Do you want to go home?"

"No," I shake my head quickly. "I wish I could stay in this moment forever." My voice is soft, but my words are honest, no matter how cliché they may be. I mean them. I am overwhelmed in the best way possible. I hear some shuffling and he is next to me, his arm is around my shoulders. I breathe him in and then smile, "Me, you, and this beautiful sunset," I whisper.

I used to love the water and didn't think I could ever bring myself to go back out on it. I guess a part of me wanted to hold on to that last happy thought as a distant memory, that going back would bring a flood of memories of the after, a flood that I just wasn't ready or prepared to ever deal with again.

But right now I am on the water and I am happy. It's a different kind of happy, but it is happy nonetheless. I am filled with joy and appreciation because my boyfriend has once again reintroduced me to something I loved, but walked away from. He is reminding me how special those old pieces of my life are while continuously adding beautiful new pieces to it.

Another tear falls and I love him.

Nine

Unexpected (adj.): not expected; unforeseen; surprising

My fingers are firmly intertwined with Barnaby's as we walk up the crowded hallway at our high school. The loud yelling and laughter from my peers is making an already uncomfortable headache even more intolerable. I was so close to deciding to play hooky today, but the thought of staying home alone all day seemed like a form of torture and though Barnaby offered to stay with me, he's already missed a lot of school. I was not going to be responsible for him being even further behind.

"You okay?" Barnaby asks, yanking me out of my thought. I sigh and roll my eyes.

"Not much has changed in the five minutes since the last time you asked me," I deadpan. He laughs, but it's a humorless laugh. "I'm fine," I continue.

"I just think you should've stayed home, you weren't feeling well last night, either. I could tell, and…" he is interrupted by someone calling his name from behind us. We stop and he tugs my hand a little to turn me toward where the voice is coming from.

"Hey," *she* says. "I wanted to ask you about that science test we have coming up."

Maybe I am insane or maybe my insecurities are just getting the best of me, but I can hear flirtation in her tone.

"Sure, what's up?" Barnaby asks coolly.

"Are you having difficulties with the study guide? I'm just all over the place trying to figure it out."

"Hmmm," Barnaby says, but my focus is still on her tone. *Is* she flirting or am I experiencing that irrational jealousy again? I mean, it is plausible. I did get jealous just imagining the names of his ex-girlfriends. I am probably overreacting. I inhale slowly.

"I haven't really started going over it in depth yet," Barnaby answers.

"Oh, well, that's what I was getting at. Maybe we can go over it together and compare notes tonight to prepare, like we used to do?"

Like we used to do…

Suddenly, what I thought could possibly be jealousy has surpassed that and is now full blown anger. She *is* flirting with him and right in front of me. It's as if I am not standing right here, as if I am just another fixture in the hallway. I am holding his hand; we are together all of the time. Everyone knows I am his girlfriend, and he is my boyfriend.

Like we used to do…

Is this girl one of his ex-girlfriends? I wonder what she looks like. I wonder what I look like compared to her.

I can feel the anger and frustration boiling inside of me, but the sudden thought of Barnaby actually agreeing and meeting with her enrages me even more. It isn't like I can forbid him from going, or can I? I don't want to be *that* girlfriend, the girlfriend who is jealous and insecure, but the truth is –I am. I am extremely jealous and insecure, especially right now.

I don't want Barnaby to think I don't trust him, but how else am I supposed to respond and act at this very moment?

Should I say something? I should say something to her, like *this is my boyfriend and you need to get the hell away from him and fail your science test*. I don't know, my mind is going a mile per minute because I've never had to deal with anything like this before. The line between rational and irrational doesn't seem to exist right now.

"I could even order pizza," she continues and now the fire once burning inside of me has engulfed my entire body.

"Actually," Barnaby says, snapping me out of my spiraling train of thought. He releases my hand and then I feel his arm around my shoulders pulling me closer to him. "That's not going to work. I'll be at my girlfriend's house studying tonight and pretty much every night." He kisses my forehead. "You're more than welcome to my notes though," he adds.

"Oh," this girl says and her tone is completely different. She's gone from flirting to sounding snobbish. "Maybe some other time?" She adds as if she hadn't heard what he said at all. "See you in class," she says and I assume she's walking away. Barnaby sighs and moves his arm from my shoulders and grabs my hand again as we begin to walk in the opposite direction.

We are walking in silence for a few seconds before Barnaby speaks. "Mazie..."

"Ex-girlfriend?" I interrupt. He doesn't answer right away which is an answer in itself.

"I wouldn't say girlfriend, exactly," he finally says.

We continue walking. My thoughts are focused on our connected hands. I can't fault Barnaby for who he dated before he even knew I existed. I can't fault him for her flirting so rudely in front of me. I should be happy and thankful that he said no to her, and let it be known that I was his girlfriend, that he would be spending his free time with me, and yet I am furious.

"What's her name?" I ask and he sighs.

"Listen, she was rude and I am sorry for that, but I need you to know that that's been done for almost a year. We don't talk in class or even sit next to each other. I don't want you to think that something is going …"

"I just want to know her name," I interrupt. My voice isn't angered, but it sure as hell isn't enthused.

"Kate."

Barnaby and Kate, *Kate and Barnaby*, yeah, it didn't work. As I add the faceless Kate to the list of names I'd paired with Barnaby, it made it even more blaringly clear that *only* Mazie and Barnaby makes sense.

"Okay," I say.

"Okay?"

"Yes, okay."

He's quiet as we are still walking hand in hand down the hallway.

"Are you mad at me?"

I squeeze his hand.

"No, Barnaby."

I never realized how territorial I am, how jealous I could be, until it had to do with Barnaby. I feel possessive. He is mine and only mine; I am his and only his. At that thought, I am actually shocking myself with how I am thinking. This can't be healthy, right? I need to finally sit down with Maya and have a real talk with her about my relationship with Barnaby, about these new and unfamiliar feelings. I think I'm doing the whole girlfriend thing wrong.

"Nothing is going on…"

"I trust you," I interrupt him again and it is true. I trust him with every fiber in my body. That girl was rude and disrespectful, but that had nothing to do with Barnaby.

"Okay," he says. "I'm sorry," he adds.

"You don't have to apologize for her, you did nothing wrong," I smile and squeeze his hand again. I am finally letting the raging jealousy dissipate. "I actually think it was kind of sexy how you stood up for me."

"Oh really?" and now Barnaby sounds like himself.

"Absolutely."

"Sexy comes naturally to me," he says in a serious tone and then we both burst into laughter and we are loud, we are *Barnaby loud*. I'm sure we are getting looks from people walking by.

I wonder how many people look at us and judge or try to figure out why he would be with me when it is clear he could probably have any girl in this school. If what my sister said is true, he is handsome, with great teeth, and beautiful brown eyes. And I know firsthand that he's funny, smart and caring. Barnaby is all of those things, and he wants me.

I smile, knowing that though there may be some that pass their judgment, no one is supposed to understand us better than we understand us. My mind drifts back to Kate and I can't help but feel triumphant and smug. Feeling this arrogant is a disgusting trait, but it is how I feel.

A small petty part of me wants to tell Barnaby to not even share his notes with her, but I am going to be the bigger person. I am going to be mature about this situation. I am not going to let Kate take up another second of my thoughts.

I really need to talk to Maya.

We are still heading toward the other side of the school building before our long period. This is usually when we make out a little or just enjoy each other's company before we have to go our separate ways to class, but I am still feeling a little off. I decide that I am going to take a detour to the bathroom so I can pop a couple of Tylenols before this headache turns into a full blown migraine. I won't be able to handle hearing my teacher drone on and on without some type of pain relief.

I am about to tell Barnaby that I have to go to the bathroom when this odd, woozy feeling overtakes my senses in a quick swoop. I try so hard to keep it together, but I am too dizzy. I am too disoriented. I squeeze my eyes trying to soothe the pain, but the discomfort is immovable. It's like a whirlwind, holding onto Barnaby won't be enough.

Before I can figure out what is happening, I lose my balance and fall, my knees slamming hard onto the ground, my cane slamming to the ground too, making a loud crashing sound in the midst of this noisy hallway.

"Shit!" Barnaby says. He is immediately helping me up, his hand never leaving mine. "Are you okay?"

"I'm fine," I say. It takes a second before I am able to stand up. I squeeze his hand to reassure him. I am thoroughly embarrassed, but his panic is the center of my world right now. "That happens sometimes," I say lowly, still feeling disoriented, still feeling like my brain is a snow globe that has just been shaken. I take long deliberate breaths to calm my racing heart.

"*What* happens sometimes?" he questions argumentatively. "I've been with you almost every day for months. You've never fallen down before? Is this because of your headache? Maybe you should tell Maya that you…"

"I'm fine," I interrupt him. Damn he jumped to that conclusion quickly. I've said *I'm fine* so many times today, that the phrase doesn't even sound like a real sentence anymore.

I can hear people walking by. I wonder how many saw me take that spill. I swallow trying to combat my nerves because I know Barnaby isn't going to let up. I can feel his eyes staring at me. I have to diffuse the situation. "I just tripped over my own feet and thank God you haven't seen me do that before. It's embarrassing."

He doesn't say anything at first and then he exhales, "You sure you're okay?"

"Barnaby, yes, I'm okay. People fall," I say simply. He puts his arms around my shoulders.

"Okay," he finally concedes, "I still think it wouldn't hurt to let Maya know about your headaches, just in general." We start to walk and I don't answer.

I inhale and try not to let my worry, fear, and panic flit across my face. People did fall, but not me, not like that. I know how I felt right before I fell, I know how I feel right now.

I exhale a steady breath and try not to let my thoughts travel to where I know they want to go. I tell myself that I've had enough bad happen in my life and now, for the first time in a long while, I am happy and I am content. I refuse to believe the universe would smack me down again. I refuse to believe that the *up there* is working against me.

"I do think I should go home early though," I say lowly. "Just to rest, since I didn't sleep much last night."

"I'll drive you," he says quickly, moving his arm from around my shoulders.

"Barnaby, you don't need to miss anymore school. I'll call Maya."

"Mazie."

The finality and seriousness in his tone lets me know that this is not an argument I want to have with him right now.

"Fine," I quickly accept. I exhale again, trying to tell myself that this is nothing but exhaustion. I will be fine after a nice long nap.

~~

I can't speak to my sister. I know she is trying to be strong for me but I can feel the fear in the room; it is engulfing me.

When I fell, I told Barnaby that I'd tripped on my own feet and it happened often. What I did not tell him was that it was the third time I'd lost my balance over a span of a few days but the first time I'd actually fallen down. Coupled with the migraines I'd been having for weeks and the nausea I'd been experiencing the last couple of days, I knew I had to tell Maya. Somewhere in the back of my mind I knew that what was going on was more serious than a fleeting headache and losing my balance, but I didn't want to believe it. I didn't want to accept it.

That is why Maya and I are both sitting in a doctor's office quietly waiting.

My phone is vibrating nonstop and I know it is Barnaby. He doesn't know that I am here. I don't want him to worry unnecessarily. I know if I answer the phone and he hears my voice he will know something is wrong and I will cave and tell him the truth and I refuse to burden him.

"How are you feeling?" my sister asks.

"Nauseated," I say. That's how we found out I had cancer before. When I was thirteen we'd gone on a boating trip with our parents like we'd done every year. I'd gotten so sick, I vomited, I felt off balanced, my vision was blurry and I had a horrible headache. I'd been having headaches for some time, but I attributed it to the fact that I never wore my glasses.

We all assumed that I was seasick, but when I got home it'd gotten worse. Maya was in her first year of medical school and insisted on looking me over. I remember being so frustrated with her because all I wanted to do was sleep away the pain and nausea. When she looked at my eyes she said something didn't seem right, that my right pupil did not react to the light like it should have.

My mother being the hypochondriac that she was, and thank God for that, made an appointment. That's when we found out I had a large tumor pressing on my optic nerve called *Optic Nerve Glioma*.

Surgery wasn't the only choice at first. I tried chemo and radiation, lost all of my hair, lost a lot of weight and I was sicker during that process than I was when just dealing with the tumor alone.

When the tumor did not shrink significantly enough, they wanted to try another round of radiation but I told them I wanted surgery, that I couldn't take it anymore. They told us that loss of vision could be a possibility, and that surgery was risky because of the location of the tumor, but I was so sick and so angry at the world that it didn't matter to me at that point.

I wanted to take my chances and my parents supported and agreed with my decision, something that meant so much to me.

I remember my father looking at me with tears in his eyes and saying, "No matter what is decided, we are a family. We will be here, you will never go through any of this alone."

His words, my mother's warm grip on my hand, and my sister's comforting aura was the strength I truly needed to go forward with the decision to have surgery.

I remember lying back on the hospital bed as the mask was put on my face. The nurse leaned in front of me and told me to *count backward from 100*. That nurse's face was the last thing I'd ever see.

Her scrub cap was dark midnight blue with tiny little yellow stars scattered all over it. I remember being so drugged up that I thought I was actually looking at the real sky. I remember wanting to reach up and grab one of the stars, but my brain was unable to signal my arm to move.

The nurse's eyes were a light hazel, she was warm and gentle. She had a small scar under her right eye that was shaped almost like a crescent and her skin was a rich cocoa.

Memories fade, they move and bounce and shift their way around and out of your conscious thought until they're unrecognizable. Sometimes, it's hard to remember what's real. That nurse's face was a memory that didn't fade, the glowing stars shown brightly as if they were lighting up a real night's sky in the midst of my drug induced semi-lucid thoughts, was an image memory could never distort.

Right now we are waiting for the results of my CT, MRI and bloodwork. I will find out any moment now if my cancer is back after five years. I'd been distancing myself from Barnaby over the last week or so, telling him I had plans with my sister or that I was busy with homework or that Maya's family on her mom's side was visiting from out of town, anything to keep him away from this part of my world.

He knows me too well and can tell something is wrong, that something is off and he has called me out on it a few times, but I just can't tell him.

Barnaby knows all about the cancer, chemo, and surgery from when I was thirteen. He knows how hard and scary it was. He doesn't need to be dragged into round two. Though I do not know for sure what this is, I have an ominous feeling. I am not going to put this on his plate; he has so much going on with his family. The last thing I want him to do is worry about his sickly girlfriend who can't seem to get into the universe's good graces.

The door opens yanking me out of my thought. I feel my heart drop, my stomach is hot and my heart starts racing. If there is a malignant tumor or tumors that would mean chemo, radiation and/or surgery. My entire world would be upside down again.

"How are you feeling, Mazie?" Dr. Nipan asks. He's been my doctor since my diagnosis at thirteen.

"Nervous," I answer honestly.

He doesn't say anything and I hear my sister sniffle. *Shit.* Is she reading his facial expression right now?

"I won't keep you waiting any longer," I hear some papers shuffling, "I regret to tell you that you do have a malignant tumor, Optic Nerve Glioma."

The words float in the air around me for a moment, the heaviness and seriousness of the words haven't found their home in my world yet. I hear my sister and it sounds like she is sobbing, on the verge of hyperventilating but me, I am just here. I am Mazie; I am eighteen, blind and have cancer again. I don't cry, I don't react or respond. I'm just sitting here waiting for the words to land. They are still orbiting, they are circling around me. I am unable to reach them.

"What does this mean?" my sister nearly chokes out. She is a nurse, and we'd gone through this before. She knows what this means.

"The good news is, it's relatively small, nowhere near as complicated as the larger tumor from five years ago. I am recommending radiation and chemotherapy; I don't want surgery to be an option right now. The location and position of the tumor does cause some concerns for me – may be difficult to remove without further nerve damage," he pauses. "We caught it early, Mazie. That is a very good thing."

I have yet to speak or move, all I do is concentrate on breathing.

Inhale, exhale, inhale, exhale…

I concentrate on the words floating around my head, frustrated to some degree that I can't make them stay still, that I can't make them stop spinning. Frustrated that I am unable to grab them and make them real. Why I need them to be real is beyond me, but I need the spinning to stop.

"I know that this is scary and it won't be easy, but you got through this once, and we will use our best efforts to get you through it again," Dr. Nipan says. "I'll go get some more paperwork and then we can discuss the treatment schedule." I hear him take a few steps then the door closes. Almost instantly my sister's arms are around me.

"It's going to be okay, everything is going to be okay," she whispers. She squeezes me tightly and I almost feel like she's trying to tell herself this. I don't say a word because there is nothing to say. If I speak, it won't make the tumor go away. If I cry, it won't keep me away from radiation and chemo. Any reaction won't stop what's happening from happening. So I continue to concentrate on what I can control for now.

Inhale, exhale, inhale, exhale…

T_{en}

Glioma (n.): a tumor arising from glial cells

I lay in my bed as Barnaby's ringtone goes off for the fifth time in the last hour. I haven't been with or said a single word to Barnaby since Friday morning. I had no clue that later on that day I would be finding out I had cancer again. It's Monday and I didn't go to school, because I just wanted to be alone. I wanted to enjoy a few more moments of being just the blind girl before I had to deal with being the cancer girl too.

I still haven't cried or really comprehended what is going on. My first treatment is scheduled for Wednesday at 4 pm and Dr. Nipan's words are still orbiting me. It is as if they are taunting me now. They know I need to make sense of them, that I need to analyze them so I can finally feel or cry or scream or have whatever appropriate reaction a person who just found out she has cancer again should have, but they keep floating further and further away from my reach.

I hear a knock on my door and then it opens. "Mazie?" my sister asks.

"Yes?" I respond lowly.

"Barnaby is at the front door."

I sigh and then inhale deeply; I knew it was only a matter of time before he'd show up here. I know that it is cowardly of me to just ignore him. I know that I should say the words to him. Tell him that we can't work anymore, that we should end this, but just the thought of uttering those words nearly paralyzes me. I can't say those things to him.

Part of me feels like if I just avoid it, the situation will just go away, but I was an idiot to think Barnaby would just accept this and not want and demand answers.

I exhale slowly, "I don't want to speak to him." It stings to say these words.

He is seventeen, it is bad enough that we can't do a lot of the things other couples do, but there is no way I am going to have him deal with the vomiting and the hair loss and the stuck in the bed for days at a time, because that's what my life is going to be during treatment.

I am helping him; I am setting him free with no hard feelings. My chest feels hollow thinking this way, but it's what needs to be done.

"You can't avoid him forever," she says softly, "He really cares about you, he looks so worried." Before I can reply I hear the front screen door open loudly, banging against the living room wall. Then I hear footsteps quickly moving towards my room.

"Barnaby!" my sister says in shock. I sit up immediately.

"Okay, so you're *not* dead." The anger in his voice is something I'd never heard from him before. I sit back against my headboard.

"Should I leave you two alone…?" I can tell my sister is trying to ask me in code if I want her to kick him out. I shake my head, I hear her leave and then I hear my bedroom door closing. It's quiet in the room for a few exaggerated moments and I am happy I can't see how angry he is. I can definitely feel it.

"Barnaby…."

"Are you breaking up with me?" he interrupts and I can feel the fear and anger in his voice. The pit in my stomach is now a gaping hole and I feel like I am going to throw up. "…because if you are," he continues, "I would at least like an explanation. I would at least like to argue my case."

"You don't have a case to argue, you didn't do anything." I am whispering and my voice is shaky. I haven't cried once since finding out my diagnosis, and I'm not going to start now.

"So you *are* breaking up with me?"

I don't answer.

The air is thick and cold. It's an energy I've never experienced when in the same room as Barnaby. He doesn't see it now but I am doing him a favor, I am saving him from having to be stuck with me through this process. I am protecting him.

I feel the weight shift on my bed and I know that he is sitting down; I take a deep breath.

"What happened?" he questions and I can actually feel my heart breaking. "Please tell me what I did or didn't do." His voice is so morose and so pained and he is my weakness. I can't do this. I have to tell him the truth, but that won't be fair. I don't want him to feel obligated to stay with me, or feel the guilt if he decides this is too much or that I am too much and he wants to leave.

Why did he have to meet me? Why did I have to fall in love with him? The pain of having to let him go is just as terrifying as all of the other things happening in my life. His pain is hurting me, swallowing me whole and it's hard to bear it anymore.

"Is this about Kate? I told you that nothing is…"

"No, it's not about her," I interrupt him. Inhale, exhale, inhale, exhale… "I don't want to burden you." It is all I can manage to get out.

"Burden me? What? Mazie, you could never burden me," he says in confusion and I feel him move closer to me. "There is absolutely nothing in this entire world that you could *ever* say to me that would make me not want to be with you. I don't understand where this is coming from. What's wrong?" he asks urgently. "Is there anything I can do?"

And in that moment I break down and cry, just like that. The tears that hadn't shown up for nearly four days are now streaming down my face. There is nothing he can do; there is nothing *anyone* can do.

"Mazie?" he asks still confused but now also panicked as he wraps his arms around me. I exhale and start to cry harder. I am now sobbing in his arms, the last thing I want to be doing.

Dr. Nipan's words that were floating and orbiting me for days have finally landed –they're finally making sense. *They are real.* My life continues to revolt against me at every corner. Childhood cancer, becoming blind, losing both of my parents on the same day …cancer again.

What had I done in a previous life to deserve this? How evil of a person was I? How many people did I hurt? Did I lie and steal? Did I kill? There has to be a reason why God or the universe or the *up there* or whatever it is that controls all of this, hated me so much. There has to be a reason why it feels like I have a target on my back.

"Talk to me," he says and he sounds so nervous, the begging in his voice is painfully clear. "I can't stand seeing you like this." Then suddenly, the energy changes in the room, it's like something finally clicks and the silence in between our words is filled with the answers he wants.

"Is this about your headaches?" his voice shakes, as if somewhere deep down he knows the answer to his question. He knows exactly what I am going to say, but he can't form the words to say them himself.

I inhale, breathing him in and realizing I can't go on lying to him for another second.

… Exhale, inhale, exhale…"My tumor came back," I say. I say it clearly, my face nuzzled into his neck; I let the words fly off of my tongue. "I have cancer again."

He doesn't speak at first. His body stiffens, his hand that is massaging my back in a circular motion stops then, after a moment, he exhales an unsteady and deep breath as if he were holding it in this entire time. Then he clutches me tighter to his chest as if I were going to fall out of his grasp. He is holding me like he will never let me go; like his arms are a part of me now or that my body is a part of him.

"Fuck," he finally says lowly, his voice gargled with agony and dread and then I hear him sniffle.

I pull away from him and I find his cheeks with my hands, his face is wet. My heart sinks as I wipe his tears away with my thumbs.

"Barnaby," I sob shakily. I wipe more of his tears and then suddenly I feel his hands cup both sides of my face, then his lips are on mine as he kisses me urgently. Every emotion, good or bad, that a human can possess is melting in the taste of this kiss.

He is kissing me like I am not the blind girl; he is kissing me like I am not the cancer girl. He is kissing me because he loves me. I don't need to hear the words to know that he loves me. I can feel it all around me, like water, like air, like *him*. I can feel it in every cell. I kiss him back because I love him too and no matter what happens after this moment, that is something that I know will never change.

Eleven

Chemotherapy (n.): the use of chemicals to treat or control a disease such as cancer. Cancer (n.): a serious disease caused by cells that are not normal and that can spread to one or many parts of the body

I am sitting in the middle of Barnaby's bathroom on a chair that he dragged in from his kitchen. My foot is tapping anxiously against the floor. I can hear him walking back and forth as if he is pacing. I roll my eyes because he is having entirely too much fun with this.

"Okay," he says in a very animated movie announcer voice. "There is no turning back, are you ready for this? Because once I turn these…"

"For the love of God, get it over with!" I interrupt and he laughs.

"Sunglasses off," he orders.

"No."

"Why?" he asks and sometimes I forget that my boyfriend is *King Asker of Questions*.

"Can you just work around them please?" I say and for once he doesn't argue with me. I don't feel comfortable without my sunglasses on. I wasn't sure how I looked or what exactly to do with my eyes when they were off. Keep them closed? Open them and possibly freak everyone out? Though I am forever in the dark, I feel like my sunglasses shield me. I feel safe with them on. Not that I don't feel safe with Barnaby because I do, but I'm accustomed to certain things and for the last five years I've needed these on when I'm around other people. It's hard to explain.

I hear the clippers turn on. I feel his hand lift the curly hair by my ear and then I feel the shadow of his hand move. My thick curls hit my shoulder before they fall to the floor.

"Again, the kick ass Mohawk is off the table?" he asks.

"There isn't even a table…" I deadpan.

I am on my fourth week of radiation and chemo and my hair is starting to fall out in small clumps. I mentioned that I thought I was ready to just shave it and of course, Barnaby being Barnaby, he jumped at the chance and offered to do it for me.

"Can I leave a patch in the back with my initials? Claim my territory?" he inquires as he is already to the middle of my head.

"Claim your territory?" I clarify. "I am not property to be claimed."

"Are you mine?" he asks and I roll my eyes again.

"Theoretically..." I say. We both laugh as he continues to shave, some song I've never heard is playing in the background and he is now singing along lowly for a few more minutes.

"Okay, final touches," he says under his breath. "All done!"

I reach my hands up and just feel scalp. I thought that I would be more emotional about this, my hair was such an important part of my identity, my culture, my personality. It was intertwined in the fabric of my upbringing. Some of my favorite moments with my mother and sister were when they'd do my hair.

I lost it all when I was thirteen and I cried for days. I was fighting cancer and in constant pain, but I was absolutely gutted and distraught about the hair loss. Right now, I feel free. I feel light, I feel like I can fly. I want to be able to.

I hear the clippers turn back on, "Missed a spot?" I ask Barnaby.

"No, it's my turn now."

"Wait, what?" I exclaim. "Don't shave your head!"

"Solidarity baby," he says with humor.

"You're crazy," I say in astonishment. "You're being funny right? You're not really going to shave your head."

"How would that be funny?" he asks as the clippers are still going and then I hear the first zip. He is doing it; he is shaving his head because I had to shave mine. Is he even real? Have I had cancer this entire time and it causes me to be delusional and I actually created a Barnaby Parks in my imagination? There had to be an explanation for him.

I'm standing in shock, while the clippers keep going. I can't believe him. This is making my heart swell.

"Okay, feel," he says after about five minutes or so. He grabs my wrist and I lift both hands to his head. His thick hair is gone. There is just scalp. Just like me.

"Oh my God," I say and then I pull his face to mine and I kiss him. "I'll miss grabbing your hair when we make out," I say breathlessly.

"Ditto," he says as we kiss our way out of the bathroom and into his bedroom.

This week has been a good week with my treatment, last week I was in bed for five days. All I did was throw up and sleep, there was nothing in between. Through the ups and downs Barnaby has been by my side. He will never know how much I appreciate him, how much I truly depend on his support.

We are on his bed and I am just so overwhelmed with how important he is to me, how special he is to me, how much I love him.

I disconnect our lips and hold his face in my hands, "It has been a very good week."

"It has..." I can hear the confusion in his voice.

"We don't know how many good weeks I will have. We can't predict the future with any of this."

"Mazie, what's wrong?"

I inhale, my hands still on his cheeks, I pull his face back to mine and I kiss him. I kiss him fervently. I kiss him as if I'd been yearning for his touch for years and now that I have it I am incapable of letting go.

After a few moments he pulls away from me and I can feel his eyes staring down at me. Our breathing even and shallow in synchronization. We don't say a word and it's almost as if you can feel the energy shift in the room. He knows what I am saying without me having to say a single word.

He doesn't know this but I've been thinking about death a lot, not in a morbid way, but in a logical, *it's the facts of life* way. I will never tell Barnaby or Maya that of course, but I've lost people I love, and I'm on my second bout with cancer. It feels like death is always looming around me in some form. But fearing it or ignoring it won't change the inevitability of it happening in the next second or fifty years from now.

I love Barnaby and life is so unpredictable. I could die from this; those are the things everyone is afraid to talk about. I am not afraid to think about it because it is a very true possibility. But Maya could die, Barnaby too. There is no way of telling when your time is up and, in this moment, I want to share with Barnaby something I've never shared with anyone else before.

I feel him move his hand and then I feel him tug at my sunglasses. "Barnaby, no!" I nearly snap. I grab his wrist tightly, my nails practically digging into his skin.

"I want to see you. I want to see *all* of you," he says quietly.

I inhale and exhale too quickly, the nerves of everything happening spinning around me at once. Though my hand is now shaky, I hesitantly drop it from his wrist. I feel him slowly pull my glasses off of my face and I stiffen feeling exposed, afraid I may frighten him. How scary do I look? How different do I look to him? Will that change how he feels about me? I have never felt more insecure in my entire life than I do right now at this very moment.

I squeeze my eyes shut.

"Open your eyes," he says serenely, his cool breath blowing lightly across my face. "Please."

I am still breathing heavily, but I eventually find the courage to open my eyes. I feel his fingertips trace the curve of my face and I know he can feel my body trembling underneath him.

"You're so beautiful," he whispers and it reminds me of how he said it on our first official date. He said it with wonder, like it was the first time he was experiencing beauty.

My body is hot to the touch. I can feel the blush cascade up and down before reflexively closing my eyes again. When I do, I feel his lips softly kiss my right eyelid and then softly kiss my left eyelid and my nerves are suddenly calmer, my breathing a little more even but now my want for him is amplified.

His lips are on mine and I kiss him back passionately. I don't feel insecure anymore and I love him. I don't feel nervous anymore and I love him. I am not afraid anymore and I love him and I love him, and I love him.

I feel his hands all over me, layers of clothing being removed, eagerness taking over all of our senses. There are no more prerequisites, there is nothing left to be said, and nothing left to understand. Everything I'd imagined since becoming Barnaby's girlfriend has come to fruition.

Time seems to be unmoving but somehow the slow seconds of anticipation manage to travel along with me as I transition from the Mazie I was before this moment to the Mazie I am now as Barnaby and I finally become one. I am connected to him in a new and powerful way. In a way that is not only carnal but cerebral, all consuming. My love for him igniting into a form that encloses me and pulls me to a world I have never been a part of until now, a new world that I now never want to leave.

"Are you okay?" he whispers. His voice strained and faint, his lips on my ear as we move slowly together, fluidly finding our rhythm.

I nod, my focus locked on many different feelings, sinking and floating, being submerged but flying in the sky all at once. I try to answer verbally but the sound I make trembles from my lips. I am unable to speak.

I am hyperaware of every single centimeter of my skin and my body. Every inch of me is affected by Barnaby's touch. All of my working senses are in override as the man I love makes love to me for the first time. For this space of time I no longer have any problems, fear does not exist. What is cancer? It isn't real in this space. In this new world, health and love are abundant. I am going to live forever. Barnaby is going to live forever.

And that is it.

Our lips, our breathing, and our longing, our wants and needs... *discovery* – our tangled bodies and our beating hearts. Barnaby has a piece of my being that no one else has, a piece of my being that I will only ever want to share with him for as long as I have left in this life.

~~

It isn't a good week.

"You have to stay hydrated," Maya says as I hear her place a glass of ice water on my nightstand. "Just take a few sips." Her voice is low and sad, she is doing a bad job of masking her emotions, but I couldn't honestly blame her.

I sit up slightly and as soon as I do, I feel the rush. Barnaby, who is lying behind me, has the bucket in front of me and in my hands before I even have to say anything. I dry heave into the bucket for a few exaggerated seconds, then lay back down with tears streaming down my face.

"It's okay," Barnaby says while he dabs my forehead with a cold cloth. I told him to go home and that I would call him but he has been lying in my bed behind me for the last three hours trying to get me to eat crackers, drink water, massaging my back, just being there.

I don't know what I would do without him and Maya. They are all I have.

"I can't drink," I whisper, my arms wrapped around my stomach because my ribs hurt from all of the dry heaving. "I'll just throw it up."

"One sip," they both say in unison. I feel Barnaby reach over me and then I feel the straw to my lips. I take a sip and I hadn't realized how thirsty I was. I hadn't really been able to eat, drink or keep anything down for nearly three days. It's by far the worst week of treatment. In three weeks I am scheduled for a CT and MRI to see if the tumor shrank anymore and if it didn't, that would mean surgery.

"Another sip?" Maya asks gently and I nod slightly. Barnaby puts the straw back to my lips. "I'm going to make some soup," Maya continues, "...you don't have to eat it all, but I want you to at least try some of it." I hear her quickly walk out of the room and I know she left quickly because she didn't want to hear my objection.

I hear the glass hit the nightstand and then Barnaby's arms are back around me.

"You don't have to stay here," I say lowly, my voice is hoarse and raspy.

"I know I don't have to, I *want* to," he murmurs as he kisses the back of the scarf that's wrapped around my head.

"Thank you," I say and I start to soundlessly cry. This is worse than I remembered it being when I was thirteen. This is worse than what my imagination drummed up. I feel like this is as close to death as I could possibly get without actually dying. Maybe this is worse than death? At least death had a finish line, I wouldn't have to suffer or feel this pain anymore.

"I can't do this," I whisper. This is my concession.

"You are strong," he says quietly in my ear, but it only makes me cry more.

"I can't do this," I repeat into my pillow, clenching his hands inside of my frail ones. "I am so tired." I am in so much pain that it is becoming foggy as to what I am even fighting for in the first place. It feels like it will be so easy just to quit, to let the cancer win. I can't go through this anymore, I have nothing left.

"You are brave," he says in the same tone as if I hadn't said a word.

"You are a fighter," his voice cracks and then he kisses my ear. "You are beautiful."

"What are you doing?" I finally ask, my tears not slowing down as he holds me tightly.

"I'm reminding you that these are fleeting moments. This is horrible, and everything in me wishes I could take this pain away, but this cloud won't hover over you forever and at the core of it all, you are still you. Strong, brave, tenacious, beautiful, smart, hilarious. You will beat this and I will be right here next to you, every single step of the way." I hear the smile in his voice. "I will always be here to remind you of everything you are. I won't let you forget."

I exhale and his words make me feel safe, his words make me regret even thinking about the possibility of just giving up. I've never given up before, why would I start now? His words alone made me feel like I could conquer anything and maybe I will.

The words *I love you* are on the tip of my tongue, but in a haze I am able to finally fall asleep.

~~

It's my first week back at school after missing two weeks. It feels good to be back, it feels good to be a part of the world again. I feel sluggish and tired most of the time, but I am moving and I am here, that's all that matters to me. My doctor, my sister, and my boyfriend all insisted that I take more time off, but I was becoming stir crazy. I need to be here, I promised them if it became too much I would go home and rest without any argument.

"I'm going to go to the bathroom. I'll be right back," Barnaby says. He kisses my cheek and then walks away. I smile and stay seated.

"Hey," I hear a familiar voice say as a hand touches my shoulder.

"Hey, Breanna," I say with a smile. She was one of the first classmates to speak to me at the beginning of the year. She is nice.

"This is going to sound so weird and hopefully not creepy, but I think you and Barnaby are the cutest couple in this school."

I start to blush and don't exactly know how to respond. It feels weird saying *thank you* but I feel rude saying nothing at all.

"I don't know if you guys have talked about it," Breanna continues, "but I'm on the Prom Committee and I think you two should run for King and Queen!"

This has to be a sick joke.

"Oh," I say, "That's not really our thing, but thank you." Even if it isn't a joke, I still don't want to be a part of something like that but, knowing Barnaby, he would absolutely love something like that, so I have to make sure he has no clue this is even an option. I have to end this conversation with Breanna before he walks back in here.

"Oh," she says and she sounds disappointed. "Well, maybe you can think about it? Discuss it with him? You guys *are* relationship goals. I mean, the whole shaving your heads together thing and the fact that he missed all that school to stay with you, it's so romantic."

Her words catch me by surprise.

"What do you mean?"

"I just think it's sweet that he stayed with you. You two must really be in love. I could only dream of something that special," she laughs, but her words aren't making any sense to me at all.

"I'm sorry, Breanna. I don't know what you're talking about," I admit.

"This is his first day back too. I'm so sorry, maybe that was something I wasn't supposed to say?" She starts to whisper, "Is it a secret that he was with you?"

Barnaby missed two weeks of school? Though he was with me every day except for two, he never came over until after school hours on weekdays and would stay with me all weekend. I can feel my face flush red.

I am angry.

"No, it's okay Breanna," I say trying to keep my voice level. "I think I misunderstood what you were saying."

"Oh," she laughs lightly. "I think it's amazing, but anyway, please give it some thought. I really think you guys would win! I'll see you later." I hear Breanna walk away and a few moments later I hear footsteps walking toward me. I know it's Barnaby.

"Okay, ready?" he asks.

I inhale and don't move from my seat. "Is the room empty?" I ask quietly.

"Yep," he says. "Let's go," he grabs my hand and I slide it away.

"Where were you?"

"The bathroom. I told you that," he answers confusingly.

"You missed two weeks of school, Barnaby," I state and it's quiet.

"I don't want to talk about this here," he responds quickly and he's angry. He has no right to be angry. I am the angry one in this scenario.

"You don't want to talk about this anywhere or ever. Were you gone because of your dad?" Maybe school isn't the best place for this. Maybe I am being too intrusive, but Barnaby never gives me any information about his life at home. I feel blind in more than one way.

"Mazie..."

"You know you can trust me," I say the words and they are so somber.

"I trust you more than anybody in my life. I wasn't lying when I told you that before, but I don't want to do this right now or here. Can you please understand that?"

I quickly wipe a tear and stand from my seat, "Yep, I understand that." I grab my cane and I walk out of the room. He doesn't say anything, but I can feel him behind me. After a few moments, he suddenly grabs my arm and turns me around tugging me in the opposite direction, and then a door slams shut.

"What are you doing? Where are we?" I demand.

"Janitors' closet," he says quickly, "I'm not trying to intentionally lie to you, okay? It's just complicated."

I don't answer right away because I don't know what he expects me to say. I take a few moments to gather my thoughts. I do not want to argue with him.

"The thing is, you *did* lie to me," I finally answer, "Every day I would ask how school was and every day you would tell me some detailed story." I pause, "But I'm honestly not even angry about the lying, I'm angry that you even have to at all. You won't talk to me and I don't understand why. What's going on with your father?"

He doesn't answer and I don't expect him to.

"Okay, I did lie about school and I am sorry, but there was something going on with my sister that was personal and I needed to be there for her."

He grabs my hand and pulls me closer to him, "I'm trying to balance both and it's a lot to take on and…"

"Barnaby, I do not want to be a burden, if you need time apart to…"

"No!" he interrupts me and pulls me into a hug. "You're not a burden and I don't want time apart. I just want you to trust me and know that if I'm not telling you something about my life, it's not because of you, it's because there's a lot going on right now and I don't want you dragged into it worrying about me unnecessarily."

I am already worrying and it is extremely necessary. I am going to worry myself and form ulcers. Doesn't he see that? His evasiveness is why I feel this way. These vague and jumbled responses make me so uncomfortable.

His words scare me because deep down, somewhere in my being, I know there is way more going on than what he will ever be willing to admit to me. It's a feeling of fear and anxiety that I can't shake, but I can't force myself into his life, into his world. He doesn't want me there and though that realization hurts, I must respect it.

"Okay," I concede, trying to hide the anger and pain I feel from his rejection. I want him to tell me what's going on because he feels like he can, not because I begged and cried for it. Barnaby is immersed in my world, he is an intricate part of my world, he is the focal centerpiece in it. And in his world when it involves his family, I feel like I am only given crumbs. I feel like an unwelcome bystander.

He kisses my forehead and the silence within our bubble, the silence within *our quiet* has a powerful emotion to it. It's the same feeling I experienced on the yacht, that same energy I felt when I realized I loved him and that he probably loved me too.

Barnaby wants to say those three words to me right now, I can sense it from his touch and from the way his lips are lingering.

I don't want to hear them, not right now, not when I am this sad and disappointed, not while I am pretending his dishonesty isn't bothering me. I want to hear those words when we are finally both on the same wavelength. I want to say them back to him when I know he can trust me with everything, like I trust him with everything.

He lets go of me and places his palm on my cheek.

"Mazie, I…"

"We should get going," I interrupt and step back slightly, "I need to get to the library. I need to check if there are any reference books for this extra credit science paper I decided to do."

He drops his hand and then grabs mine, "Okay," his voice is low, "are we okay?"

"Yeah," I smile and squeeze his hand, "We're okay."

I know he can hear the off note in my voice, but if there is one thing we both know it's that we will always be okay even if we aren't okay.

I exhale and try to push my very true and very loud feelings to the back of my mind. In this moment I realize, I'd rather have any fraction of Barnaby than no Barnaby at all. It is in this moment that I decide against my gut and let my heart lead the charge. I love him and a few moments ago he was going to tell me he loved me too.

I don't want to jeopardize what we have because I keep pushing him to tell me things he isn't ready to share. I can't make this about me because it is clearly more than that. I do trust Barnaby and I have to trust that he knows what he is doing. He will come to me eventually and I will be here ready and willing to help him in any way I can.

Twelve

Burden (n.): something that is carried (1) a load (2) duty (3) responsibility

"You're making me nervous," I say to Barnaby. I can hear his foot tapping anxiously, every couple of minutes he exhales slowly. Maya is eerily quiet. We are waiting to find out if I need surgery. The surgery is high risk because of the location of the tumor, but I would honestly prefer surgery if it means I don't have to start a new round of radiation and chemo.

"Sorry," he says and even his voice isn't quite right. I sigh and reach out my hand. I hear him stand up and then his hand is in mine as I sit with my feet dangling off of the hospital bed.

"Surgery is not the end of the world," I say, but making sure they both can hear me. "I would prefer surgery over anymore treatments," I spoke my unpopular opinion out loud. They do not want me going under the knife, Maya especially.

"The tumor shrank. You won't need surgery," Barnaby states as if he's spoken to my doctor already and is privy to info no one else in this room has. I want to say something along the lines of *Oh excuse me, I must've missed when you got your medical license* but there definitely isn't a joking vibe in this room right now, so I don't respond.

"Maya," I change the subject, "are you even still here?" I ask. Of course she is; I can smell her fragrance and sense her presence.

"Yes, I am, sorry."

"Why are you apologizing?"

"I'm just sitting here thinking …"

Her words trail off and I immediately know where she was going with that sentence. She is thinking about mom and dad. After my first surgery, I was cancer free and blind for all of six months before our parents died. Thirteen was not a good year for me. Twenty six was not a good year for my sister. Our world came crumbling down without warning. With my illness the dynamic of our family had changed so much already and now we were parentless on top of everything.

We didn't have many family members and my sister took it upon herself to take care of me. She quit medical school so she could be with me more. She drove me to my appointments, my classes, anywhere I needed. She helped me learn Braille, she helped me learn our house inside and out so I could get around on my own. She worked two jobs at one point in order to afford special tutoring for me my freshmen year of high school. She helped me learn that I could be self-sufficient and independent with cooking and cleaning and taking care of myself to the best of my abilities. She taught me that just because I was blind didn't mean I was limited; the same opportunities were still available to me. The road would be bumpier and tougher to navigate, but the destination would remain the same.

My sister was my rock, she still is my rock. She gave up so much of her life for me. I am forever indebted to her. When I was sick before, we had our tiny tribe and our parents took the brunt of the work. But I know my sister, she is thinking that the responsibility is on her now and that we have to go through this, just the two of us. I wish I could make that feeling go away. I am glad Barnaby is here and has been here. Maybe his presence will help her see that she doesn't have to do every single thing. His words about the cloud not hovering forever were words I'd like to believe are true.

"Everything is going to be okay, Maya –me," I say with a soft smile.

"Why are you the one calming us down?" she asks and I am happy to hear a little life in her voice now. "It should be the other way around."

"Good point," Barnaby interjects. "What sorcery of turning tables are you using right now?"

I laugh and shake my head, "My one request from my amazing boyfriend is that you leave your weird *Barnaby babble* at the door." I squeeze his hand and I hear both him and Maya laugh. Then the door opens and I know Dr. Nipan is standing in the room. It's crazy how quickly the atmosphere goes from light to intense.

"How are you all?" Dr. Nipan inquires as I hear the door close.

"We are doing well. How are you, Dr. Nipan?" I ask calmly speaking for all of us.

"I am actually doing very well, Mazie. I get to tell one of my long time patients that her tumor is nearly gone and that there are no signs of any new growths."

"Thank God!" my sister blurts out in an excited sob, the relief oozing through both syllables.

I feel Barnaby's arms around me instantly. I remember this type of hug, he's squeezing me like he's afraid of letting go, like I may drift away and disappear if he doesn't hold on for dear life. This is the hug he gave me when I first told him I was sick.

I exhale and let Dr. Nipan's words sit in my being for a moment. These words don't float away and orbit around me like last time. These words are real, so real that I feel like I can reach out and touch them if I wanted to.

"What's the next step?" Maya queries. I hear her walk over to me. She grabs my hand squeezing it securely.

"Finish the last two weeks of treatment and we will test again, but I am confident we will have good news."

I smile, but I don't say a word. I did not want to get my hopes up like my boyfriend and my sister. This is far from over and I've learned a lot in my eighteen years. Always expect the worst case scenario, especially if you're me.

I'd made a conscious decision to be as upbeat as I could be on the days treatment didn't get the better of me. I vowed to be positive and happy around my two favorite people because I'd come to the realization that my life could be over at any moment. I'd accepted that, but I didn't want to waste however many days I had left in this life of mine being angry at the world or depressed or afraid. I want to live and I am going to do that for as long as my body will allow.

Though Barnaby and Maya have no clue of my thought pattern, it did overjoy me to hear and feel the joy they are experiencing right now. Despite what I feel my own conclusion to my life's story will be, I did truly feel like the cloud was moving, very slowly and calmly, but it is no longer hovering and if that is enough to give my sister and my boyfriend hope, then I am happy.

It's a week later and Barnaby and I are in my room editing two chapters I'd finally had time to complete. I hadn't been able to write much in the last few weeks because I was just too sick or had too much school work to catch up on. It feels good to be back at it again.

I hear the printer go off, and then I hear Barnaby grab the papers. He's really quiet and I realize the only time I can get him to shut his mouth is when he is reading and editing one of my chapters. I giggle quietly.

"What?" he asks distractedly.

"Oh, nothing..."

I don't hear anything for a moment and then suddenly, in the quickest movement, he has pushed me back on my bed. I can feel him hovering over me. I ignore my urge to laugh.

"You know the rules!" I yell at him, but the amusement is too blatant in my voice.

"We are all born to break the rules," he says teasingly.

"We still have twenty-two minutes of editing time, Barnaby," I say, even though my body is saying something else. My hand is gripping his shirt and my knees are up and spread apart, his body resting between them.

"What were you laughing about?" he asks huskily as his lips leave a trail of gentle kisses down my neck and to the top of my chest. I am suddenly extremely thankful that I decided to wear a plunging V-neck today.

"You're ten seconds away from being fired," I say, but now I am almost breathless, my entire body is a flame and he is the match.

"Can this be my severance package?" he asks and his lips are on mine.

Will this ever get old? Will I ever tire of how he tastes, of how he feels against me? Will I ever want someone different? I know the answers to these questions and the answers are a resounding *no*. I will always want him, all of him, every second of every day, all of the time, forever. Even if *my forever* is shorter than it deserves to be.

He finally lets me up for air and kisses my cheek. I don't feel him against me anymore.

"Barnaby?" I say breathlessly. Without even thinking, I put one hand up reaching for him, wanting to pull him back down to my lips.

"Yes?" he asks but he is sitting too far away from me.

"What's wrong?" I ask. "Come back," and I am embarrassed because I sound like I am begging him.

"We have twenty minutes to finish the edits on this chapter. You need to focus and keep your head in the game." He says and, though his tone is very serious, he is clearly enjoying teasing me.

"I hate you," I say as I sit up from my bed. My body is still hot and tingling and *wanting* and he is sitting there laughing at me. Jerk.

He chuckles, and then he pecks my cheek quickly. I wipe my cheek immediately, which makes him laugh harder. I can feel that he's gotten off of the bed.

"I was laughing before because the only time I can get you to shut up is when you're reading my work and concentrating on editing. I need to write much more frequently ..." I say tauntingly with a scowl and, not thinking it was possible, his laugh gets even louder. He is so damn annoying, *oh my God*! I try to hold in my own laughter as best I can.

"That is true," he says. "And the only time I can get you to stop arguing with me is when I put my tongue in your mouth," he says back coolly.

My jaw drops and I gasp in mock anger, "You ass!"

And we both start laughing. He is back on the bed next to me, but I can hear that he has his laptop, so no more funny business.

"Now that we are done insulting each other, I have a serious question for you that will require an actual answer," he says.

"What is it?"

"How is this going to end?" he questions. "We are only on page 118 and I have this nagging feeling your main character is going to die."

I don't say anything.

"Am I right?" he asks after a beat of silence.

"We are only on page 118," I repeat. "Don't you want to wait and see?"

"If I did, I wouldn't have asked," he says. "Plus as your editor, your best friend, your boyfriend, and someone you're sleeping with, I feel like I should get special privileges."

I sigh. "There isn't another way for the novel to end for it to stay real to the storyline and the character. The lesson learned would be missed and the whole book wouldn't make sense," I say honestly.

"Her dying isn't the only way this book could end, Mazie." He sounds upset.

"How?" I ask because I can't envision any other way.

"It could be a happy ending. That never occurred to you?" he asks and I am a little surprised by how clipped his voice is. Is he *actually* angry with me?

"Not for her," I answer anyway. "It wouldn't work..."

"What do you have against simplicity? Against happily ever afters?" he interrupts and I am sensing a double meaning in his angry words, but I don't acknowledge it out loud. I keep my voice even and emotionless as I answer.

"I don't have anything against simplicity or happily ever afters, but I will always go with the realistic ending first." We are definitely talking about something else. "Life isn't simplistic, it's messy, scary and unpredictable. I can't just write the easy and pretty parts. The uncomfortable parts are what make the story relatable. They are the parts that make these characters real…"

"So a happy ending isn't realistic to you?" he interrupts again, ignoring the second half of my statement.

"Not always. Not in this case. Not in her case," I emphasize. It's quiet and the air is thick and turbulent between us. There are unspoken words and though I am not sure what those words are exactly, I can feel them igniting. They are invading *our quiet*. I can feel their weight boiling over. I need to be the first to speak.

"Barnaby…."

"You're not sick anymore Mazie and the scans are going to come back cancer free. If you allow me to stay in your life, you are *going* to have a happily ever after," he blurts the words out angrily; he says the words like they are weapons. Those beautiful words don't match his anger.

I inhale and ignore the prickling of tears I feel trying to come out.

"This book isn't about me," I say lowly because this is not a conversation I want to have right now or ever for that matter.

"The hell it isn't," he nearly snaps. "What are you trying to tell me? Are you trying to tell me something?" and I can't ignore the pain and agony I hear in his voice, it's gripping.

"It's just a book," I say and my voice shakes, "…and you can't guarantee me a happily ever after, you can't guarantee me anything. I admire that you want to, but it's not realistic, not for me at least." I did not know I was going to say that, but it's true.

Just look at my scorecard, besides meeting Barnaby I did not have the best of luck. My life constantly revolted against me in more ways than one.

"What the fuck does that even mean?" he questions exasperatedly, his sadness overpowering his initial anger. "You have gone through so much, more than anyone I have ever known and you've come out the other side, but …"

"But what?" I ask. He doesn't answer right away. He takes so long to respond that I almost ask the question again, but then he speaks.

"Reading your book, I feel like you're preparing for the end of something. Like you're writing your own conclusion, trying to predict your future and the future you're predicting right now is sad and painful and that terrifies me, Mazie."

I bite the inside of my cheek, realizing that I am now unable to keep these tears at bay.

"I've been given too many chances!" I snap, surprising myself. I am not even 100% sure of what I am saying, but with Barnaby I usually don't have or need a filter. I just let the words flow out of me. I don't want my very real fears and thoughts to terrify him, but this isn't about him. It's about me and how I view my life.

"I was told that I had a 33% chance of survival when I was thirteen, but here I am." The tears are streaming down my face, but I don't even bother wiping them because more will just replace them.

"I was in the car the night my parent's slid off of an exit ramp. They're dead and I am still here. How is that fair? How is that right?" I inhale a big gulp of air, the words nearly caught in my throat. This is the first time I've mentioned to Barnaby how my parents died.

I vaguely remember the details of that night, a night that I don't often think about and never talk about.

The memory I have of that night is waking up to the sound of my sister's sobs. I was newly blind, still trying to figure out my other heightened senses and how to find my bearings.

"Maya?" I remember saying, my voice was all but gone and my entire body was sore. I could feel bandages on my arm and head.

"Mazie," she choked out in a whaling shriek, then seconds later I feel her arms around me. I remember trying to figure out why Maya was in my bedroom crying, why I was sore. Was the cancer back? Had I dreamt about the surgery? Impossible because I was still blind, but confusion took over me, wrapping me in its tight unrelenting blanket.

"Why are you crying?" I managed to ask as I sifted through the fog of my thoughts. I tried to remember the last thing that had happened in my life, but I was coming up short.

"God!" she screamed and I jumped. Something was wrong; something was seriously wrong and just in her one word cry my emotions quickly went from confusion to fear. I didn't know what to be fearful of, but I felt it in my chest, an ominous feeling that something very bad had happened, something that would hurt, "I'm so sorry, Mazie!" she screamed again but her words were nearly unintelligible as they were hidden within her sobs. Sorry for what?

I remember hearing a door open and hearing a woman's voice say, "It's okay, it's okay."

Who was this stranger in my bedroom talking to my sister? "Miss Day, come with me, we are going to give you something to calm you down."

What?

My thoughts were now jumbled mush, my sister's loud hysterics weren't helping. I'd never been more afraid than this very moment. Not even when I found out I was sick. What was going on?

"Nurse Tia, could you please take Miss Day to an empty room?" I hear the woman say referring to my sister. Were we in a hospital?

"Maya!" I yell out but her screams seemed to be further and further away until I could tell she was no longer in this room with me. I could hear the woman who'd had my sister taken away typing into what sounded like a laptop.

"Where is my sister?" I asked panicked as tears began to stream down my cheeks. The ominous feeling was no longer a feeling; it was now a part of me. It rested within every cell of my body and seeped into every thought that I had. Something bad happened, something very, very bad happened. "Is this a hospital? Why am I here?" I choke out.

"How does your head feel, sweetheart?"

"Call my mom!" I yelled at her because my confused and anxiety ridden body could no longer handle this level of fear. I hated being blind so much then, it was so new to me, it took away my ability to assess a situation or adjust to a situation. I'd never heard my sister cry like that before. If I were able to see her, to see where I was, to see the woman who is in this room but not answering my questions quickly enough, maybe I'd be able to calm myself in some way.

But I was in eternal darkness, I was lost and I would never be able to escape it. "I want my dad!" I yelled at the woman, when I felt her hands gently grip my wrist.

"You were in a car accident, Ezmerelda."

"Mazie," I corrected her before I allowed the words to make sense in my mind.

I was in an accident?

Then flooding my mind like a broken dam, I remembered getting in the car leaving a doctor's appointment. It was raining; I remember getting soaked while getting into the car and then hearing the loud prattles of the raindrops smack against the car once we started moving.

My dad was driving; my mom was in the passenger seat. She was talking about the baby, a new little sister was on the way in four short months. The baby started kicking the day before and I remember how fascinated I was by it. She and I talked about going shopping for the baby's room later that week and I was so excited.

I remembered hearing my father suddenly yell out an expletive. I remembered feeling the car swerve and then jerk which caused my head to bang roughly against the backseat window. I heard my mother yell my father's name, the panic laden shriek of her voice stunned me. I was confused at the loud and excruciating sound of screeching tires.

Then I woke up to my sisters sobs.

Frozen, paralyzed, engulfed by fear, I tried to force my lips to ask the question, but deep down in my conscious thought, I knew the answer and it couldn't be real, not yet, not ever.

"Where are my parents?" my voice was a shell of what it was. It was shaky, scared, and it regretted asking the question, because it *knew* what was to come. I wanted to somehow freeze that moment, the moment before my life would erupt in flames. I wanted to hold onto the last seconds of having living breathing parents.

"I'm so sorry," the woman said to me.

What was she sorry for? Had she killed my parents? Had she run us off of the road? What the hell was she sorry for? How would her apology or sympathy make this any better? How would this empty and mechanical apology bring my parents back to me?

I don't remember what happened after that. I don't remember if I cried and screamed like Maya. I don't remember if I yelled at the nurse and called her a liar. I don't remember if I just laid there in that hospital bed, numb and unfocused mentally on the world around me. I don't remember.

And I don't ever want to remember.

I have to bring myself back to real time. I have to finish telling Barnaby how life has never been on my side. How my life has always found a way to throw a wrench at me without remorse or regard. I inhale and continue, inwardly marveling at my boyfriend's patience. I hadn't realized it until this very moment that he's grabbed my hand and linked our fingers together. How long had I been silent? How long had I been sitting here in front of him crying at an almost memory of the day I lost my parents?

"I have cancer again," I finally say and he squeezes my hand, "…and yes, we can celebrate and act like all is good in the world because the tumor shrank, but I am not out of the woods and that is a very real thing. I am sorry if I can't be all rainbows and unicorns. I have been through a lot and I have made it through, but one of these times the universe or the *up there* is going to realize that I have been given too many chances and that will be it. I rather be prepared for it than pretend it isn't a reality."

I said all of that in one breath. I inhale and exhale slowly, "I *want* a happily ever after. I *want* simplicity, but that's not how the cards fall for me." My words are bitter and I am not sure why I am putting all of this on Barnaby. He doesn't deserve this, but I am angry and sad and frustrated and my only outlet besides him has been writing this book. I need to be honest with and to both.

It's quiet and I have absolutely no idea what reaction I am going to get from Barnaby, our hands are still connected as I wait for his response.

"I don't believe that," he says softly. "You haven't been dealt the best hand, I won't argue that but there is a reason you are still here. There is a reason that with everything you have been through, you are still this magnificent human being that you are. You are here because you are supposed to be here and the fact that you can't understand just how much this world needs a Mazie pisses me off. You're not cheating death; you're beating it because of your strength and resilience."

I feel him move closer to me placing his free hand on the side of my face. "I want to be in your life and I want to *stay* in your life. I *am* promising you a happily ever after. I am guaranteeing it because you deserve that much, more than anyone."

His words make me warm all over because I believe that *he* believes he can do that for me, so I won't dare tell him he's making promises that he absolutely has no way of knowing he can fulfill. But, nevertheless, his wanting to make me happy, his vow to me that he wants to stay in my life puts a smile on my face through the tears and I am going to tell him I love him. I am finally going to tell him I am madly in love with him with every single fiber of my being but then I feel his lips press against mine.

After a few moments we both come up for air and we sit in silence, my hand still in his. "The book, it isn't about me in that way," I add.

"In *that* way?"

"It's like a parallel universe, my life in many circumstances," my voice is quiet. "I haven't been trying to tell you anything."

That is the truth. I am not trying to tell him anything, I am telling myself how to prepare. I am telling myself that there is an end and it's important to accept it, not fight it. I don't think I am lying to him, I think I am protecting him because Barnaby is the headstrong love of my life and I know there is nothing I can tell him that will help him understand why and how writing my life *in many circumstances* is cathartic and a form of release for me.

He exhales and I feel his arms wrap around me. "I just want you to know that everything is going to be okay. Alright?" he says softly. I don't say a word as I lay my head on his chest, and I nod slightly. In his arms is and always will be my favorite place and if my story were to end right now, this very moment would be the conclusive *happily ever after* that he so desperately wants me to have.

"Okay, seriously, where are we going?" I ask for the umpteenth time while sitting in Barnaby's car. One would think I would actually get used to the fact that my boyfriend specializes in grand gestures and finds joy in whisking me away on surprises. As much as I enjoy our little adventures, I am an impatient person and I always get frustrated wondering what we are going to do. I truly believe because he knows this about me, he does it on purpose.

He does not answer my question –again – and then the music gets louder.

I laugh, "Wow! You're not going to drown me out with the radio," I yell over the music. "My voice is very loud."

"I am extremely aware of that," he says and I flip him off.

"We've been driving for over forty minutes," I add. "Are we going out of town or something?"

"Ezmerelda, relax," he says calmly. He says it in that tone that he knows I hate. The tone he uses that makes me feel like a child who is on the verge of having a tantrum in public.

"Mazie…" I grumble.

"And we've been driving for so long," he interrupts as if I had not said anything, "because I got lost, but we're all good now."

"We're lost?"

"*Were* lost..."

I inhale and tell myself that whatever he has up his sleeve will be worth it because it usually is. I tell myself to not be annoyed or pissed off that I am starving and we've essentially been driving in circles to nowhere for nearly an hour.

"Don't do that..." he says and he's turned the volume down on the radio.

"Do what?" I ask flatly.

"You're making that face you make when you're pissed off."

"I don't have a face that I make when I'm pissed off."

He laughs and then the radio is off completely. "We are five minutes away." He grabs my hand and I intertwine our fingers, resting them on the armrest between us.

We are driving in silence, enjoying *our quiet*. The windows are slightly cracked because it's pretty nice out for this time of year. I wonder if Barnaby knows that holding his hand is one of my favorite pastimes. I wonder if he knows that all of my favorite pastimes involve him…

"Okay," he says, letting go of me. "We are here."

I fight the urge to say where, but instead I just unclip my seatbelt. I don't open my door because Barnaby makes a big deal if I attempt to open the door before he can get to it. I've learned to pick and choose my battles with him. A few seconds pass and he is helping me out of the car.

"Right this way," he says while handing me my cane. We walk only for a few seconds and then I hear a door open, quickly followed by a little ding as we walk in. I think we are in a store.

I lose my battle and ask again, "Where are we?"

Before he can respond, I hear a woman greeting us, "Hi, I am Stacey. How can I help you?"

"Hi, I am Barnaby and this is my girlfriend, Ezmerelda. We are looking for something to wear to Prom."

My head immediately darts in his direction. "What?" my voice louder than I intended it to be. He grabs my hand and squeezes it.

"Oh, how exciting!" the woman says. "It's so important to get an early start on it. What color scheme are you both thinking?"

"Hmmm," Barnaby says, "It'll actually be up to Ezmerelda, whatever she wants. We both look great in any color."

The woman laughs, "Of course! You two are just adorable. Okay, Ezmerelda, what did you have in mind? Were you thinking about going traditional or perhaps trendy? Trendy seems to be the go to with your generation. We also have a custom designer on call who…"

"It's Mazie," I interrupt her and I am not trying to be rude, but too many things are happening right now and I haven't had a chance to think. "I'm sorry, can I get a second to talk to my boyfriend?" I ask trying with all of my might to temper my mood.

"Oh, well absolutely. I'll be in the back. Again, the name is Stacey. Just holler when you need me."

I nod and try to smile. I wait a moment until I believe she is out of earshot. I tug Barnaby back a few paces before I speak. "What the hell?" I whisper forcefully.

"Surprise?" he says and of course he thinks this is funny because he thinks everything is funny.

"Barnaby..."

"Why don't you want to run for Prom Queen?" he asks.

Shit.

"You talked to Breanna?"

"Yeah, she told me that you said it wasn't our thing."

Breanna is a traitor.

"...and," Barnaby continues, "imagine my shock at hearing that because we never once discussed it. I was unaware that Prom wasn't my thing."

"Okay, well it's not my thing."

"Why?"

King Asker of Questions...

"I don't know."

"Yeah, you do."

I clench my jaw. "It's just stupid," I finally say and he is quiet and I hope I didn't just offend him.

"Hmmm," he finally says and of course I take the bait.

"What is that particular *hmmm* supposed to mean?"

"Honestly?"

I nod.

"I personally don't believe you think it's stupid at all. I think the attention freaks you out," he says easily.

One of the scariest and highly annoying things about being so in sync with someone is the fact that he can call you out on your bullshit so effortlessly.

"Okay, fine. I don't want to run for Prom Queen because I don't want to win because of the pity vote."

"The pity vote," he repeats.

"Yes. The pity vote…"

"Okay," he says after a quick moment, "I don't want to belittle your feelings or anything like that because how you feel is how you feel, but we are an adorable couple, just ask Stacey. She saw it right away."

I'm trying not to smile because I am trying to be serious.

"Maybe some people will vote for you because of that and that is something we cannot help, but Mazie, I promise you that your hardships are not what everyone sees. You know it's sure as hell not what I see. I just don't want you to miss this special day and regret it later on. You only get to be a senior once."

"Not true. If I don't pass my science final, I will definitely be a senior again.;"

Barnaby laughs, "You know what I mean. This is something I want to experience with you, but if you honestly don't want to go, let it be because you just don't want to, not because of what you think everyone else is thinking." He sighs and continues, "Running away from it doesn't make you invisible. You are seen. You just need to understand that you are being seen for so much more than what you think."

Barnaby always knows what to say in almost every situation. He is a pretty wonderful human being and he has a point, I guess. Maybe one day I would think back on it and regret not going. Prom is like a rite of passage and I know that even if all eyes are on me, the only pair of eyes that matter will be Barnaby's.

"You always say you don't want people to pity you or notice your handicap first and I agree, but you have to stop noticing it first, too, or at least stop making it seem like you're less of a person because of what someone might think or say. You don't need me to tell you how amazing you are because you already know that, but I did tell you I feel like it's my job to keep reminding you. This is me reminding you."

And he does. He always reminds me. Everyone has their moments of insecurity and everyone is allowed to sit in their very real feelings and try to make sense of them, but with someone like Barnaby in my life, it's hard to stay in those moments for too long.

I sigh. "You lied to Stacey," I finally say.

"What?"

"I don't look good in every color. We have to scratch green off the list of options, immediately."

He laughs and it's such a guttural and infectious *Barnaby laugh*, "I know for a fact you can pull off green."

And I roll my eyes.

"Okay," he says, "Bringing you here was mostly payback for not telling me about the Breanna thing, but there's a new coffee shop/jazz place I am actually taking you to across the street. But I do want to formally ask you."

I smile and I know I'm blushing. The fact that I still blush around him blows my mind. There's no human in this world who knows me in the ways Barnaby does and yet he can still make me feel like it's our first date.

"Ezmerelda Constance Day, will you go to Prom with me?"

I don't correct him, "Yes, Barnaby *no middle name* Parks, I will go to Prom with you."

"Okay!" he says excitedly and I feel his warm arms wrap around me and then he pulls away to kiss my forehead.

"Alright," he says loudly and he grabs my hand and we start walking. "I need to find Stacey and tell her to point us in the direction of all of the green dresses."

I laugh and intertwine our fingers, enjoying my favorite pastime thoroughly.

~~

"This is nice," Maya says.

"I'm freaking out," I say, as I squirm in my seat.

"Calm down!" she laughs.

We are getting pedicures and I can't handle it. I don't like people touching my feet, with the exception of Barnaby and that is still difficult at times. I made the mistake of telling him I didn't like my feet to be touched, so now he makes it his mission to touch them as often as possible so I've had to learn to somewhat tolerate it.

"If you don't think about it, it's really soothing," she says.

"How can I not think about a stranger's hands on my bare and exposed feet?" Is she crazy? And why the hell did I agree to this? She laughs, ignoring me as I continue to tense and squirm in my seat.

"Maya, why are we here?" I ask her and I don't mean for my voice to sound so annoyed.

"I just wanted to spend time with you," she says. "It was very dark there for a while and now ..." she drifts off, and I know she is smiling. I wouldn't be surprised if some tears are falling from her eyes right now. "Besides, I am always working and when I'm not working, Barnaby gets all your time. We have to make time for each other, I miss my Mazie- My."

At that thought I realize she is right. Even when chemo was getting the best of me, Barnaby was always there and I never once considered or wondered how she felt not having to do it all. I assumed she liked not having to carry the load on her own. It also made me sad realizing that she works so hard and so many hours so she could keep a roof over our heads. I was allowed to come and go as I pleased with Barnaby 100% of the time. I would get sick and then go back to my life but nothing changes for her. She works, comes home and is there for me. My sister doesn't have a life that doesn't revolve around helping and or protecting me in some way.

"I'm sorry," I say and I cannot hide the anguish in my voice.

"What?" she says surprised. "No, no, no! I didn't mean it like that. I just know that things are going to change the older you get so I want to make sure we carve time out for one another."

"…but are you carving out time for yourself?" I ask.

"What do you mean?"

I sigh because this is something we never talk about and I don't know why, "You should go out and date and have fun and not worry about me so much."

"Mazie..."

"I'm serious," I interrupt her. "The last five years of your life have been all about me and taking care of me and doing more than anyone should ever offer to do without getting something in return. Now that I am a little older it isn't fair that I just get to go back and live an almost normal teenage life and you still have to do what you've been doing because of me."

She doesn't say anything so I keep going, "I think you should go back to medical school. I think you should date and party and get drunk and do all the things you couldn't do in your twenties because you were too busy being a mother to me."

She sniffles. I didn't mean to make her cry, I am just being honest.

"I don't know what I did to deserve such a wonderful little sister," she says between sniffles "…but I promise you I am okay and that I love my life, I love my choices, I love you and I don't regret a thing." She says softly, "I wish you knew the joy I feel seeing you happy, seeing you healthy and full of life. That's all I wanted and it is all I will ever want. So please stop thinking like that okay?"

I want to counter her, but I believe her words and I just want my sister to have a life that is separate from mine. I've taken up so much of hers already and here I am having my own world with Barnaby, a part from her, it just doesn't seem fair.

After our horrendous early morning pedicures, we went to brunch and now we are walking in the park. It feels so good talking to Maya about school, about my fear of getting my new scans, about my novel, about Barnaby.

I don't tell her that I think about death a lot. That will only scare her, and I'm past that now, it doesn't scare me anymore. If there is one thing we all know universally is that we all die, but I've realized that my focus shouldn't be on actually dying. My focus should be on the life I am living in whatever time frame I am given and when I focus on that, I am genuinely happy.

I don't feel like I am forcing myself to navigate through life and this world anymore. I don't feel like I am begging the world to accept me, I am in it. I am walking alongside everyone else now, finally. I don't need to be constantly reminded of everything I am because I am learning more and more about myself as the days go by, as my love for Barnaby grows, as my appreciation for the small things helps me muddle through the difficult days.

"We have to do this once a month," I say to Maya before I even realize what I am saying, my words trailing off. My thoughts can't help but think about the possibility of me being sicker or worse, not alive. It's a tricky feeling to describe, knowing that you've accepted a certain version of your life that you simultaneously have to protect your loved ones from.

They won't understand.

"Of course," she says lightly. She is happy and I have to ignore the knot that forms in my stomach. I have been extremely careful about not making concrete plans too far in the future. I have been vigilant about not committing or making promises so if my time comes sooner than any of us wants, it would be one last thing for her or Barnaby to agonize about.

"Even if you're at MSU," she grabs my hand and the sadness is blatant in her voice. I inhale because as we walk together, as my emotions flood my thoughts, I can't imagine being at MSU in the fall. I can't imagine being anywhere in the fall and my only fear is hurting the two people I love more than anything in this world.

"Even if I'm at MSU," I say softly as we continue to walk hand and hand.

Maya clears her throat, and before she speaks, I already know she is changing the subject, "I found an old letter Dad wrote to Mom. It was in some boxes in the basement. He was telling her that he missed her. I think it's from when they first started dating and couldn't work in the same department anymore."

I don't say anything right away, because I am not exactly sure how to respond. Maya and I never really talk about our parents. I don't know why, but that's how it's been for pretty much most of the last five years.

"Oh," is all I say. The quiet that engulfs us is a heavy quiet and I know it won't last long.

"Do you think about them a lot?" she asks.

I swallow and nod. "Every single day," I admit.

"Does it get easier for you?"

"Amaya, what are we doing?" and I can't keep my voice at the proper octave. I don't understand why we need to talk about this right now. Why out of the blue is this a conversation that needs to be had?

"It's okay to talk about them. It's okay to talk about painful things, Mazie."

It's almost as if she's been reading my mind. All the things I've said to myself about my cancer and my upcoming scans, about not running from the scary parts of life, about not pretending bad things can't happen in order to preserve some type of sanity and normalcy. Everything I have been saying to myself, she is saying to me.

I take a moment and try to find a way to word this without getting too emotional.

"It doesn't get easier for me, but I've accepted it. I just learned to deal with it because I don't have a choice." I exhale, "In the beginning, it was like I had to relearn how to exist all over again, every single day trying to understand this strange new world that they were no longer physically a part of. It will never be easier; I'm just well-practiced in this routine."

I realize that my words could almost be used in the same context as when I went blind. Having to relearn a strange new world, every single day having to fight with the universe to remind it I was there.

She squeezes my hand and I squeeze hers.

"Looks like I am the naïve one," she sniffles, "I was convinced it would get better. I've been waiting for it to start."

In her words, I realize that this conversation isn't for me. She is asking these questions because she wants to talk. I just got done talking about how her whole life has been about me and never once did I truly comprehend what she goes through in other areas. I am barely able to suppress the lump growing in my throat.

"Have you found peace?" I ask, and just saying the words sends a calming sensation through me. "I didn't know that's what I was searching for until Barnaby said he hoped I'd found peace. I think that helps."

She doesn't answer right away and I am transported to that day when Barnaby said that to me. Back when I was in denial about my feelings for him, back when I tried, and quickly failed, to keep him in the friend zone.

"I'm so happy you have him," she says, and though it's subtle, her avoidance of answering the question makes me so sad. "I'm glad you have each other."

"I'm glad too," I smile and I hate how somber this outing has become. I don't want what little time I spend with my sister to be shrouded in sadness and fear and whatever other emotions are flowing between us.

"Are you two being safe?"

I almost choke on air; she asks the question so casually. It's clear that she wants a subject change as well, but *damn*.

"I ..." and I don't know how to answer this. I think at this very moment I would much rather talk about my scans.

"Mazie, you're eighteen and I'm your sister. I just want to make sure you're being smart and safe. You look like you're going to throw up." And though I am mortified, I am happy that there is humor in her voice.

"Yes, we are," I mumble. I'm actually not sure if the words fully came out of my mouth. "Being safe..." I add so there's no confusion.

"Good," she gives my hand a quick squeeze, "Have you both been tested?"

"Amaya!" I snap and she laughs. Of course she does.

"If you're mature enough to have sex, you should be mature enough to have this conversation."

She has her mom voice on right now and I am pretty sure it's one of the most annoying things in my life. The mom lectures always pop up with no warning.

I am finally able to structure a full sentence. "Do I need to have the conversation with you in a park?" I whisper and she lets go of my hand and puts her arm around my shoulders.

"You need to go on the pill, but that doesn't mean he stops using condoms. Birth control doesn't protect you from STDs." Why is she still talking? Why won't the words stop coming out of her face? "I have some condoms in my room, the second drawer in my nightstand. Just in case you're ever in a situation where Barnaby doesn't have…"

"Oh my God," I interrupt, "Okay, I get it! Please stop."

If we were in her car right now, I would jump out of it while it was still moving.

I expected Maya to be understanding, but what I did not expect or particularly want is a sex education course. I can't handle this conversation with her and she knows it.

"Okay," she finally says, "We can talk about this later."

Thank God.

"I love you, Mazie –My."

I sigh and roll my eyes, "I love you too, Maya –Me."

～～

"Barnaby," I whisper breathlessly as his lips travel up and down every inch of my neck and bare chest.

"Mmm hmm," he mutters as his lips never disconnect from any given part of my skin. My skin that is sensitive to the touch, sensitive to his touch.

I don't say another word as I enjoy his body moving with mine. There aren't too many things I enjoy more than being this connected to Barnaby, to be able to express how we feel about one another without proclamations. Sometimes what is known doesn't need to be said; Barnaby was right about that.

"Stay," his words are mumbled as his lips move back to my neck. "All weekend."

"You're …trying to kill me," I giggle breathlessly as I grab his hair. He and I are both starting to grow our hair back, mine –small spiraling curls, his –just a bit longer than a buzz cut.

"No, the exact opposite of that," he says strained. "We have so much to celebrate …" and then neither one of us can speak any further. His lips are now on mine and I am lost. I am always lost in some other euphoric world when we are together like this. Every moment is something out of a dream, a dream that I never want to wake up from.

Afterwards we lay on his bed wrapped around each other's naked bodies on top of his covers. He is tracing his fingers up and down my back.

"When someone says she wants to celebrate your birthday and the fact that I am officially cancer free I assumed that meant cake and ice cream," I say with a smile. He laughs and pulls me closer to him.

"We can always add cake and ice cream if you like that kind of thing."

I nudge him as we both laugh.

I am cancer free.

All of my scans and bloodwork came back negative. It's the news I'd been waiting for –we'd all been waiting for. It's the news that was supposed to stop these intrusive thoughts about death I'd been having. That cloud would disappear for good and I could stop trying to fulfill and condense so much of my life into a small frame of time before reaching an arbitrary expiration date.

Finding out that I am cancer free for the second time in my life should have been one of the best moments in my life, but that stubborn cloud is still here. I have this feeling in the pit of my stomach that something is still looming, that there is a clock I should be racing.

The future scares me, death doesn't. The future scares me more now than anything else. It's dark and unpaved and I've had enough surprises in my life to fill many lifetimes. I hate that I don't understand why good news is causing me to react this way, maybe it's muscle memory. When so many unfortunate things happen to a person and then good finally happens, maybe the body starts to panic, waiting for the other shoe to drop.

"How does it feel to finally be of age?" I ask Barnaby, because I am getting too into my thoughts. I don't want him to sense that anything is off with me because he'd call me out on it and then pry it out of me if he tried hard enough. I reach out to run my fingers along his jawline.

"I feel refined," he says sarcastically. "Wiser than usual. How does it feel to not be a cougar anymore?" he asks and I laugh.

"Five whole months of not having to feel ancient around you…" I smile and he quickly pecks my lips.

"Have you heard back from MSU yet?" he asks.

"If I had, you'd be the first one to know," I say.

He and I decided that we will go to MSU together. It wasn't really an official talked out plan, but I told him I applied even though at the time I didn't think I'd be healthy enough to attend. Then he said he would apply the following week and then we agreed that MSU would be our first choice, AMU would be our second choice, and staying here in state would be our third and last choice.

So without actually saying the words, we'd plan to go wherever the other went.

Last week he told me that AMU isn't really prepared for blind students because the dormitories and Braille selection are lacking. I thought it was so sweet of him to go out of his way to look into that for me. I honestly hadn't even given it much thought which annoyed him.

"I have an idea," he says, yanking me from my reverie. "An idea that I am sure you'll argue with me about and try to come up with a million reasons as to why it won't work."

"You want to tell me what you're talking about before you put words in my mouth?"

"I want to travel all summer," he says, "...out of the country."

"Oh..." is all I say.

I wasn't expecting the sadness to take over me so quickly. I had this idea that our summer was going to be spent together, not having to have school carve out a six hour block where we can't be cuddled up somewhere together. Maybe I shouldn't have jumped to that conclusion; we would be together even more when we went away to college than we are now.

Maybe he wants and needs a break. No matter how I try to rationalize his decision, my feelings are hurt. "If that's what you want to do, I can't stop you. Where will you go?"

He laughs and holds me to him. "We. Mazie," he says. "I want us to go; you think I can go two and a half months without you?"

The sadness I felt quickly turns into happiness and joy, then I am finally able to comprehend what he said.

"Wait, you want to leave the country for the entire summer?" and the shock in my voice is much stronger than I intended. "I can't afford that, Barnaby."

"I can."

"Absolutely not!" I say and damn it he knows me well. I *am* going to argue this. He is insane! That's not something you offer to someone you haven't even known a year whether you're in love or whether you have the money or not. It's illogical. Barnaby is completely absurd if he thinks for one second I'd go along with this.

"And here we go. Classic Ezmerelda," he laughs, and I can't squelch the fire that ignites in my chest at his words. He knows how much it bugs me to one, call me Ezmerelda still after all of this time and two, when he laughs when I am trying to be serious.

"Yes, here we go!" I snap. "You can't be serious right now!"

"As a heart attack," he answers immediately. "And calm down before you have one. Listen, I have the money and I have the right and the choice to do whatever I want with it and I want to get one major life experience under our belts before we are stuck in classrooms and study halls and lectures."

"I can't let you spend that kind of money on me. I'm sorry." It is out of the question. This isn't going to be like our arguments where we go back and forth and finally I concede to whatever it is he wants or vice versa. I am not allowing him to spend a single penny on me toward this trip and there is nothing he can say to make me change my mind.

"I've never left the U.S. You went to Mexico a million years ago and don't even remember it. You know deep down you want to do this. We'd be together every single day, just us. Think about how good you always feel every time you throw caution to the wind."

I sigh because I know what he is doing. Tracing my back lightly, holding me close to his chest, his words soft as his cool breath touches my skin when he speaks. He is trying to seduce me into going. He is trying to smooth talk me into letting him spend ridiculous amounts of money on me. "You'll be throwing money to the wind," I say.

"You cannot put a price on happiness and fun. I want to do this and I don't want to do it without you. I really don't think I would survive a whole summer without you."

"Are you going to go either way?" I ask and the sadness manages to seep into my tone. I hadn't really considered the fact that my not going didn't mean he wouldn't go.

"I don't want to, but this is something that I really feel like I have to do. I have to get away for awhile."

I lay quietly in his arms weighing the options. It's just so hard trying to wrap my head around him spending that kind of money on me. It's overwhelming actually. I probably have about $400 I could possibly contribute and that would be a drop in a bucket compared to how much two and half months out of the country would cost. But I also can't wrap my head around being away from Barnaby that long. I'd go mad.

"Where do you want to go?" I say quietly and I feel his grip on me tighten. "This is not me saying yes," I say quickly trying to stifle his premature excitement. "I just want to know your plan."

"First, visit your family in Mexico for as long as you'd like," he says. "Then I want to travel all over Europe, just take trains and visit as many countries as possible and eat as much food as possible."

He's holding me so close to his body that I can feel his heartbeat thumping against me. What he is planning is a lot and in this moment I realize that I am really not going to go. I feel my chest getting warm because not only am I sad at the thought of a summer without Barnaby, but I hate that I'd be disappointing him too.

"I want to make love to you in every single country we visit. I'm going to cherish every inch of you and your body all over the world," he says lowly, pulling me out of my slumber. The way he says the words and the vicinity of our bodies makes me shiver.

"I can give you $400 toward it upfront," I blurt out.

He is easily able to make me negate every single thought I'd just had. He truly is my biggest weakness, damn it.

"Mazie, no…"

"…and I'll make $50 payments a month to you until I pay off my half," I interrupt. "That's the *only* way I will go, I can't let you take on the entire bill." I had to give myself some type of a spine in this situation.

He's quiet for a moment. Then he sighs, "How about this, you save the $400 and the $50 payments in a separate savings account and on this date next year you give it to me in full?"

"Barnaby…"

"Compromise with me," he says and I sigh.

"Fine."

"Deal?"

"Deal."

He bear hugs me and I can't stop the giggle that escapes my lips.

"I'll start booking stuff tomorrow!" he says. "What are you going to tell Maya?"

"I didn't think about that," I say honestly. "I'm eighteen, she trusts you. I'm sure it won't be an issue."

We lay in comfortable silence for a few moments. I honestly could stay like this forever. I want to; maybe I'd take him up on that offer to stay the entire weekend. I'm sure Maya won't mind and at that thought something gets my attention…

"I've been here at different times almost every day this week," I say. "Where has your dad been?"

He doesn't answer right away and I feel bad for bringing him up, but Barnaby is open with me in many aspects of his life except for his relationship with his father. It still makes me so sad that there is a part of him he doesn't feel comfortable sharing with me. We keep having the same conversation, but I can't help it.

He basically forced himself into my life and when I tried to push him away he wouldn't allow it and now he knows me in ways no one else does. Not just sexually, but I feel more myself with him, I am not labeled or different, I am just a girl with her boyfriend. I want to be that for him, someone he can come to with everything and he won't let me. He is more than enough for me, but I can't help but feel like I am not enough of what he needs

I need access to that restricted area.

"I know you told me that you don't want to talk about your dad but," I say quietly because I know that I am opening a can of worms, "I just…I still worry…"

"I told you there is nothing to worry about," he says and his voice is almost clipped. "This is something you shouldn't even be thinking about."

"Why can't you talk to me?" I ask honestly and I hate that this isn't the first time I've asked him this question. I wasn't expecting so much sadness to fill my words. I thought I had let it go. I thought I was okay with him keeping this huge part of his life locked up away from me, but I clearly am not.

I can feel the atmosphere in the room changing. This may turn into an argument and that is the last thing I want right now. We were having such a good day and it's his birthday, but I can't stop myself from asking the question.

"I do talk to you, every single day. We talk for hours."

"Don't patronize me, Barnaby," I almost snap. He stops tracing my back and I feel his body tense. "You know what I am talking about, how bad is it?"

"Mazie, God…" he snaps and then I feel him get up from the bed. Though he has seen my naked body on more than a few occasions, I suddenly feel self-conscious and exposed. I search for his sheet with my fingers and pull it over me.

There have been times when he has missed school. There are some days that we are together and for the first few minutes he is this other person; he isn't my tornado, my full of life, burst of sun rays and energy. He's this sullen contemplative version of Barnaby and that version makes me sad because I don't know anything about that Barnaby.

"What if the tables were turned?" I say. "What if I was being abused and wouldn't talk to you? I wouldn't let you in?"

"What?" he nearly barks, confusion saturating his words. "I'm not being abused! It's not like that."

I shake my head and can feel my eyes prickling, "He hits you and probably Mel too. What would you call that, Barnaby? And this is not just physical abuse, this is emotional abuse too. He…"

"I don't know what the hell you want from me!" he yells, interrupting me. And I jump, not expecting that from him. He's never yelled at me before, I don't think I've ever heard him raise his voice at all, not like that. I hate that I can't stop this tear from falling down my cheek because I am more pissed off than I am sad but, once again, in true Mazie fashion, my body betrays me.

"Don't speak to me like that," I say assuredly. I don't raise my voice because I know it will get us nowhere. He is angrier than I've ever heard him before and there is no point in fueling the fire even more, especially if I want to get some answers. He sighs.

"I'm sorry," he says quickly, but the words are cold. This is truly bothering him, this is bigger than he is leading on. I think I've known that all along, but I let my fear of losing him stop me from questioning him.

We are in love and though we have never said the words out loud, I know he will see that I care, that I am only trying to be there for him. I know that I'm not being a good girlfriend if I don't make him talk about it. He is going through things and I am left in the dark in more than one obvious way.

Maybe I can help him or maybe Maya can. Maybe a school counselor can step in? He doesn't know and I don't know, but I at least have to try.

"You know what," I say calmly, "you don't have to apologize. You can scream at me until you're blue in the face and hoarse, but I am not going to let this go. Believe it or not, you need to talk about this. I am right here and I always will be, just talk to me. *Please*."

He's quiet and I hear him pull out a chair from across the room. I wait, wishing I could see his expression, wishing I could decipher if he were coming around or if he is just stewing in his anger toward me.

"I don't know where my father is," he says slowly. "Well, not this week anyway."

"Okay..."

"He uh," he clears his throat and I have never heard Barnaby struggle for words before. "He disappears a couple times a month for days at a time and he usually calls me to pick him up from wherever he wandered off to. Most times he's at a drinking buddy's house and I leave him there a couple days just to have him out of the house. Sometimes I go out and look for him if he's gone longer than a week. When I find him, he's so drunk that he doesn't even know who I am, he doesn't know my name," he pauses. "He probably doesn't even know his own name. The only reason why I bring you over here is I know he can't get here without me picking him up."

I don't say anything because I want him to keep going; I want him to get it all out.

"That's why my mother left. He hit her a few times. One day they got into an argument and he pulled a gun out on her and shot at the door she was standing next to. I haven't seen her in five years; we speak on holidays and birthdays though."

The shock I am feeling listening to his words is overpowering. I'd never heard him sound like this before. This Barnaby I am listening to is a deeply broken child with an absent mother and a father who is an abusive drunk.

What kind of mother would leave her children knowing that this man was abusive, knowing that he was capable of pulling a gun out and firing it in his own home? Did she really think just giving them an account with access to large amounts of money would make it all better? I never knew I could hate two people so much whom I'd never met before.

I want to get up and hold him, but he keeps speaking.

"Mel looks just like my mom, they even have the same mannerisms and when he is drunk, it confuses him." I hear movement and I expect him to sit back down on the bed, but he doesn't.

"He's still bitter that my mom left so a lot of the time she gets the evil end of his anger and that is why I have those bruises sometimes and miss school or have to go home abruptly, because he calls and I have to get him before he gets arrested or I have to protect Mel from him, or drive her somewhere so their paths don't cross when he's …" he pauses again and changes the direction of his sentence. "There's always something I have to do." He adds softly, defeated.

And the pit of my stomach and the center of my heart are set ablaze. I am angry that he has to live this way, and I am mad that I don't know exactly what to do to make this better. How can I protect him?

"He's only like this when he drinks," he adds as if it were an acceptable excuse. As if I should think it's okay because there is a logical reason. "He's not a bad person."

"Barnaby," I finally speak and my voice is distant and pained. What is this world he's living in, how is he able to separate the Barnaby I know from this Barnaby that is in front of me right now?

"That's everything, okay?" he says exasperatedly and, almost like a light switch flipping, his aura changes at once. "I told you and now you need to drop it."

"*Drop it?*" I repeat in shock.

"Yes, drop it."

His tone is making me so angry, his flippant way of speaking to me is rubbing me the wrong way and I know he knows it. It's unbelievable what he and Mel are going through, but using his body as a human shield to protect her from their father is not the solution.

"If you can't leave Mel alone with him, how do you expect to leave the country for three months?"

At this point, I feel like the only way I can make him understand where I am coming from is to poke holes in his logic.

"She'll be at summer camp," he states immediately. His anger is blatant, but I ignore it. How am *I* the only one between the both of us who can see how wrong this is?

"And what about college? If we go away, are you going to drive hours back home every time something happens? Are you planning on taking Mel with us? What if your father calls and he…"

"Mazie."

"This isn't okay, Barnaby!" I am overwhelmed with fear, confusion and frustration. Barnaby is one of the easiest people in the world to talk to, but right now I feel like I am speaking to a brick wall. He is not comprehending how dangerous this is, that how he has been handling this is not productive. He is theoretically putting multiple Band-Aids over deep flesh wounds that won't stop bleeding, wounds that need a different type of attention in order to heal.

"Or safe," I continue. "You have to tell the police!" He is telling me these horrible things as if they're normal, as if I should accept them because he told me to. "Your father is clearly dangerous and he needs help! Barnaby, *you* need help so that…"

"Damn it!" he yells, interrupting me, "You don't know anything about my family, you wanted me to tell you so I did. Every day I am getting pulled in different directions, I can't keep giving you *every fucking thing* that I am! I can't give you anymore of me, Mazie! This is all I have. This is my life!" his voice is booming as if I weren't in the same room with him. His anger and frustration toward me is so evident in his tone that I feel like cowering away.

The words sit there, my conscious thought dissecting them immediately. He isn't just talking about this particular situation. Through my blindness and my cancer and treatment, he feels like he is giving too much of himself, just like I suspected. I am taking from him, more than he has to give, but he gives it anyway. My biggest fear in the beginning was this very moment, the moment I realize I am a burden to him.

"That's…" he stutters to say, realizing the impact of his words. "That's not what I meant…"

"I think I'm going to go home," I say calmly. I stand from the bed and I ignore the fact that I am still completely naked and feel exposed.

He sighs and then I hear him walking closer to me. "Here," he says softly. He hands me my clothes, and a tear falls because, buried deep down inside of me, I expected him to beg me to stay. I expected him to want to explain what exactly he meant. Barnaby is never short on words and his quietness now lets me know that he meant what he said, he just didn't mean to say it in that tone or in this particular moment.

I get dressed in silence, and I hear him getting dressed as well.

"I'm driving you," he says and I nod, assuming he is looking at me. I feel for the nightstand and put my sunglasses back on. I get to disappear now. I get to remove myself from this room and his presence and be by myself again. I am protected.

The ten minute car drive is excruciating. I've never felt this way with Barnaby. I've never felt so alone when with him. I do my very best to keep myself from crying. I am going to save that for my pillow.

I feel the car stop and he puts it in park. He doesn't say a word and neither do I for a few moments.

"Mazie..."

"Thank you for driving me home, Barnaby," I interrupt as I open the door and step out, grabbing my cane and walking up the walkway, clinking right and clinking left until I got to the steps. I am at my door when a car door slams and then I hear footsteps almost running toward me.

I turn around and immediately have my hand up. "Just go home," I say and the flood of tears I was saving for my pillow come streaming down my face. I can't hold them in anymore.

"I am sorry," and this time he doesn't sound cold and distant, he sounds sad and passionate. "I don't know why I said that. I'm just…I'm frustrated and stressed out and I took it out on the wrong person."

"You said what you've been feeling; I never wanted to burden you. I told you in the beginning that I …"

"No," he interrupts urgently grabbing my hand. "You're not a burden. You're the most important person in my life. I don't think you understand how important."

I am facing the ground, letting my tears splash wildly. I feel his hand lift my chin. "Mazie, believe me. Please."

It's quiet for a moment, while I play back our argument, his words resting angrily in the center of my chest. Words are powerful. His words were powerful. I take a step back. "I believed you when you said you wouldn't break my heart."

"Mazie…"

"I have to go, Barnaby." I turn around and walk in the house closing the door and leaving him behind.

Thirteen

Redamancy (n.): the act of loving the one who loves you; a love returned in full

Saturday

I keep telling my brain to not think about him. I keep trying to rationalize with her that she-us *–we* were the ones to walk away from Barnaby, that we had no right to think about him and miss him and wish he were lying next to us. It all spun out of control so quickly that I didn't really understand what was happening until it happened. I never thought being without Barnaby would ever be an option.

I've been in my bed, locked in my room going on twelve hours and I am discovering that there is no limit on how many tears I can shed. I'd come to grips that I will never stop crying, that it is a part of who I am now.

I even tortured myself by thinking that maybe Barnaby would be better off with a girl like Kate. He didn't have to direct her where to walk or sit with her when she's vomiting from chemo. He didn't have to sit with her in doctors' offices and attend appointment after appointment. He didn't have to argue with her all of the time because she was probably agreeable and nicer than me. They could go to the movies with subtitles only and text and play video games without the audio.

He wouldn't have to describe a sunset to her.

It would be easier, stress free, care free and light, exactly how a relationship with two teenagers should be, exactly what a person like Barnaby deserves.

I miss Barnaby, but I am so hurt. I need Barnaby, but I am angry he spoke to me that way.

I love Barnaby and there is no but. I love him so much, maybe too much and my brain once again has failed to follow directions. I wipe more tears away and bury my face further into my pillow.

Sunday

I hear a knock on my bedroom door and for a fleeting moment I hope it's Barnaby, but deep down I know it's not and a new wave of tears fall.

"Mazie," I hear Maya say, "I'm coming in." I hear the door open slowly and then there is nothing but silence for a few exaggerated moments. Then I feel her sit on the side of my bed.

"I know you don't want to tell me what happened and I am not going to force it out of you but all I will say is that you're young and whether whatever is going on between you and Barnaby is permanent or just a little bump in the road, your life will go on and you will not feel like this forever."

I know she meant for her words to make me feel better but they make me cry harder. Is this permanent? The thought is nauseating. She is trying to tell me that I am young and that there are plenty of fish in the sea and whether that is true or not, I don't care. I want the fish I have already, I can't imagine there being anyone else for me. I can't fix my mouth to say that, so I just let more tears fall as I feel Maya rubbing my back in a gentle circular motion.

"You know I am here for you," she says softly and I can hear the sadness in her voice. She's never seen me cry like this over something that didn't have to do with my health or our parents. "You can say whatever you want and I won't say a word. Sometimes talking through something, getting it out of your mind, can make a world of difference."

I don't respond for nearly five minutes. When I feel Maya about to get up, I reach out and grab for her, pulling her back down to keep her next to me.

"Okay," she says softly. After about five more minutes, I finally sit up and exhale.

"How much have I burdened you?" I ask her and my voice is a little raspy, but filled with emotion.

"What?" she asks and she almost sounds angry. "You are not a burden!" she's nearly yelling. I shake my head and face down as I wipe more tears from my cheek.

"Wait," she says, "did Barnaby say you were a burden?" and now she is angry and I feel the need to protect and defend him.

"No!" I say. "I mean, not those words exactly. I don't know…" I trail off.

"Well, what *exactly* did he say?"

"He has a lot going on in his life and I was trying to help him, help that he clearly didn't want and it kind of turned into an argument when I was being persistent and he yelled at me. He said he couldn't give anymore of himself to me, that he couldn't give me 'every fucking thing' that he is," saying the words burn my lips because they cut right through me.

It isn't just the words, it's how he said them. It's still hard imagining him speaking to me in that tone let alone what he said. It isn't the Barnaby I'd grown to know and love.

Maya doesn't say anything at first, then she sighs. "Did he try to explain what he meant? Did he try to apologize?"

I nod. I am not sure I am able to relay exactly what he said on the porch two days ago because if I am broken now, I'm sure saying the words will turn me into dust and rubble.

"What is going on in his life that would get him that upset with you?" she asks. And I almost want to smile because my sister just promised she wouldn't say a word, she was just going to let me vent. I knew when she said it she would be incapable of listening without commentary.

My thoughts go back to everything Barnaby told me about his family and the last five years or so of his life and my stomach feels like it's going to reject the little bit of food I have in it.

"It's really not my place to say," is all I offer because it's Barnaby's business and whether we are on the same page or not, he trusts me to not say anything and I am going to keep that promise no matter the status of our relationship.

"Okay, my perspective," she says calmly. "I don't think he meant it the way you took it. He is young and you have to admit he has been there by your side in very difficult times and that would be a lot for any seventeen year old to take on, not a burden but just…" she pauses. "It's difficult stuff Mazie. He clearly cares about you and

I am sure his words were from anger and frustration with whatever is happening in his life."

That is pretty much what he told me. Am I overreacting? Whether I am or not it doesn't change how the words made me feel, how they are making me feel right now as I think about them. Or how he yelled at me like I was not worthy of being a part of his world even though he is completely immersed in and connected to mine.

"Do you love him?" she asks and I swallow. I've loved him for a while now, but I have never said the words and even if I would be saying them now just to Maya, it still frightened me. Once I put these words out into the universe they will be floating there forever and I won't be able to get them back. If Barnaby and I can't find each other again, if we continue to drift from one another, my words will be out there weightless and meaningless and I don't want that because they mean so much to me.

I put my head in my hands and start crying harder and I cannot believe who I have become, I'm not just lovesick, it's much more than that. It's that and a combination of something else. Something that makes me feel like I am alone, that I am wandering and not connected to something that has been ingrained in me. And then I realize I feel homesick, I feel like I have gotten lost and can't find my way back to the world that I know, the world that I am comfortable in. I am homesick because Barnaby is home.

My sister has her arms around me and I am so embarrassed. I never thought I would be the girl crying over a boy because we may or may not be broken up, but I know deep down in the depths of my being that what

Barnaby and I share is different, it's stronger and palpable. We both have our own reasons why we need each other and right now those reasons are in the void.

Monday

My alarm is going off for the third time when I decide I am not going to school today. I want to talk to Barnaby. I want to forget everything that happened Friday and just go back to how it was but I know I am unable to right now. I know that even though everything in me wants to drop it, I can't and I hate myself for not being able to let it go. I'm not ready to not be sad and mad yet which is the most childish and idiotic thing to do, but it's a true emotion that I can't shake.

I hear my door slam open.

"This is where I draw the line," Maya says, her tone is harsh and surprises me. "I know you're sad and I am sad for you, but you are not missing school. You are not going to stay in this room for God knows how long, you're stronger and smarter than that. You are a beautiful and amazing girl so, no matter what happens today or tomorrow or next week, you will be okay. You will always be okay. This is a lot for you and I know he is important, but you are still you with or without Barnaby! You've never been weak a day in your life and I'll be damned if you start now because of a boy!"

"You need to truly understand that your life will move forward and you will have more happy times and, unfortunately, more sad times, but that's life. If anybody should know that I think it would be you. You have to roll with these punches and pick yourself up no matter how hard it may be at first. I won't let you fall into this dark spiral because you and I both know you're embarrassing yourself. You have twenty minutes to get dressed, there's a bagel on the counter for you. I'll be in the car." She doesn't wait for me to respond and then I hear my bedroom door slam shut.

I inhale and, for the first time since Friday afternoon, I smile, even though a few tears are streaming down my face. I am smiling. My sister has never been that assertive with me and in all honesty she is right. I am sad, that I know isn't going to change right now, but this is humiliating. I am strong and smart. I can own my feelings and feel them profoundly, but I can't let them control me. I exhale slowly then get up from my bed to get dressed.

I walked into English class timidly. Barnaby and I had a routine ever since the first week we met. When I would walk into English, if we weren't already together, he would say *good morning* to me and when we started dating he would lean over and kiss my cheek once I was seated.

Right now as I walk into the room I am not greeted and there is no kiss. Is he here? Is he still giving me space? Is he pissed at me and doesn't care if we ever speak again? My stomach gets hot and my cheeks are burning. What if his dad is back and he is not here because he is protecting his sister?

I am resisting the urge to stand up and yell *Barnaby are you here? Let yourself be known!*

Less dramatically, I take a deep breath. If there is one thing I know in the world, it's Barnaby's scent. It rained today so all I smell is wet grass and outside. I am frustrated but I have no right to be and I know that. I walked away from him.

The day goes by in a slow haze. I can't concentrate, so much of my days in school have been scheduled around my time with Barnaby. First period English together, free period together, lunch together, him walking me to math, then picking me up from math to walk me to science, history and Spanish, sneaking behind the fire exit stairwell during extended period before my Spanish class to make out for fifteen minutes –we only got caught once. Then, us walking hand and hand to his car at the end of the day where we'd make out more and he would drive to my house and I would force him to sit ten feet away from me so we could work on my novel without distractions.

Today, I am just alone. I am clinking left and clinking right up these crowded hallways. I don't go to the library because now the Braille section is synonymous to him and so is Strauss' classroom. I sit outside and just wait for the hours to tick by so I can go home and cry some more. I don't care about how embarrassing I am being. I miss him, but I am not ready to forgive him and that war within me is torturous.

Tuesday

I was practically up all night. I slept a total of two hours. I am so tired of crying. I am so tired of wanting Barnaby, though I know that is something that is never going to change. But I realized last night that my anger is deriving or at least morphing into something else. He hasn't called or come by. If he was at school he didn't try and speak to me and that hurt almost as much as his words from Friday did. Am I being irrational? Maybe, but I would be lying if I said I didn't expect him to call or show up at my house, and he did neither of those things.

I won't allow myself to think something bad happened, the anxiety of knowing how crazy his father is, is almost enough to paralyze me.

I somehow manage to make it through day four without Barnaby. I picked up my phone to call him probably six times once I got home from school today, but then I put the phone down to cry some more.

Because I am so exhausted, I decide to take a shower and call it an early night. I finished all of my homework outside during my free period. I am not really hungry and I can barely keep my eyes open. I pick up my phone one more time to call him and then shake my head and throw the phone on my bed.

I stand in the shower letting the hot water nearly burn my skin. Subconsciously, I think I can wash all of the bad and sad feelings away. I am wrong. God, I truly love him. I love him so much, but I never thought he of all people could hurt me, even if it was unintentional. It's hard to let go of that feeling, that pain... that sadness of knowing that I am overextending him. That I am taking *every fucking thing* he is and have little to give to him in return. It's such a hopeless feeling of unworthiness.

I get out of the shower and, as soon as I sit down on my bed, I hear my phone buzz three quick times, which means I have a voicemail. I put the phone on speaker and listen:

"I know that we are in a weird space ...I don't know if or when you will want to speak to me again..."

It's Barnaby and my heart reacts in a strange way – stopping, starting, flipping, skipping. I inhale and continue to listen.

"...but I am sitting here rereading Pride & Prejudice and since it's your favorite book I wanted to share with you my favorite lines," he clears his throat and takes a deep breath before he continues, *"I cannot fix on the hour, or spot, or the look, or the words, which laid the foundation. It is too long ago. I was already in the middle before I knew that I had begun – In vain have I struggled. It will not do. My feelings will not be repressed. You must allow me to tell you how ardently I admire and love you."* He pauses. *"Mazie, sometimes proclamations are needed."*

And then the voicemail ends.

I play it three more times before I can process and think clearly.

For the first time the words are spoken, *"how ardently I admire and love you."* I can't control my tears and the butterflies in my stomach. *"Mazie, sometimes proclamations are needed."* Before I realize what I am doing, I speak into my phone, "Call Barnaby."

"Ezmerelda," he says answering after the first ring, he's surprised.

"Mazie," I correct softly and I can hear him exhale in relief and I do too.

"How are you?" he asks cautiously.

"I was actually calling because I wanted to tell you *my* favorite line in *Pride & Prejudice*." My voice is low and nervous.

"What is it?"

I inhale, *"It has been coming on so gradually, that I hardly know when it began."*

There is a pause and then softly, he speaks, "Lizzy and I have that in common."

I smile and it's quiet, *our quiet* and all the feelings swarm around me like a hurricane. I miss him. I want him. I need him and I can't remember anything else. So the words come easily and naturally.

"I love you too, Barnaby."

Fourteen

Numb (adj.): unable to think, feel, or react normally because of something that shocks or upsets you

We have been on the phone for nearly three hours, and he's apologized so many times that I had to tell him to stop. I believe him. I believe that he loves me and every sacrifice he has made has been because he loves me. I am forever grateful for him, but I am not going to let him overextend himself anymore, I will find a healthy balance for the both of us.

"Excuse my language but I really fucking missed you," he says and he sounds like a man searching for water in the desert.

"I missed you too," I say. "More than you'll ever know."

"I don't want to fight," he says and his voice is low and I can't help but laugh.

"Barnaby, all we do is fight."

He laughs too, "You know what I mean." He corrects. "…and we don't fight, we have passionate discussions."

"Umm maybe that's what you're doing…" We both laugh again.

"So, is it safe to start booking our trip?" he asks.

"Yes." I smile.

"Serious question, will you be packing bikinis?"

"Oh, I thought there were nude beaches in Europe," I say jokingly.

"Ezmerelda, do *not* tease me like that!" he says and again we are laughing and I am no longer homesick.

"Can I ask you something?"

"Of course."

"Were you at school?"

"Yes," he says and his voice is low.

"Oh."

"I sat in the back. I figured you wouldn't want me by you and frankly it would've been too hard to be that close to you and not talk to you or reach over and touch you…or kiss you," he pauses then exhales. "I'd never seen you that mad or sad. I wanted to give you space. I didn't want to give you space but I thought it would be the best thing."

I don't say anything at first as I think about the fact that he was there the entire time, I missed him with all of me and he was in the same room.

"It wasn't the best thing," I say lowly and I wipe a tear because the thought of us actually breaking up and not being together is such a horrible thought. I feel so stupid for even reacting this way because our four day standoff is my fault. How long would I have let this go on had he not called? My stubbornness could have completely ruined this.

"I didn't know how much space to give you and today you looked..." he pauses, "I'd never seen you like that and it took everything in me not to just run up to you and hold you and kiss you until I could make that look go away. I hated that I was the reason you were like that. I never want to be the reason you're unhappy, ever."

"You make me happy," I say as I wipe another tear. "I've never been happier." My words are raw, open, and honest. I love Barnaby Parks with all that I am and feeling like this isn't scary or intimidating. It is beautiful and euphoric.

"Me too," he says and I can hear the smile in his voice. "You make me better, Ezmerelda."

And I don't correct him, I smile and take a deep breath because he has no idea how much he has made me better.

"You see me more clearly than anyone has ever seen me," he says softly after a beat of silence.

"The irony isn't lost on me," I say, while sniffling. We both laugh quietly.

"I mean it, and I guess that's why I tried to keep all of this from you, away from you. I never wanted to talk about my situation at home," he continues, "… because I didn't want you intertwined with that part of my world. You're my happy place, where I can run to when that world is too much, where I want to escape and just be alive and carefree; you're my light at the end of the tunnel."

I exhale, letting his words wrap around me as he continues.

"Talking about the murky things in my life with you, my light , I didn't want any of that near us, near what we are together. I didn't want what we have tainted by all of the things that I don't have and it was stupid because all it did was push you away."

He pauses. "I am *so* sorry," he finally says. He says it almost desperately and I didn't think I could cry any more than I had the last four days, but I am definitely gunning for my personal record.

"Stop apologizing," I sniffle in the phone and he chuckles lightly. "You're my whole world, Barnaby," I admit softly, not realizing I was going to say that and, as terrifying as that concept is at eighteen, it's true. "I just want you to be happy and safe."

"Ditto," he says and I laugh again and it feels so good to hear that sound coming from the both of us. It didn't feel melodramatic at the time, but I was pretty convinced I would never laugh again if he and I weren't together. That thought makes me laugh even harder because it was indeed melodramatic as hell.

"What?" Barnaby asks.

"Nothing," I answer while wiping the continuous flow of tears from my cheeks. I probably look like a sociopath.

Then it hits me that he isn't the only one who has something to apologize for. He wasn't and isn't the only one at fault here.

"Actually, I want to apologize to you," I say softly.

"Mazie, no, you didn't do…"

"Wait," I interrupt him, "I shouldn't have forced you to talk about something you weren't ready to talk about. I was selfish in thinking that your silence was a direct dig at me or had anything to do with me at all. I ended up making it about me and my feelings and it wasn't fair." I exhale, pausing for a second before continuing.

Honesty and transparency will be the only way he and I can continue to work and build this relationship further. He and I have already been through a lot of heavy situations early on and though he knows me better than anyone and I know him better than anyone, we still have a lot to learn about each other, a lot to understand, a lot to grow from.

"We are all broken, we just shatter differently," I finally say.

And that is something I never really thought about before. We all experience pain and loss, just like we all experience happiness and joy, but we don't all process these emotions the same way. It's not fair to make people express themselves the way you expect, the way *you* would.

"Maybe that wasn't the best analogy…"

"No, it's perfect," he interrupts gently and it's quiet again –*our quiet*. All I can hear is Barnaby's faint breathing.

"What are you, like a writer or something?" he finally asks and we both laugh, slowly changing the energy. "I won't keep anything else from you, Mazie. I promise."

"Okay," I say softly.

"I mean it."

I believe him. I love him, and more importantly, I trust him.

I relish in how right this feels, how right it always feels. It's so right that when we aren't together, when we are battling to be on the same page, it's a foreign feeling, a confusing, seemingly unnatural feeling. I am overwhelmed at how perfectly our imperfections and faults mesh together, how every sharp edge of our shattered pieces fit together like a puzzle.

"I want to come see you tonight," he says, his voice snapping me from my thought.

"I thought you said your car wouldn't start?" I wanted him to come over hours ago. I need to be near him, I want to breathe him in, but he said his car was on the fritz again.

"You live ten minutes away, I'll jog over. I just want to see you, right now."

And I smile, the urgency in his voice makes my heart react.

"Okay."

"Is Maya there?" he asks. I can hear shuffling in the background. Knowing him, he is probably already halfway out of the door.

"She's working for a couple more hours. She won't care…" it is getting late, but it has been four days and I want him here by my side more than anything.

"Maybe we can walk to the football field," he says and I smile, we haven't been in a while. I miss it. It feels like it's ours, even if only for a few hours out of the month.

Before I can answer, his tone changes. "Wait," he says abruptly and then I hear a bunch of noise in the background. It sounds like crashing and things falling.

"Shit," he says. "My dad is here. Lenny must've dropped him off." The anger in Barnaby's voice is deeply engraved. I hear yelling, a man's voice deep and booming. I can't make out what he is saying, but he is clearly angry and loud.

"Lenny? Who is Lenny? Barnaby, call the police!" I say in near panic and I almost bite my tongue, not wanting to upset him like I'd done four days ago. I'm realizing that through all of the making up and apologizing, this situation hasn't been solved. Nothing in regards to his home life has changed.

This can't continue, but what else can I do?

"It's okay, but I have to go." Barnaby says. "I'm sorry. I won't be able to come over tonight because Mel is here, but I'll see you in the morning, bright and early. I love you." He hangs up before I can respond.

My anxiety is at an unprecedented level, knowing that his dad is back and that angry. I can't understand how he is living like this. Now that I know the pattern, I know that Barnaby may have a new bruise or miss school. This isn't right.

I want to call the police, everything in me is telling me to dial the number and send the address but he and I nearly broke up because of this, I can't imagine what he would do if I sent help over or interfered in any way, especially after the conversation we just had. Though it is distressing, Barnaby dealt with this way before he knew I existed. He said it was okay and I had to trust and believe him, right?

I sigh and lay back down wishing there was something I could do to make this better, to make all the bad and sad things in his life go away. Barnaby is the type of person who deserves nothing but laughter and joy and spontaneity. All of the things he's provided for me, he should have tenfold.

He spends so much time reminding me of everything I am, but I don't think he truly understands everything he is. Something I am going to make sure he realizes. Something I should've been doing from the very beginning of our relationship.

After about an hour of restlessness I am finally able to fall asleep, but all too quickly I am startled awake.

"Mazie," I hear Maya saying as she is shaking me. "Mazie, wake up."

"What?" I nearly snap.

"I tried to call you; please don't panic."

I sit up immediately, "Maya, what's wrong?"

"When I was leaving my shift I saw Barnaby being brought in on a gurney, I don't know any details because they rushed him straight to the O.R."

Before she can finish her sentence I am out of my bed. It is like I am moving in quicksand. I am hurried and frantic, stumbling into walls and doors as I rush out of my bedroom door in only seconds, but my mind is on a delay. My mind is still retaining the words that came out of Maya's mouth.

We rush out of the house and are on the freeway in minutes. I didn't have a reaction, I haven't said a word. I just need to be by his side. I need to make sure he is okay. I won't allow any other thoughts to invade me.

We get to the hospital and Maya asks someone, who I assume is another nurse, if she has any information on a Barnaby Parks.

"Oh, the GSW? He is in surgery."

"Shit," Maya says and it sounds gargled like maybe she is crying.

"What?" I ask and it's a mixture of shock, and pain and confusion. The panic in my voice spills out in a shrill. I didn't even recognize my voice. I am not even sure if the sound I heard came from my mouth.

"He was shot," she says and then I feel her arms around me.

I think I am numb because I can't understand her words, I can't feel their meaning. It is similar to when Dr. Nipan told me I had cancer again; I heard the words, they were there, but they were orbiting. I couldn't reach them. I can't reach these words either and I never want to.

"I'll go see if they'll let me back there," she whispers and then she is no longer holding me. I am standing there unfeeling, all emotion void.

"Young lady," I hear the nurse my sister was talking to, say. "Why don't we have a seat?" I feel her grab my elbow and she helps me sit. She offers me water and coffee but I cannot answer her because I am numb. My lips won't move.

Five seconds, three hours, ten days —who knows how much time goes by, but I just sit here. Waiting. Numb. Lost.

I need Barnaby. That's all I want, then everything will be okay. All the planets will be aligned and all of the stars will continue to shine, the sun included. My world will still be alive and thriving.

"Mazie," I hear Maya say and her voice, the despair, the fear in it, almost cuts right through the bubble I'd created.

This bubble where Barnaby did come over and we laid in each other's arms and he apologized again and I told him to stop. In this bubble he kisses me and I kiss him and we make love and I get to tell him I love him for the second time and I can feel his smile against my lips as he says it to me for the third time. In this bubble, we joke back and forth to make up for the four days we spent apart and then we leave in the middle of the night to break onto the high school football field and lay under the night's sky while he starts to go on one of his *Barnaby babble* rants about life and the stars and their meaning and I giggle and tell him he is weird, confusing and crazy and my words evoke a laugh out of him. The laugh that nine times out of ten will make me laugh too because it was infectious. And then I would tell him I loved him for the third time and our lips would meet *somewhere in the middle like heaven and the up there* and I would feel safe and whole.

Everything would be okay. Everything would make sense.

"Mazie," Maya says again and she is crying, she is crying so hard. She is unable to get her words out clearly because they are fighting against a sob. I am trying very hard to acknowledge her, but I am stuck in this bubble. I never want to leave it, this bubble is warm and happy and beautiful and love and *home*. I feel her hand on my shoulder as she sits down and wraps her arms around me and now I know.

This is the dark cloud that kept hovering, this was the feeling in the pit of my stomach all of this time, that something was looming, that I was right to be terrified of the dark and unpaved future. It is starting to seep in, the jagged and razor thick edges of the truth have punctured my bubble, *our bubble*. I know that it will be real if she says the words. I know that nothing will ever be the same again.

Planets will crash. Stars will burn out, the sun included.

My world, unrecognizable.

"Mazie, I'm so sorry…" she chokes out.

"Don't," I say and my voice is stoically calm.

I am calm because the best thing about the numbness is that every feeling that can destroy you, ruin you, send you spiraling into the deepest and darkest parts of your being –all of those feelings, can't touch you. They can't reach you because you're unable to feel anything. The idea of unrivaled pain is there lingering like a distant memory, but it isn't palpable.

It's temporary, but at this moment I am safe and, more importantly, he is safe and our bubble is impenetrable.

Fifteen

Death (n.): the end of life: the time when someone or something dies (2) the permanent end of something that is not alive: the ruin or destruction of something

The word infinite is an adjective that is defined as immeasurably great. This basically means great without bounds, limitless in its greatness. It's a heady word, powerful, and intimidating but it's also beautiful. To have a word describe in just three syllables how it feels to want something so badly that you never want it to end. The other side of that is the loss of something or someone, and then the word infinite takes a dark turn. Its permanence is overwhelming, the pain will always be there *infinitely* changing small pieces of who you are until your own time is up.

I think we have a tendency of looking at life in patterns. It's like we get comfortable with whatever specific order is laid in front of us, accepting the overall complacency of life. When we read books, watch movies or whatever it may be, we subconsciously try to piece together clues that will lead to the big conclusion. What will the finale be? What is this character foreshadowing? Will this character have a happy ending? Does this character deserve one? Is he or she doomed? That's how we treat life in a sense. What will our finale be? I don't think you will find too many people who can honestly say they are prepared for any and everything life is capable of throwing at them.

We rarely consider the things that come out of left field, the things that smack you down so hard into the ground that you don't think you'd ever be able to get back up. We never take the time to actually understand that this could be our last day, our last words, our last breath.

We don't have those terrifying thoughts about the end every single day because it is too depressing to live life that way - to expect the worse out of every situation, to wait for the bad, the shocking, to wait for death. So we live, love, learn, breathe and keep breathing until we can't breathe anymore.

So, life may not be infinite, life can indeed be measured but the love you give and the love you receive is infinite. It's immeasurably great and, like love, make the mark you leave here in the world immeasurably great too, even if the mark you leave is only to be felt by one person.

*(**The Improbable Infinite**, pg.118)*

Epilogue (n.): a section or speech at the end of a book or play that serves as a comment on or a conclusion to what has happened

I am sitting on our couch tapping my foot impatiently. I am irritable and ready to go.

"I'm coming!" Maya yells out. "Ten more minutes!" she says and I sigh because she said that ten minutes ago. Today is my orientation for my freshmen year of college. I am finally ready to be on my own, the college I am attending has a program for the hearing and visually impaired. Those dorms are more accessible than the average dormitory but I will still have the independence that I crave.

After graduating high school I took a year off. If it weren't for Maya I don't think I would've been able to keep my grades at a passing level. After Barnaby's death I shut down. I didn't speak much, I barely left my room, I missed a ton of school, and I lost a lot of weight. I was unable to *feel* for the first two months; I was just there. I was present physically, but that was it.

I didn't cry at his funeral that Maya forced me to attend. I didn't cry at the dedication the school gave him and, though I obviously didn't attend Prom, Barnaby and I were voted King and Queen, definitely receiving that pity vote after all.

I didn't cry at the speedy hearing when his father was sentenced to life in prison. I didn't cry when his father testified and said that he was so drunk that he thought he was shooting at an intruder. I didn't cry when he cried and said he loved his children more than anything and that he wished he were dead and not Barnaby. I wished that too.

I didn't cry when his mother, the woman who abandoned him and ultimately left him with the man who would fatally shoot him, tried to speak to me about how amazing her son was though she had no right to say anything about him. She didn't know him. I didn't cry when a sobbing Amelia gave me Barnaby's notebook that was full of poems and things he wanted to say to me. She offered to read it to me, but I didn't want her to. I wouldn't ever want to hear those words if they weren't coming from Barnaby's lips.

I finally cried when my phone alerted me that my voicemail box was full. I listened to the messages, all of them were from people who had gotten my number from Maya and wanted to tell me how *sorry* they were about Barnaby's passing, that they were keeping me in their thoughts and prayers. All of the typical things people say when someone dies.

Sixteen deleted messages in and I heard *his* voice, my Barnaby. I heard his voice for the first time in two months. I'm listening to him quote my favorite book and him telling me he loved me for the first time.

I fell to the floor choking on my sobs. I couldn't breathe; I was suffocating. I was practically screaming as if I were being burned alive. Hearing his voice sent a jolt of pain straight to my heart so fierce and overpowering that I actually grabbed my chest to make sure it was still closed, to make sure that my heart was still in there beating. No matter what I did, there just wasn't enough oxygen in the room. I sat there clutching my chest screaming for and at Barnaby. I screamed as if he could hear me. I screamed expecting him to respond and come back to hold me and tell me it was just a bad dream and that he would never leave me.

That he would stay in my life like he promised.

I didn't know what emotion tormented me more, the sadness or the anger, maybe the guilt was in the lead? They were all encompassing me and they were all burying me rapidly. The numbness had finally worn off and I was feeling everything at once. I was feeling everything intensely and viciously. The deep dark areas that every human should be afraid to ever go to –I was there. I was sitting in it, sinking quickly, the dark covering every inch of me.

Maya rushed into my room and didn't say a single word, she just knew and she held me while I cried for two hours sitting on my bedroom floor. I didn't think it was ever going to stop. I was finally realizing in that moment that I would never be with him again; I would never touch him again; I would never argue with him and be annoyed by him again.

I would never be that version of me again.

The following months were the deep depression months where all I did was cry. I couldn't understand, I honestly still don't understand. I wasn't able to really function; it was the first time in the last six years that I was thankful I didn't have my sight. I couldn't imagine having to go through this world knowing that Barnaby was no longer in it. It was already painfully unbearable to handle *feeling* it, I couldn't fathom *seeing* it too.

I fell in love with the dark, with being alone. I fell in love with the grief because in those moments of agonizing pain, it was the only thing reminding me that I was even alive. I could feel it all, so profoundly ingrained in my being. With therapy and counseling I was able to find some type of balance, but I was always drifting out of orbit, having to fight my way back to this world. A world that was foreign to me now since my Barnaby was no longer in it.

It's been a little over a year and I still have my moments, many moments actually. That's something I don't think will ever change, but I have been able to slowly and steadily come back to being me in some form again. I hurt, I cry, I yell at God, but I am living and Barnaby once told me that was always a special occasion.

"Okay," Maya says bringing me back to real time. "All set?" she asks me.

"I've been *all set* for the last twenty minutes," I say rolling my eyes and getting up from the couch. She laughs.

This college is only twenty two minutes from my sister which is good. Though I want independence, I still need Maya; she is all I have.

We are finally at the college. All I hear are chairs moving and so many different loud voices talking over each other. It sounds incredibly crowded for a small college.

"Hi!" I hear a female voice say. It's high pitched and chipper.

"Hello!" my sister says immediately, matching this woman's excitement.

"I am Lisa," the high pitched chipper voice says to us. "I'll be your tour guide for the first half of the orientation."

"Okay, great! I'm Maya, and this is my sister, Mazie, she will be a freshman here."

"Hello Mazie, you're going to love it here!" Lisa says enthusiastically. "I'm going to get you both nametags. Mazie, how do you spell your name?"

"Hi, and actually I would like to go by Ezmerelda with a Z."

"Of course!" she says brightly as I hear her walk away. Maya grabs my hand and she squeezes it.

I drift back to the first day I met Barnaby, he told me, *"It's a beautiful name. It's very commanding. Anybody with a name like Ezmerelda is ready to take over the world. Agree? Ezmerelda's don't guess, someone with a strong name like that knows there are no in betweens, she knows who she is. You should wear it proud, you should own it."*

I remember at the time thinking he was crazy and that his obsession with my full name was annoying, but now I want nothing more than his words to be true in my life. Yes, I am still battling demons of guilt and sorrow and though the deep dark places are never too far away, I want to take over the world. I want to believe there are no in betweens. I want to discover who I am after having the human form of energy and light that is Barnaby, in my life.

I want to leave my stamp in this world the way he'd left his. I want to own it and I am going to wake up every single day with the hopes of being closer to that feat, with the hopes of being better than I was the day before.

I am not only doing this for Barnaby or because of Barnaby. I am doing this for myself because I've learned on multiple occasions how precious, fragile, and fleeting life is and because of this, I want to get the most out of mine.

I want the time I have left to count.

~ A few years later~

Maybe I should've picked a warmer day, but this can't wait and I really need to be with Barnaby today. I sit down next to his grave with a big coat on and a blanket wrapped around me.

"Okay," I say and the smile on my face is so big that my cheeks are burning. "I have an hour before Zachary and Ebony pick me up." I get situated and exhale, "It's officially here!" the words leave my lips in an excited flurry.

I open up my bag and grab the book. It is my first novel, published and ready to be sold and shared with the world, the book that I started with Barnaby almost four years ago, *The Improbable Infinite*, a book that I didn't touch for two years after he died.

I hold the book to my chest, take a deep breath and then I place it sitting upright against his headstone.

"I didn't think this day was ever going to come," I drag my hand over the engraved letters of his name and smile. "…but you did."

He apparently knew something I didn't know. We weren't even halfway done when we'd worked on it together, but he made sure to tell me every chance he got that I had tapped into something special, that I would be published one day. I always took his words as extremely biased; I never imagined this coming into fruition.

"I wanted you to have the first official copy," I whisper to him.

I sit there for a moment imagining his reaction if he were still here. He would've jumped up and grabbed me, spinning me around until I demanded he put me down. He would kiss me and then say something like *and to think you were going to waste this talent?* Or maybe something along the lines of *so you're not a shitty writer after all!* I would roll my eyes and he would laugh and, in true Barnaby fashion, he'd remind me of *everything I am* and tell me that he was proud of me and that he loved me.

I can't help but smile knowing that his last words to me were – *I love you.* That memory used to make me cry. The first and last time he would ever say *I love you* were on the same day. That knowledge stung for a while and though that thought can get heavy sometimes, I smile when I hear his voice saying those words to me in my thoughts or, when I desperately need him, I play the voicemail and I am immediately transported to a simpler time.

I replay his words in my head often, words that forced me to think, words that encouraged me to finish this book, words that helped me face fears, words that motivated me to be everything we both believed I could be, a *me* that was always there but he helped flourish. Words that used to infuriate me and confuse me but made me absorb things in a different light. I remember every single conversation I've ever had with him and it has helped me through so much in the last four years.

The book was originally supposed to be fictional, though for the longest Barnaby didn't see it that way and again, in a way, he was right. With all that had gone on in my life, when I picked it up again to write two years ago, it morphed into a book about overcoming pain, very real pain. It ended up being about trying to find solace in a world that was hell bent on breaking you. I'd used what Barnaby said to me when I told him my parents were dead. I wrote about finding peace, what exactly peace is and how can you obtain it when all you want to do is curl up in a ball and hide from the world long enough for the world to not miss you, long enough for the world to forget you ever existed.

I'm not going to lie, it was hard for me to find peace after he died, one of the hardest processes in my life. I was too angry and depressed and guilt ridden. Wishing I would've done something, the guilt drowned me for a long time. I could not forgive myself knowing that I had a bad feeling, knowing that I should've told my sister the first time Barnaby told me his father hit him or *that night* when he hung up and I talked myself out of sending the police over. With the guilt and anger I felt within myself, I knew I wouldn't be able to stay afloat if I didn't find peace somehow.

I had many thoughts about whether it was even worth going on. Aside from Maya it was as if everyone I loved died and that feeling was a feeling that tormented me day and night. It was hard to find reasons to want to wake up in the morning.

Writing this novel that he and I started together helped me, the peace I was searching for was hidden in my words *–our* words. The solace I needed to forgive myself and to forgive Barnaby was in between the lines, screaming at me, telling me that whether it felt like it or not, the sun would still rise and the sun would still set.

"Thank you, Barnaby," I say quietly as I wipe one stray tear from my cheek.

I take the blanket from around my shoulders and spread it out so that I can lie down next to him.

"I would read *The Improbable Infinite* to you but there aren't any Braille copies yet," I laugh lightly.

I'm quiet for a moment, letting the cold air pinch my exposed skin. "She doesn't die at the end," I admit very quietly. Remembering how angry he'd gotten with me when I told him that I couldn't envision it ending with her being alive, that she, this character, couldn't possibly have a happily ever after. He believed that I was writing about myself, that I was trying to tell him something...

"She's happy at the end. She's found a way to be some parallel version of happy despite it all."

I can feel myself getting emotional and I am not here to have a sob fest on his grave, I'd done that plenty of times in the past. I change my thought process and force myself to think of something else to talk about.

"Sorry, it's been a while since the last time I was here. This semester has been kicking my ass."

I'm tapping my foot, bobbing my head to the faint rhythm. "Oh and Maya," I sigh. "You would think being a nurse and in medical school she would know the difference between contractions and Braxton Hicks." I shake my head.

Maya is almost nine months pregnant and we've rushed to the hospital three times in the last month because she thought she was in labor.

Her fiancé, Michael Whimer, is a doctor at the hospital where she works and I had no clue she'd been dating him on and off for over *six* years. I was so worried that her life was all about me, that she wasn't living because she'd given up so much for me, and the entire time she did have a life outside of our world together. She did have her own world that I wasn't a part of.

It pissed me off at first that she'd kept it from me. She claimed she didn't think the relationship would be serious so she didn't see the point in bringing him around or mentioning him. At the end of the day, I am happy that she is happy, she deserves it. He's a great guy and perfect for her; I truly feel like I've gained a big brother.

I'm lying on my back facing the sky and I imagine Barnaby lying next to me holding my hand and squeezing it tightly like he always did. He's letting me know that he is here, that he isn't going anywhere. I miss him, I miss him every second of every single day and I will always love him from the depths of my being.

Some weird and reflective version of my psyche has processed and accepted that he is no longer here with me, my heart understands it. She still hurts and aches for him but she understands.

Barnaby and I didn't get forever but we got each other in a very small, but beautiful and life changing window. That alone is more than I could've ever imagined for myself, a love like that isn't something many people get to experience in a lifetime. There's nothing that will be as meaningful to me as that discovery.

I knew that I had a choice, we all have a choice. When bad things happen, when the unexpected destroys everything you thought you needed in order to survive, there is a moment when you have to decide exactly who you are and if you're okay with who you are becoming.

Barnaby's death was that final dagger. That gut wrenching moment that had the power to extinguish me. I had questions that couldn't be answered, I had feelings that couldn't be described, and I had pain that no one should have to ever experience.

I could've chosen to believe I was cursed. I could've chosen to believe that there was an omen following me through my life, making sure all of the bad things happened and happened frequently. I could've fallen into the dark and stayed, accept that it had defeated me and always would. I could've lost faith and lived the rest of my days miserable and angry, never letting any of the light back in.

Or...

I could take that pain and that loss and turn it into strength. I could feel all the bad things deeply, but learn how to feel all of the good things just as intensely too. I could be a willing participant in life even if it didn't always play fair.

I remember the football field; I remember his hand intertwined with mine. I could feel his pulse in his fingertips and I am sure he could feel mine too. Barnaby said that what if everything had to have a reason or a rhyme? He thought that maybe no matter what direction our lives went, that there was a map with many roads leading to the same place.

I argued with him because that's what we did. I said that maybe sometimes things just happen for the sake of happening. I now know that we were both right. Our points of view met *somewhere in the middle like heaven and the up there.*

He was right because I did think one thing happening affected the next thing, that the twists and the turns were all to keep life moving and the world turning.

And *I* was right because not everything needed a reason, not a reason we were all supposed to understand anyway. Not everything had to follow a specific code so that it would make sense. Life wasn't supposed to make sense. You couldn't force life to show you symbolism from every single thing that happened to you or the ones you love.

Barnaby's death made no sense at all and it never will, but I don't think it's supposed to, not for me or anybody who truly loved and knew him. It is horrible and terrifying and the anger that fills me when I think about how and why he died has enough force to knock a plane out of the sky.

But that's exactly what life is, it isn't here to make us comprehend. It just happens and it's up to us to figure out how we react and respond. It's up to us to find our own symbolism if we want it. Even in the midst of the most horrific things, life is giving us an opportunity to learn and grow and expand to another level of consciousness and understanding.

I found mine, and it was him. Barnaby, just simply existing and loving me the way he loved me, is the symbolism I pulled from the excruciating and mind numbing pain of losing him. Knowing him taught me more than I thought I would ever know about the pureness of love. It hurts to think about him sometimes, but most of the time I can smile and still feel connected to him in an integral way.

This was never about me, this was never *my* story to tell. It was always Barnaby's. He tried with everything that he was and everything that he had to get the most out of every day, out of every moment, even when his life was glum and hard to muddle through. He never let it hold him down for too long. He managed to keep going when it could've been much easier to give up. I want to continue to live my life that way.

When I dream of him, I never get to see his face, but he is beautiful. I know this because *you don't need to see beautiful things to know that they are there, to know that they are beautiful.*

His energy preceded him. His humor and laughter wrapped around me and held me close. In those dreams I could feel his love and that was much more important than anything else.

Vibrant, loving, beautiful in mind, body and spirit –I believe he is in the sky glowing brighter than the stars I so often wish I can reach up and grab to bring back down to the earth with me. After all of this time, he's still illuminating every part of my many universes.

He is still a tornado, bigger than life, *all consuming*. He is still my Barnaby and he always will be.

"You were right," I whisper, *still* hating to admit that to him.

There isn't a limit to the love we share. Even in his absence it's potent. It cannot be contained by time or space or even death. It did not weaken or diminish. It's infinite and we reached it, we obtained the one thing I thought was unobtainable.

I smile, imagining the sky staring down smiling right back at me. I am thinking about the football field again, the first time we kissed. I am thinking about our hours spent writing and editing this book. I am thinking about our many arguments and all of the laughter in between. I am remembering every moment I shared with Barnaby and I am realizing we never needed an empty football field to be seen or to be felt. We were *never* insignificant. We were *never* specs or trivial beings in this big, overwhelming, and confusing universe.

We are Titans. We are giants. We are beautiful. We are at full capacity.

I smile brighter and speak proudly and loudly to the odd boy who stole my heart, to the weird and blunt boy whom I will always love deeply, "We *are* immeasurable."

I exhale and I am transported. He *is* lying right here next to me, our fingers are intertwined. The trust present between our tightly gripped palms is a feeling that hasn't diminished with time or faded with the fickleness of a memory.

There is no ending to my story; there is nothing finite about Barnaby's story either –it is boundless, *he* is boundless. So, I whisper and make sure he *feels* the last of my proclamation. I make sure I feel it too, "We are, we are, we are…"

End (n): a final part of something, especially a period of time, an activity, or a story

ACKNOWLEDGMENTS

Thank you to Andrew McGrew Jr., Constance R. Smith-McGrew, Rachael Norfleet, Samantha Blackwell, Colleen Samura, Kay Blake, Channon Nation, Samantha Kis, Steven Kis, Theresa Gill, Mansour Jadallah, Leanne Kocian, J.V. Kocian, Kimberly Greytak, Ervin Williams and Tammara Webber.

When I started writing my acknowledgements, I broke it down individually and ended up with over five pages. I have so many things to be thankful for, but the people in my life are number one. You all have contributed to my dreams in different and impactful ways and I can honestly say this book wouldn't be what it is or published if it weren't for you all. Whether it was your time and energy, your words of encouragement, giving much needed advice or simply being a sounding board when I needed guidance, you were there and never wavered and for that I am forever grateful.

Thank you from the bottom of my heart!

Made in the USA
Lexington, KY
10 September 2018